Sometimes Naughty, Sometimes Nice

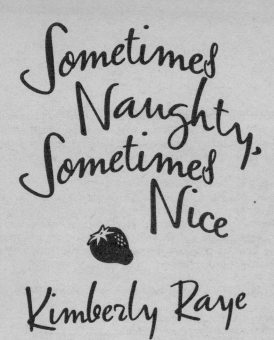

Kimberly Raye

WARNER

FOREVER

NEW YORK   BOSTON

Cover art and design by Shasti O'Leary Soudant
Book design by Giorgetta Bell McRee

Warner Books

Time Warner Book Group
1271 Avenue of the Americas
New York, NY 10020
Visit our Web site at www.twbookmark.com

Printed in the United States of America

First Paperback Printing: October 2004

10 9 8 7 6 5 4 3 2 1

"YOU LOOK REALLY GOOD."

The words were out before Xandra could stop them. "I, uh, mean the house looks really good." She tore her gaze from Beau's and glanced around. "Great."

Beau gave her a puzzled look. "We're in the process of stripping it and tearing out the rotting wood."

She licked her lips and gave herself a mental shake. "I'm sure the house is going to look great when everything is done." She was stuck on his grin. His mouth crooked at the corner and his face softened and his violet eyes sparkled. Her stomach hollowed out and her fingers trembled and damned if she didn't have the insane thought that she wanted to kiss him. And touch him. And feel him kiss her. And touch her. And—

"When am I going to get inside?"

"I'm wondering that myself," she said.

Boy, was she ever!

ALSO BY KIMBERLY RAYE

Kiss Me Once, Kiss Me Twice

In loving memory of my sister, Janet Denise Cole.
I love you to the moon and back,
And I miss you more than words can say!

Acknowledgments

I would like to extend an extra special thank you to those who helped during the writing of this book. *The Big Bang*-er ladies: fellow authors Nina Bangs, Lynn McKay and Donna Maloy, for their professional insight, and for turning me on to a great research tool! My husband, Curt Groff, for his love and enthusiasm when it comes to helping with said research. My agent, Natasha Kern, for being my touchstone and keeping me focused. And my editor, Melanie Murray, for her continued encouragement and support. Y'all are the best!

Sometimes
Naughty,
Sometimes
Nice

Chapter One

This was *not* happening.

She was an attractive, sexy, vibrant sensual woman in the prime of her life. Not to mention she was the owner and head designer for Wild Woman, Inc., a leading manufacturer of erotic toys and sexual enhancement products for women. Attractive, sexy, vibrant, sensual women who made their living by selling the whole attractive, sexy, vibrant, sensual image to other women didn't have gray hair.

Not *down there*.

That's what she told herself as she set aside the King Kong Ultra Deluxe Number Five vibrator she'd been trying out. She always tested her own products during the development phase and perfected every flaw before handing a prototype over to her manufacturing division.

Her hands trembled as she closed her eyes and tried to calm her pounding heart.

Maybe it wasn't really gray at all. Maybe it was a very light, silvery blonde hair that just happened to spring up among its very dark counterparts. A fluke, like the one hard, dark, skinny french fry always found at the bottom of a hot, piping order.

Or maybe it was the fact that it was ten o'clock on a Friday night—*the* Friday night that had followed the Friday morning when her live-in boyfriend of eight years had walked out on her—and she was still working, thanks to the King Kong Five that went into production first thing Monday morning. The new version of a tried-and-true product would, hopefully, bring back the dozen or so accounts Wild Woman had lost in the past few months to Lust, Lust, Baby!, the number-one ranked company in the industry that had recently been attracting even more attention with a new line of multicolored, multispeed, musical vibrators.

At five that afternoon, she'd noticed that the King Kong head wobbled more than it rotated. After six hours of going back and forth with the engineering department, she'd managed to perfect the movement. Trying it out had been the last step before calling it quits. She was tired. Mentally and physically worn out. No wonder her mind was playing tricks on her.

Then again, it could just be the poor lighting in her office, where she not only designed her latest products, but tested them as well. She had no fluorescent squares overhead like the ones that lit the suite of Wild Woman, Inc. Rather, she'd traded the bright fixtures for several small lamps strategically placed throughout the large room. The light played off the dark, mahogany-paneled walls and rich, lush pink carpeting to create an overall effect that was soft, subtle, *sensual.* The perfect atmosphere to relax and tune in to her body, and unleash the wild woman within.

Usually.

She forced her eyes open, eased her reclining leather

chair upright and smoothed her skirt back down. She double-pressed the button that controlled the red privacy light above her door to make sure that it blinked. It was one thing to be disturbed during a trial test, and quite another to face the world when she was *this close* to a major life crisis.

Close, but not quite there. Not yet.

Pushing to her feet, she rounded the desk. She was not going to panic. Or kick. Or scream. Or cry.

She was going to get a better look.

Fifteen minutes later, she sat on the thick carpet, her skirt hiked up to her waist, her lace panties pushed aside and her legs parted in a V. She adjusted the neck of the desk lamp she'd pulled to the floor with her. A pencil cup toppled over as the cord stretched tight and she went in for a close-up view.

Please, she prayed to the Big Lady Upstairs. *Don't do this to me. Not now. I'll change my ways. I'll smile at that snotty lady up on the tenth floor who spilled cappuccino on me last week. I'll even stop scowling at that guy down on the second who wears the blue leisure suit every Thursday and offers to bend me over like a shotgun. I'll give up my pot of coffee every morning and stop eating those Snickers bars for lunch and I will never, ever tell the salesclerk at Saks that I found something on the sales rack when I really didn't.*

Hope renewed, she gathered her courage and drew in a deep breath. Sixty watts of light illuminated the area in question. Her gaze zeroed in on the hair and a lump formed in her throat.

It was there and it was gray, and it was now officially the worst day of Xandra Farrel's life.

*   *   *

"Knock, knock!" The deep voice rang out as the door to Xandra's office opened.

Xandra lifted her head from her desk, where she'd collapsed after hauling herself off the floor ten minutes earlier. Her gaze went to the man who stood in her doorway.

Albert Sinclair was the head engineer for Wild Woman, Inc., and a bona fide walking, talking Ken doll. He was tall, tanned, and blond with sparkling blue eyes, a white smile, and an athletic body honed from hours of racquetball.

He'd beaten her more times than she could count. Then again, she'd never really played to win. Just to talk. He could talk and listen even better than he could play, thanks to hours of sensitivity training courtesy of his gay parents. He was kind and compassionate, and he was the closest person to her besides her two older sisters.

"Your light was off, so I figured you'd finished the test run. How did it go?"

"Fine."

"We still don't think the rotating head is smooth enough and so a few of us are working late on a new gear. Not to mention, we're brainstorming ideas for the Sextravaganza next month. Have you come up with anything?"

"Not yet." How could she focus on the biggest marketing convention of the year when all she wanted to do was crawl into a hole and never come out again?

"I'm making a midnight food run. Can I bring you anything while I'm out?"

"A gun. Or a noose."

"I was thinking more like Chinese or Thai."

"Only if it's loaded with rat poison and guaranteed to put me out of my misery." She reached for a tissue and swiped at the traitorous tear that slid down her cheek.

Albert's smile faded into a concerned frown. "Oh,

honey, what is it? What's wrong? You're not upset about the Sextravaganza are you? You'll come up with something. You always do."

"I . . ." Xandra shook her head and blinked. "No, no. I mean, I'm concerned, but I've already started my brainstorming list for the convention." She eyed the familiar notebook where she kept her prized lists. She penned them for everything, from What to Do Today to Creative Ways to Kill the Competition to New Condom Colors. "Not that I can really think about that right now. Or a new product. And I doubt I'll be able to think about it tomorrow. Or ever. I might be all washed up professionally as well as personally. I might as well call it quits and go file unemployment. I'll lose my new house and my car and end up bagging it on some street corner, my face all wrinkled up from the elements." At Albert's puzzled stare, she added, "I'm just having a moment, that's all."

"One of those life-is-passing-me-by-and-I'm-cooped-up-watching-from-the-inside-out moments?" He nodded. "I know the feeling. I had one of those myself not more than a few hours ago when I watched the marketing girls head off to happy hour at one of those hot dance clubs, while I stayed here with the rest of my team to work on the gear."

"Not that kind. This one's more of a wait!-this-is-going-too-fast! moment. Like when you ride a bike for the first time without the training wheels. Or when you climb behind the wheel of your first car. Or when you climb into the backseat with the hottest guy in high school who turns out to be a total dud in the sack. Or when you find your first gray hair."

"A gray hair?" Albert walked in, closed the door behind him and perched on the corner of her desk. "Is that what this is all about? Relax, honey. That's why God invented Bjorn over at Bolo's. That man works wonders with bleach and foil. He'll blend it in so you don't even know it's there."

"I seriously doubt that."

"He did mine and I've got *seventeen* of the stubborn little sons of bitches." He pointed near his temple. "Right here. And here. But you can't see even one of them thanks to Bjorn."

"I'm not doubting his ability. I just don't think the hair in question is long enough to foil."

He gave her a get-real look. "Why, your hair is way below your shoulders."

"You've got that right."

"So stop worrying. All you need is a little careful bleaching and bam! problem solved."

"I wish it were that easy." Another tear slid free and then another. "But it's not exactly on my head."

"Let me get this straight." He gave her a we'll-get-to-the-bottom-of-this look. "You've got a gray hair, but it's not exactly on your . . ." Albert's words trailed off as the truth settled in. "Oh. I guess Bjorn's out of the equation now. He only handles the hair up on top."

She bit her lip and blinked, trying to hold back a new flood of tears. "Not that it's the end of the world, mind you."

His smile seemed forced. "That's the spirit."

She blinked frantically. "It's all in the way you look at it."

"Exactly."

"Gray, doesn't have to mean old, right?"

"Right."

"It can also mean mature. Experienced."

"Seasoned," Albert offered, handing her another tissue. "Weathered." At the last word, she cut him a watery stare and he shrugged. "Sorry. Poor word choice. How about . . . knowledgeable?"

She nodded. "Knowledgeable. That's good." She dabbed at her eyes and sniffled. "I'm not losing my youth. I'm merely starting a whole new phase of life."

"You're evolving."

"Right. My life isn't over just because of one silly gray hair. I mean, I think it's just one." Panic rushed through her and her gaze caught his. "What if it's more?"

He shook his head. "I'm sure it's just one."

She nodded and tried to calm her churning stomach. "It's not the end of the world," she said again. "It's not like I'm going to shrivel up and die just because I have a gray hair and I'm alone for the first time in eight years. Alone doesn't necessarily mean lonely. It can mean free. Untethered. Ripe for the picking."

Albert nodded. "You're so ripe, you're about to burst— what do you mean, *'alone'*?"

"I'm in my prime," she rushed on, eager to focus on the positive. "I'm enlightened. I'm mature and knowledgeable and weathered." As soon as the words popped out, a tear squeezed past her lashes. She shook her head. "Hells bells, who am I kidding? I'm past ripe. I'm *this close* to my expiration date. No wonder Mark packed up his laptop and walked out."

"He *left* you? He really left you?"

She nodded and whacked her forehead on the desktop. "Right after he told me I didn't do it for him anymore."

"He *didn't*!"

"What does that mean anyway?" She glanced up through tear-filled eyes. "I don't *do it* for him? If he's talking sex, it's his own fault. He works more than I do, even with the Sextravaganza only a month away. When I initiate, he's always too tired. And when he initiates . . ." She shook her head. "Come to think of it, I can't remember the last time he initiated." She slumped back in her chair. "It's me. I'm old and unattractive and fat. Do you know that I've gained ten pounds since I stopped smoking six months ago?" She pulled open her top desk drawer to reveal several Blow Pops, a roll of SweeTARTS, six packages of Bubble Yum, and some Mentos. "All this extra sugar is killing me."

"Ten extra pounds makes you voluptuous, not fat."

"What about twenty?"

"Chubby."

"And thirty?"

"Metabolically challenged, which you're not. You're attractive and nicely rounded, and Mark is an idiot."

"Mark is perfect. We're perfect. We both like the same things, we both respect each other and we have great sex. Or we *had* great sex. In the beginning. In between his meetings and business trips." Her gaze met Albert's. "It's not supposed to happen like this. We had it all."

"Maybe you just thought you had it all."

She eyed Albert. "What's that supposed to mean?"

"That you love Mexican food and Thai and any and everything spicy, and Mark lived for tofu."

"I eat tofu, too."

"But it doesn't make your mouth water. Deep down in your soul," he tapped his chest, "you don't lust after tofu. You don't yearn for it. You don't *crave* it."

"You're right," she blurted after a long, contemplative moment. "It's me. I tried to hide it, but Mark finally saw past the front to the spicy food junkie who dwells inside."

She shook her head. "I'm a fake. And I'm fat. And I'm old."

"You're not a fake and we've already been over the ten equals voluptuous issue."

"But I *am* getting old."

"You're *only* twenty-nine."

"I'm this close to being thirty. Two months and bam! I'm there."

"It's just another year."

"It's *the* year." She eyed him. "Do you know that a woman's number of fertile eggs decreases by fifty percent when she hits thirty? That's half."

A knowing light filled his blue gaze. "So that's what this is all about. You want a baby."

"Of course I do. I mean, not *now,* at this very moment. But I definitely want one before I hit thirty-five. Or I at least want to be pregnant by then."

"What catastrophic event happens at thirty-five?"

"The measly fifty percent of fertile eggs I have left decreases by *another* fifty percent. Each year thereafter, it's downhill. Fast." She shook her head. "I invested eight years. *Eight.* Mark and I were stable. Comfortable. We'd actually reached the no makeup phase of our relationship. I could walk around the house in nothing but my ratty warm-ups and sparkling personality."

"Maybe that's what scared him off." When she cut him a glance, he grinned, "I'm trying to make you laugh."

"We were so close to the next step in our relationship," she went on.

"Marriage?"

"Are you kidding? You know how I feel about marriage. It's the most archaic form of oppression," Xandra repeated the words that had been drilled into her as a child.

Her widely popular, Harvard-trained sexologist mother and her quiet, conservative conservationist father had been together for thirty-seven years now without benefit of a formal license, their longevity due to her mother's infamous Holy Commitment Trinity. Jacqueline Farrel preached her three-part recipe for relationship success—great sex, shared interests, and mutual respect—every night on her late-night talk show, *Get Sexed Up!*, and Xandra had learned long ago from watching her own parents in action that her mother was right on the money.

"It's a man's way of enslaving a woman," Xandra went on. "And I value my freedom far too much to just give it up just like that." She snapped her fingers. "No thank you."

"I just thought that since Skye finally took the plunge, you might have mellowed to the whole marriage thing."

Xandra's oldest sister, Skye, had walked down the aisle six months ago and enslaved herself to the hottest, hunkiest driver to ever race a NASCAR series. Worse, she'd been ecstatic about the whole thing. She still was.

"Skye's suffering from a major case of lust," Xandra told Albert. "It'll wear off eventually and she'll realize she's made a mistake."

That's what Jacqueline Farrel kept saying to any and everyone who would listen. But Xandra had her doubts. Six months and her sister seemed happier with each day that passed. Content. Complete.

A pang of longing went through her. "My life sucks," she sobbed. "It's crapola with a capital 'CRAP.'"

"You'll find someone else."

"I don't have time to find someone else. Do you know how hard it is for a woman to meet men? Even a single, heterosexual, financially solvent woman with no STDs and all of her teeth? It's nearly impossible. Dorothy from marketing has been dating for the last five years since her divorce and she still hasn't found anyone."

"Dorothy has all of her teeth?"

"Most of them. She's missing one in the back, but she's getting it capped. Anyhow, that's beside the point. I don't have five years to waste on dating, much less another eight years on top of that to get to my comfort zone." She shook her head. "My life *really* sucks."

"So do something about it."

"I am. I'm crying, and in another minute I'm going to go for the stash of cigarettes in my desk and start smoking again."

"That will make the past six months of torture all for naught."

"I either light up, or head for the candy machine down in the lobby. They've got Snickers bars. Lots of Snickers bars."

"That's just a temporary fix."

True. Chocolate, even a lot of chocolate, would only *ease* the pain. It wouldn't make it go away entirely, and it certainly wouldn't change the fact that she'd been dumped *and* she had a gray hair and after eight years, she still hadn't managed to push her company into the industry's top spot—she sat at number two.

She had to *do* something to get her life back on track.

"You're right. I'm sitting here crying when I should be thinking about the future."

"The convention is next month. We need something to really wow everyone and make those boys over at Lust, Lust, Baby! look like amateurs."

"I'm wasting my time agonizing over this relationship business when I should be washing my hands of it entirely."

"I wouldn't go that far. I was thinking more in terms of concentrating on work as a distraction until the pain eases. Then you can get back in the game with a fresh mind and find a new man."

"Forget it. That's the last thing I want. But I am going to come up with something really spectacular and kick this company up a notch. In the meantime, I'm going to find the man."

"But you just said you didn't want a man," Albert reminded her.

"I don't." She smiled as she reached for her notebook and pen and scribbled the heading for her newest list. "I want *the* man." Her smiled widened. "The perfect man to father my baby."

Chapter Two

American women are on a quest for the perfect man!"
Barbara Donnelli's voice sounded in the doorway of the
dressing room.

Jacqueline Farrel glanced up and caught her executive
producer's reflection in the large dressing room mirror.
The makeup artist who'd been powdering Jacqueline's
nose turned to dab at her palette, giving Jacqueline a full
view of her producer and the current issue of *Entertainment Weekly* she held in one perfectly manicured hand.

"He's sweet, sensitive, sexy," Barbara went on, reading
the cover of the issue, "and he's out there waiting for you."
Her gaze met Jacqueline's when she finished. "Guess what
I just read."

"A pile of rubbish used to perpetuate man's desperate
quest to be the center of every woman's universe?"

"Theoretically, yes," Barbara agreed. "But I was speaking in professional terms." As well as being the executive
producer of *Get Sexed Up!*, she was also one of Jacqueline's biggest supporters and one of the smartest women in
the talk show biz. She'd worked on several hit shows, from

Oprah to *The View*, before turning her attention to Jacqueline and the Womanist cause. "This is the front-page headline advertising the review for the first episode of Cherry Chandler's new show *G Spot*."

"I saw that show," said the young brunette who stood in the far corner of the room filling the coffee machine with fresh ground Colombian. Alexis Dupree was a twenty-something graduate of the University of California—Berkeley with a wide smile and an eagerness to please. "It was so cool." When Barbara and Jacqueline turned et-tu-Brute? looks on her, she shrugged. "I mean, it was okay. It could have been better if it hadn't promoted the whole man as a perfect animal image—which he's not. Not by a long shot. And, of course, the only reason I watched was to see what we're up against—which isn't much since the show is so totally unrealistic."

"Man, because he *is* a man, is completely imperfect," Jacqueline said as she held up her chin for the makeup artist who dabbed her with blush. "Donovan is the closest thing to a perfect man that I've ever come across." Donovan Martin was her significant other for the past thirty-seven years and the father of her three daughters. "And even he falls sadly short, despite the fact that he makes apple muffins and gives a really great foot massage."

The muffins and the massages just weren't enough to make up for the fact that she had to put the toilet seat back down and resqueeze the toothpaste from the bottom up and pick up his dirty socks that he insisted on leaving near the coffee table.

Of course, that was only for the six months she actually spent at the home they shared in Georgetown, Texas, the small college town where she'd been born and raised. For the rest of the year, she lived in her own apartment in L.A.

where she taped *Get Sexed Up!* and worked on her new book projects. Meanwhile, Donovan stayed home, lectured at Southwestern University, and added to his mountain of dirty socks.

"Never met a perfect man myself," said Connie the makeup artist as she reached for a lip pencil from her tackle box. "I've met crazy men, perverted men, funny men, depressing men—the whole shebang—but not a one of them has even come close to perfect. Except maybe that hunky son-in-law of yours."

Jacqueline ignored the reference to Clint MacAllister, the famous NASCAR driver who'd corrupted her oldest daughter, Skye. She wasn't going to angst anymore over the incident. She still had two daughters left. Her youngest, Xandra, was a walking, talking example of the Holy Commitment Trinity. Her middle daughter, Eve, wasn't as on track as Xandra, but she was single and successful and a Farrel, so there was hope.

"The whole concept of a perfect man is completely far-fetched," Jacqueline went on. "It's ludicrous."

"Unfortunately, there are three-and-a-half million viewers who don't agree with you." Barbara stepped inside the room and walked over to lean against the wall-length vanity. The woman wore a navy suit and trendy pumps. She had classic Italian looks with her dark brown hair, olive complexion and rich brown eyes, and a classic Italian attitude thanks to five older brothers—meaning she was tough. And intimidating.

Especially when she started quoting viewing statistics.

The last time she'd recited statistics, Jacqueline had found her no-nonsense beige and chrome set redecorated in a bright, vivid, blinding red.

She'd been living on Tums ever since.

"Three and a half," Barbara went on. "That's one-point-five million more viewers than we currently have, and the show's been on less than a month. Cherry Chandler has the right idea."

"Cherry Chandler has set women back at least a hundred years," Jacqueline said.

Cherry Chandler was the author of the *New York Times* best-selling *Sensitive* series. She was Jacqueline's polar opposite when it came to advising the sexes—namely she urged every woman to bend over backward to please her man. Cherry had written everything from *The Sensitive Wife* to *The Sensitive Girlfriend* to *The Sensitive Mistress* to the current best seller *The Sensitive Seductress*.

She was the same age as Jacqueline—they'd graduated together at Harvard—but she looked at least ten years younger thanks to a fortune spent on cosmetic surgery. She had long blonde hair and straight white teeth and breasts big enough to float several people to safety should she ever find her Passion Plane—the hot pink 747 she'd bought the previous year—plunging into the ocean during one of her numerous publicity tours.

"Her show is a hit." At Jacqueline's outraged look, Barbara shrugged. "Look, I'm not agreeing one way or another with her doctrine, per se. I'm talking about the way she promotes that doctrine. Her show is fun and practical. She gives advice that women can use in their daily lives."

"Urging a woman to apply for financial aid to fill out a few butt cheek dimples so that she looks better in a swimsuit is not practical. Women don't need to hear that nonsense."

"Maybe not." Barbara's gaze zeroed in on Jacqueline. "But women don't need to hear a lecture on the dangers of wallpaper either, which you gave last week during Monday's episode."

"Weren't you listening? Wallpaper isn't dangerous in and of itself," Jacqueline said before blotting her lips on the Kleenex that Connie handed her. "It's the act of picking out wallpaper that poses the threat. Women, all too often, find themselves bending and molding their tastes to match those of their significant other. It's a terrible process that can become a deadly habit in life. First you're compromising on the wallpaper pattern. Then you're missing your favorite show so that he can watch WWE on Monday nights. Then you're eating pizza when you would rather be having a nice Greek salad with extra olive oil. One thing leads to another, and before you know it, you're rotting away in an emotional prison, while he's enjoying his freedom."

"So go with paneling instead of wallpaper. Or paint. Or stucco."

"The point is not the wallpaper. It's to stand firm in your opinions."

"Which is *my* point. You can't stand firm in your opinions if there's no one to stand firm against. Our viewers don't just need relationship advice, they need advice on how to get into a relationship in the first place. They need tips to help them find their Holy Commitment Man. They need Smart Dating."

"Smart what?"

"Smart *Dating*. It's going to be an ongoing series on the show where we'll feature four women from major cities across the country. We'll have our cameras follow them during a typical evening out to meet prospective men. Then we'll have you review the tapes and give them dating advice. What they're doing right. What they're doing wrong."

"I don't think so." Jacqueline shook her head. "It's all wrong for the show. We're about freedom. About rejoicing in your femininity. About loving yourself first and foremost."

"Eighty percent of our viewers are single."

"Then we're doing our job."

"They're single, but not by choice. Our average viewer is a professional, college-educated career woman who believes in love and marriage and family, and wants all three."

"Says who?"

"Our polls. See, our show is justification to all those single women who don't have a significant other. They're busy in their careers and they're looking for validation for all the Saturday nights they spend at home working rather than dating. But when they reach the settling-down point, they're going to turn us off and turn on Cherry because she validates their longing for that special someone. She feeds the notion that he is out there and that they can actually find him." Barbara shook her head. "We have to feed that need before she steals all our viewers. We're doing Smart Dating."

"And if I object?" Jacqueline's gaze met Barbara's.

"Objection noted, but majority rules."

"It's one against one right now."

"One against three." She gestured to the other two women in the room, who gave Jacqueline a sheepish look before sliding their hands into the air. "Not to mention I've polled everyone from my boss, down the loop to the bagel guy. It's a unanimous yes so far." Barbara's voice softened a notch. "You're a wonderful host, Jacqueline, and you have a wonderful message. But if we don't keep up our ratings, then there'll be no show, which means no forum for your message."

"Just do it, Dr. Farrel," Connie said as she recapped several tubes and deposited them into her tackle box. "It sounds fun."

"Fun and cool," Alexis added. "I think it's a great idea."

Barbara smiled. "We're already taking applications for the first batch of daters. We'll start here in L.A., then we're airborne for the other cities on our list. I'll get you the profiles as soon as we've narrowed them down. You can select the final four for each episode. You're the host, after all."

"Sure, I am," Jacqueline grumbled as Barbara turned to leave.

"I can't wait for the new show," Alexis said as she refilled the sugar dispenser. "It's so *now.*"

"'Now?' Why, it's positively archaic. Not to mention stressful and pointless. Imagine getting all dressed up to go out and impress a man." Jacqueline shook her head. "It's ridiculous."

"Not the Smart Dating show. Cherry's Mr. Perfect segment." Alexis left the sugar dispenser, walked over and picked up the copy of *Entertainment Weekly* Barbara had left on the vanity. Flipping open the magazine, she found the review. "It says here she's going to talk about physical characteristics that lend themselves to the perfect man."

"For the last time, there is no such thing."

"Amen," Connie said as she hefted her tackle box and started for the door. "Have a good taping, Doc."

"Okay, so maybe the perfect man doesn't exist," Alexis said when Connie left, "but the notion is sort of fun. What if he did? What if he was standing just on the other side of that door? My life could change just like that. No more Friday nights out with the girls. No more Saturdays doing laundry. No more Saturday nights with my *Braveheart* DVD."

"No more closed toilet lids."

"Exactly." Alexis grinned. "Sometimes I lift my own lid and pretend a man—my man—left it up. Check this out"—she turned her attention to the magazine—"'Cherry's going to have some really big-name hunks on the show—perfect man specimens. Brad Pitt is going to be there. And Sean Connery. And—ohmigod—Mel Gibson!" Alexis held out the magazine. "You really should look at this lineup. It's incredible."

"I don't want to look."

Looking would mean that she might actually care what big names Cherry managed to lure onto her propagandist show.

Even more, looking would mean that Jacqueline might actually see the woman as serious competition. Which she didn't. Not back in college when Cherry had won an apprenticeship at Johnson & Johnson helping the company conduct their newest sex study, thanks to her short skirts and flirtatious smiles and the fact that the final three judges had all been men. And she certainly didn't care now. "The only thing I want is a cup of coffee," Jacqueline said. "And a Tums."

Smart Dating.

The title echoed in her head and her stomach heaved.

She drew in a deep breath and tried to quiet her nerves. So it wasn't the greatest title? The concept *was* good. It wasn't enough to know the secret of long-term relationship success—namely the Holy Commitment Trinity and its three all-important points. Her viewers deserved to know how to find a Holy Commitment mate. They needed to know where to look and how to present themselves and, overall, how to recognize someone with Holy Commitment potential.

Her viewers needed her—poor Alexis was proof of that.

Jacqueline drew in a deep breath and squared her shoulders. She could endure an upset stomach if it meant helping needy women like Alexis. If she refused to work on the series, there would be a whole mass of desperate, misguided women out searching for a myth—Mr. Perfect, a man who actually put the toilet seat down after he flushed.

No such creature existed, and it was her duty as a teacher and a womanist to enlighten the masses.

But first she needed to know what she was up against.

"Maybe I'll just take a little peek," she said as she reached for the magazine.

Chapter Three

Xandra buried her head beneath the pillow and prayed for the ringing to stop.

Rrrrrring!

She felt for another pillow and added it to the growing pile on her head.

Rrrrrring!

Groping for the covers, she hauled them up over the pillows. There. Ah, blessed si—

Click.

"This is Xandra. You know what to do . . ." *Beep.*

"Hey, sis. I know you're there. Pick up."

"Maybe I'm not here," Xandra grumbled to herself.

"Moping won't help. Mark's a jerk and you're better off without him."

"I'm not moping, I moped last night. Now I'm sleeping," Xandra replied to the machine. At least she was trying to sleep. She'd been trying all night long, in fact. With very little luck. Despite her resolve to shape up and get her life back on track, she'd slumped home, collapsed into a pint of the only thing she had that was even close to chocolate ice cream—a pint of fat-free raspberry sorbet. She'd ended up with a stomachache, a splitting headache, and the sudden urge to cut up what was left of Mark's things. The problem? He'd taken everything except the bedroom and living room sets—both of which she'd brought into the relationship.

As if Skye read the thoughts racing through her head, her sister said, "At least you were smart enough to keep your financial situation separate from his. Otherwise, you would be in for a battle over the house."

"It's *my* house," Xandra grumbled. They'd decided six months ago to trade their apartment for a bigger place. They'd wanted to plant roots. To grow a family.

At least that's what she'd wanted, and she'd assumed that he'd wanted the same because he'd never said anything otherwise.

Still, she should have known something wasn't right. When it had come time to actually look for a house, he'd always been too busy with his job. Too tired from his job. Too stressed over his job. Too . . . something. So she'd picked it out all by herself. Applied for the mortgage by herself, and now she was here.

All by herself.

"Stop wallowing in self-pity and pick up this phone right now, Xandra Michelle Elizabeth Farrel."

"I'm not wallowing." She'd done that last night and now she was too exhausted to haul herself out of bed and walk the few feet to the cordless phone she'd left on her dresser the night before.

"Then don't say I didn't try to warn you when the doorbell rings in about five minutes and it's Mom. It'll be your own fault because you didn't have the common courtesy to answer the telephone and talk to your big sis—"

"Mom's on the way?" Xandra blurted into the phone after throwing off the covers and sprinting to the dresser.

"I knew you were there."

"Why is Mom coming here?" Xandra shook her head and tried to think. "Did she have a layover? Or is she coming on purpose? Please tell me she's not coming on purpose? You didn't tell her about Mark did you? Because then I'll have to pull myself together and act like nothing's wrong and—" Her words stumbled to a halt as she glanced in the mirror. "Yikes, I can't do this now. I look like death and she'll think it's over Mark—a man—and she'll totally freak out because I let him do this to me." She glanced out the window at the street below before reaching for her warm-ups. "I've got to get out of here."

"Slow down."

"You don't understand. I can't do Mom right now. I'll have to act like everything's okay and then I'll have to listen to what's wrong in her life—namely you and Eve who constantly monopolize her attention by not being the perfect Farrel children."

"Hey, I've got a Holy Commitment Man. I've just got love and marriage to go along with it. It's Eve who totally rejects the idea of *any* lasting relationship."

"You're both driving her nuts, which means she drives me nuts."

"Because you're the only one who listens to her."

"I don't have a choice. She's my mother. It's listen or live with the consequences."

"Namely?"

"A load of guilt that I don't need since I'm already feeling rotten right now. I can't take Mom in person. I can't even take her on the phone. I need peace and quiet and several aspirin and a big chocolate doughnut and a cigarette. Oh, God. I'm not just craving one or the other now. I want to eat *and* smoke. Life totally bites—"

"Mom's not coming."

The sweatshirt stalled over Xandra's head. "What do you mean?"

"I wanted to get you to the phone."

She pulled the shirt off and tossed it to the floor. "You're the devil." She stumbled back and collapsed onto the bed.

"Don't I wish. Then I could shoot a few flames out of the nearest orifice and I wouldn't be in such a mess."

"What are you talking about?" Xandra stretched out, pulled the covers up to her neck and closed her eyes.

"I'm making dinner."

"It's . . ."—Xandra lifted her head long enough to squint at the clock on her nightstand—"eight o'clock in the morning."

"Already? The last time I looked, it was only seven."

"Why are you making dinner at eight in the morning?"

"Because I'm cooking for Clint's entire family. All sixteen of them, plus his great aunt Myrtle who eats like a horse. I'm doing Italian."

"And the problem is?"

"Chicken tortellini *and* spinach pasta *and* baked ziti *and* five-cheese lasagna *and* chicken Parmesan *and* stuffed ravioli *and* sweet pepper bruschetta. Seven dishes, less than eight hours before everyone arrives, and I can only do two dishes at once because my oven is too small. That's why I had to get an early start. I have to bake everything first, then start reheating because while one dish is in the oven, another is cooling off."

"Life's a real bitch sometimes."

"Exactly. But I really want things to go well for tonight's announcement."

"Skye, why are you torturing me the morning after the worst day of my— What announcement?"

"Well, since you can't make it for dinner, I might as well tell you now."

"I'm in Houston and you're in Dallas. Dropping by for dinner isn't exactly an option. Besides, you didn't tell me tonight was that important. I thought you were just nervous to have Clint's entire family at your place for the first time since the wedding."

"I am, and I only agreed to do it because I wanted everyone here when Clint and I break the news."

"Which is?"

"We've decided to procreate."

"Come again?"

"We're going to have a baby!"

Xandra's eyes snapped open and she bolted into a sitting position. "When?"

"Nine months from the date that his sperm manages to fertilize my egg, I suppose."

"So you're not pregnant now?"

"Not yet. But we've decided to try. My business is going well and Clint just found a driver for the new car he's been working on—it's Linc Adams, who's every bit as good as Clint ever was, even if he is sort of a womanizer. Things are great and the timing couldn't be more perfect for a baby. Isn't that wonderful?"

"Absolutely."

"I didn't think so at first. I was actually a little freaked out by the idea. I mean, I've always wanted kids. Some day. But now Clint's nieces and nephews have really made me see what I'm missing."

"I thought you hated the little buggers."

"I didn't *hate* them. I just didn't *like* them. They're loud and obnoxious and they've always got stuff on their hands, and Clint's youngest brother's daughter—Suzee—always beats me at Monopoly."

Xandra laughed. "A six-year-old beats you at Monopoly."

"She's practically seven, and she cheats. But you're missing the point."

"Which is?"

"When you get past all the sticky hands and runny noses and Monopoly cheating, the kids can be really sweet at times. Even Suzee. She made me a card for my birthday out of painted macaroni."

"Not exactly a new pair of Jimmy Choos." Xandra's oldest sister lived for trendy shoes.

"No, but I liked it anyway," Skye said. "Can you believe that? I liked it even better than a pair of new shoes. That's when I knew it was time to give the whole baby thing a try. So Clint and I talked, and here we are: on the verge of making our very own baby boy."

"A boy?"

"Clint really wants a boy. I'd be happy with either, but I'm keeping my fingers crossed that a male sperm hits the finish line first."

"That's great." Xandra sniffled and blinked back a wave of unexpected tears. "I'm happy for you." Another sniffle and several more blinks. "I'm really happy."

"You're crying."

"Yes, but I'm still happy for you. Mark and I were this close to making our own babies."

"You and Mark had decided on children?"

"Yes. Well, sort of. I decided. He didn't exactly know it. Yet. But we were there. We'd gotten the house. Filling it with babies was the next step."

"After eight years of dating and then living together, marriage was the next step."

"You sound like Albert."

"Albert's a smart guy."

"I don't *do* marriage."

"Don't knock it until you've tried it."

"I haven't tried cabbage, but I still know I don't like it."

"Marriage isn't like cabbage. It's like a foreign dessert whose name you can't pronounce. It's wonderful once you work up the nerve to take the first bite."

"Don't let Mom hear you say that."

"I've said it to Mom."

"And what does she say?"

"That I'm still delirious with lust. That, or I've got a bona fide medical condition that's affecting my cognitive abilities. I swear every time I see her, she holds her hand to my forehead to check for a fever. When she doesn't find one, she rolls around to possibility number three—Clint has me brainwashed. She even told Dad she was thinking about hiring one of those deprogrammers to kidnap me and undo the damage. Of course, he killed that idea. At least he understands."

"Clint as a cult." Xandra sniffled and wiped the one traitorous tear that slid down her cheek. "I can definitely see that. He has charisma. Mark had charisma, too."

"Mark had a selfish streak. He wanted what he wanted, and to hell with you."

"That's not true."

"What happened to all of your eighties rock CDs?"

"I still have them. They're in a box in the back of my closet." Along with her favorite Madonna pillow and her pink fuzzy bathrobe with Jon Bon Jovi silk-screened across the back and a dozen of her other favorite things she'd saved from her teenage years.

"That's what I mean. You love eighties music and Mark liked jazz."

"And?"

"And which type of CDs do you keep on the shelf next to your stereo?"

"The jazz. But I like jazz, too."

"Maybe, but you don't love it, and you certainly don't love Mark."

"I don't do romantic love. Besides, love isn't the point. We oozed long-term commitment. We liked the same things. We respected each other. We had great sex." At Skye's silence, Xandra added, "Okay, so it was so-so sex most of the time, but we were comfortable."

A sincere note crept into Skye's voice. "There is more to a relationship than the Holy Commitment Trinity, whether you believe it or not. And when you least suspect, it'll jump up and bite you on the butt."

"Now that Mark's gone, there'll be no more butt-biting. Not that he ever actually bit my butt, but at least there was hope." She shook her head. "I'm through with men and relationships." Despite her words, she felt a small sense of hope steal through her. As if Skye were right. As if there were more to a relationship and Xandra had yet to find it.

As if.

She shook away the thought, said good-bye and punched the OFF button on the phone.

"She was right about one thing," she told her reflection when she hauled herself back to the mirror to face the horrific-looking woman staring back at her. "You're not solving anything by lazing away in bed with raccoon eyes and hair straight out of a Don King promo. "It's time to get moving. Personally and professionally."

Starting with a shower, a good blow-dry, and some water-proof mascara. Then it was on to her most important order of business—the Sextravaganza project. She planned to spend the morning researching various products on the Web and compiling a Hot Prospects list based on what the market already offered, and what it lacked. After that, she would run the ideas by Albert during racquetball.

First things first . . .

Fifteen minutes later, she'd unearthed her favorite Aero-smith CD from the Favorite Things box in the back of her closet. She'd just slid on her Bon Jovi bathrobe and fed a disc into the CD player downstairs when the doorbell rang.

Aerosmith's "Cryin'" filled the air as she pulled open the front door to find her neighbor standing on the front stoop.

Leslie Vandergarten lived just across the street to the left. The petite blonde was typical of the thirty-something married set that dominated one of Houston's oldest neighborhoods of restored turn-of-the-century homes. Educated, well-off, with a steaming latte in one hand and a set of Lincoln Navigator keys in the other.

Today, the latte and keys dominated one hand while a large white bakery bag overwhelmed the other.

Her gaze swept Xandra from top to bottom and she shook her head. "It looks like I'm just in time."

"What are you talking about?"

"You poor, poor, *poor* thing," Leslie rushed on as she shoved the bag at Xandra and pushed her way inside. "Why, it's a travesty, that's what it is."

"You said it." How anyone could bounce around and

look so perky at eight A.M. on a Saturday morning was a sin against womankind as far as Xandra was concerned.

She eyed Leslie who wore black spandex biker shorts and an itty-bitty tank top that wouldn't even come close to housing even one of Xandra's sizable D-cup breasts.

"I couldn't make my Pilates class without stopping by first to see how you were doing. Just so you know, we all thought he was a jerk. A scoundrel. A *loser*. Even if he did know how to dress."

"I take it you're talking about Mark."

"Of course I'm talking about Mark. I saw it all myself yesterday morning. I was on my way to my yoga class, when I saw the moving van." She shook her head. "Why, you must be stunned. Devastated. *Destroyed.* Imagine, having your man just up and walk out on you." She snapped her fingers. "Just like that. Why, it's terrible. Tragic. *Horrific.*" She gave Xandra a smile. "But the good thing is, you don't have to go through any of it alone. I've already activated the neighborhood phone tree. It's part of the ladies' neighborhood watch association. We use it for emergencies only. Situations that require a multitude of emotional support. The men's neighborhood watch handles the actual physical stuff like patrolling for strange people or suspicious goings on."

"I didn't know that."

Leslie smiled. "You won't go through any of this alone. We're all here for you. And don't you worry. You'll find someone."

"I don't want anyone."

"Denial," Leslie sang out, refusing to comprehend the fact that Xandra truly had given up on men. She had her belief system and it revolved around the old if-you-fall-out-of-the-saddle-you-climb-back-on theme.

Not Xandra. Who needed to sit in a saddle when she could bypass the horse entirely and get herself a nice, comfy sports car with leather interior and a kick-ass sound system? She was coasting solo from here on out, focusing on her business while she perfected her Perfect Daddy list. Then she would do the procreation thing and bam! she would be adding a car seat to the whole sports car scenario.

"Once you grieve," Leslie went on, "you'll graduate to the healing phase. Then you'll be ready to dive back into the dating pool. And I know just the guy."

"Thanks, but no—"

"Why, he's perfect for you." Leslie waved off her objection. "He's a stock broker, good-looking, and itching to settle down. I know he'll take one look at you and fall hard and fast. Why, you've got so much to offer a man. You're beautiful, successful, and financially independent. You've got your own house—albeit a house in sore need of renovation—in one of the oldest and most well-kept neighborhoods in Houston. Speaking of which, when do you suppose you're going to start the actual renovations? I hate to ask at a time like this, but as well as chairing the ladies' neighborhood weight watch, I'm also chairwoman for the neighborhood renovation committee." She glanced around before whispering, "I hate to tell you, but people are asking."

"The project starts first thing Monday." At least that's what the message on Xandra's answering machine had said when she'd hauled herself home late last night after finishing the King Kong Ultra Deluxe.

"You did choose someone from the list I gave you? A bad contractor can be your worst nightmare. The neighborhood is an investment for us all and we wouldn't want a substandard house dragging down everyone's property values, albeit completely unintentionally." Any more than they wanted a single woman upsetting the coupled status quo that dominated the neighborhood.

Xandra had chosen the third contractor on the coveted list since she'd seen their work firsthand and been very impressed.

Great work. That's why she'd chosen Hire-a-Hunk. Her choice certainly had nothing to do with the fact that the company was owned by one Beau Hollister. A blast from her high school past and the hottest looking guy to ever ride a motorcycle down the streets of Georgetown, Texas. It wasn't as if she actually expected to see him again.

Sure, she'd caught a glimpse of him eight months ago when his company had remodeled the apartment directly above her old place, but that had been pure luck. She'd come home to change thanks to a diet soda that had fallen into her lap and a run in her sheer black stockings the size of the Grand Canyon. She'd just let herself into the apartment when she'd heard his voice. She'd turned in time to see him walk toward the staircase to inspect the work his team had just completed.

She'd seen him, but he hadn't actually seen her. Thankfully. Because then he might have recognized her and she would have had to talk to him with a huge cola stain on the front of her skirt and a run in her panty hose, and then she would have had the worst day of her life months ago rather than just yesterday.

Besides, she'd had three planning meetings with his company so far, and he'd yet to attend any of them. Instead, she'd met with his assistant, Annabelle Marshall, who dealt with all the residential renovation projects while Beau handled the commercial side. At least that's what Annabelle had told her when she'd asked.

"The company architect is supposed to drop by the final plans later today for my approval. Then it's full speed ahead on Monday," Xandra said.

"Great." Leslie smiled. "That's just great, and it's perfect timing, too. Why, you just concentrate on whipping this place into shape and you'll forget all about what's-his-name. Anyhow, have a nice bran muffin"—she indicated the white bakery bag—"and don't go near any sharp objects or fat-laden food. Hugs and kisses." She gave a wave and walked out into the bright morning sunlight.

Xandra took one look into the bag and got a good whiff, and then crumpled it closed. It was definitely too early for visitors and especially too early for bran. She set the bag on a magazine stand near the door and turned to head upstairs.

The bleakness of the room stopped her and she simply stood there for a long moment, her gaze fixed on the sofa and coffee table that occupied the center of the living room, the small stereo system in the far corner. There was nothing else in the room. He'd taken his Chanel lamps and his stainless steel end tables. And the framed print from the Museum of Modern Art he'd brought back from one of his business trips to New York. And even the authentic Persian rug he'd brought her as a gift from one of his trips overseas.

The cold hardwood floor seeped through the soles of her feet and creaked when she shifted her weight. He'd hated the hardwood floor. And the frieze work that lined the upper portion of the walls. And the wooden staircase. And the entire house in general.

But she'd fallen in love with it at first glance because its wraparound porch and gingerbread shutters reminded her of the house where she'd grown up with her sisters and her grandmother. Her parents had lived in the five-bedroom, two-story house, as well, but they'd always been off somewhere. Her mother had had book tours and speaking engagements and her college professor father had been away fighting for animal rights or doing research for one of his textbooks. And so it had been Xandra and her sisters and her grammie.

She'd loved that house because she'd been safe there. Safe from the boys who'd chant "Here comes Mrs. Boss Hogg"—the overweight wife of the villain in the hit TV show *The Dukes of Hazzard*—when Xandra had always longed to be sexy, svelte Daisy Duke.

At home there'd been no one judging her or ridiculing her. There'd just been Grammie and the sweet scent of vanilla extract and acceptance.

She blinked back a sudden rush of tears and squared her shoulders. She wasn't going to get caught up in the past. It was all about the future now. Time to be proactive. To take charge of her life again. To turn back the clock, pick up where she'd inadvertently left off, and *make* things happen.

She headed up the stairs, into the bathroom and over to the medicine cabinet. She eyed the extra large box of un-used condoms sitting inside and burst into tears. Not because she loved the person who'd purchased the box or because she wanted him back, but because she'd wasted eight years on a man. The wrong man. Eight long years with the wrong man. Eight of her best years with the wrong man.

She wasn't wasting another minute.

Downstairs she cranked up the Aerosmith CD to a level that would have driven Mark nuts, lit the log in her fire-place, and watched the flames flare to life.

"Here's to new beginnings." Tearing open the box of condoms, she pulled a package free and tossed it into the fire. The plastic curled and sparked as she listened to Steven Tyler wail about lost love.

She hiked up her Jon Bon Jovi robe around her calves and sat down on the stone ledge that extended from the fireplace. She positioned herself near the grate, facing the fireplace, the box next to her.

"You're a jerk," she said as she tossed another condom into the fire. "And a commitment-phobic control freak. You're insensitive. You're juvenile. And overall, you suck."

By the time the song had faded into the next, she'd tossed a handful of condoms and called Mark every name she could think of. She actually felt a little better.

"You definitely suck," she said again as she leaned in with another condom package. Flames licked at the plastic. "You suck, you suck, you *really* suck."

"I've never liked that brand of condoms myself, but don't you think you're being a little harsh?"

The deep voice came from behind her, just above the wail of music. She half turned. Flames licked at her fingers and she dropped the package with a loud yelp.

Pain shot through her and scrambled her brain for the next few heartbeats until the voice sounded again and jerked her back to reality.

To the fact that she had a stranger standing not more than a few feet away.

Her gaze swiveled from her singed fingertips to the shadow outlined in the bright morning sunlight spilling through the bay windows behind him. Her heart revved faster than her brother-in-law's infamous #62 Chevy at the starting gate of the Daytona 500. But the cause had nothing to do with excitement and everything to do with fear.

There was a stranger in her house. *This* close to her. Towering over where she sat on the ledge of the fireplace. Planning to do only God knew what.

She opened her mouth to scream, but all that came out was a frenzied yelp as heat licked at her thigh. Her attention snapped back to her lap.

Fear faded into full-blown panic as she realized she wasn't just facing off with an intruder.

She'd dropped the flaming condom into her lap and now she was on fire.

Chapter Four

Okay, so she wasn't actually on fire.

The condom package was on fire, flaming right there in her lap, the flames licking at the terry cloth of her robe, turning the faded pink a crisp black . . .

Cripes, she *was* on fire!

Her heart jumped into her throat as she slapped the package out of her lap and swatted at the sparks. But it wasn't enough. While one spark died, another flared. And another. And—

The thought stalled as the Madonna pillow she'd unearthed from her box of treasures hit her square in the lap and smothered everything beneath.

"Christ, I'm so sorry. I didn't mean to startle you," the deep voice sounded far away this time and barely penetrated the frantic *bam, bam, bam* of her heart.

Her gaze hooked on the back of Madonna's head and she slowly turned her favorite pillow over to see the damage to her robe. The material was so thick that the flames hadn't reached her skin, but her robe was a mess. Several spots had been singed. Madonna didn't just have black ringing her eyes now. Half of one cheek was singed and burnt spots mottled her Marilyn Monroe hairdo.

Xandra had the sudden insane urge to cry.

Not that she was going to. It was just a pillow and a robe. Granted, her favorite pillow and robe. The pillow and robe, in fact, that she'd curled up with every Saturday night to watch TV with her grandmother while she'd been growing up. Meanwhile, all the rest of Georgetown High had been keeping company at Uncle Funkel's Bar-B-Que out near Interstate 10. *The* hangout for all the popular kids.

Xandra, of course, had been there only once and that was on a weekday when she'd gone with Grammie to pick up sliced beef sandwiches and potato salad for dinner.

"I knocked, but you didn't answer," the voice went on, drawing her attention away from the past and back to the present. "I don't normally walk into anyone's house, but we're on a time limit with this project. The plans have to be approved by Monday morning, or we lose an entire day of work."

Project. Plans. Work.

The words registered in her mind and sent a rush of relief, followed by a wave of anxiety because she knew he wasn't some anonymous intruder. His voice was too deep. Too stirring. Too familiar.

Memories pushed and pulled at her brain and images rushed at her. A tall teenage boy wearing a Dallas Cowboys jersey and worn Levi's. A sunny Saturday afternoon. A flat tire on her grammie's old Bonneville. Strong, tanned fingers working at the wrench. A twinkling, violet-colored gaze that caught and held hers and made her stomach hollow out. A deep, rich voice that made her hands tremble.

Like now.

She clutched the throw pillow, glanced up and found

herself eye level with the zipper of his jeans. She meant to look north. She really did. But he was so close, and it was right there and she wasn't exactly thinking straight thanks to all the memories buzzing inside her and her near death experience with the flaming condom.

Soft, worn denim cupped a rather impressive bulge. Her stomach fluttered and she actually swallowed.

A crazy reaction for a woman who'd seen more than her fair share of male members. Sure, most of them were rubber reproductions, but they were so realistic—thanks to her fabulous engineering department and Wild Woman's quest for perfection—she might well have been staring at the real thing. She was a seasoned veteran when it came to penises. Her stomach simply did not flutter, particularly when the penis in question was completely concealed beneath the faded denim.

Then again, maybe that was the charm. A penis-in-hiding opened the door for tremendous possibilities. It made her think of a hot, moonlit night and slippery bodies and lots of gasping and moaning and . . .

Him.

She forced her gaze upward, and the stomach fluttering only got worse because the view got even better.

He wore a soft, white cotton T-shirt, the ends tucked into the waistband of his pants. The material clung to a wide, impressive chest. The faint outline of his nipples pressed against the cotton. The chest spread into a broad set of shoulders. A dark, tanned neck extended from the neckline of his T-shirt. The neck gave way to a broad jaw covered with dark stubble, a strong chin and lips that would have seemed a tad too large if they hadn't been so damned sensual at the same time. His mouth crooked up at the corner and a dimple cut the side of his face. Her heart actually skipped a beat, and then it stopped altogether when her gaze collided with his.

Okay, finding the gray hair last night had been bad enough. Humiliating. *The* worst moment of her life.

Until now. It *was* him.

"My life *really* sucks," she murmured, and then she did the only thing a woman could do when faced with the man who'd given her the worst five minutes of her sexually active life.

She started to laugh.

Beau Hollister loved women and so the hard-on pressing tight against his jeans came as no surprise.

He'd fallen hard and fast years back the first moment he'd set eyes on Susie Thorton's Malibu Barbie. Susie had lived next door to Beau's family—an all male household that consisted of his father and three younger brothers. Since Beau's mother had passed away from breast cancer when he'd been seven years old, the only female he'd ever kept company with had been a wheat-colored lab named Honey. But then Susie had moved next door. He'd done his best, like any ten-year-old boy when faced with a cootie-carrying *girl,* to make her life a living hell. He'd trampled her baby doll with his bicycle, shot spit wads at her while she played tea party on the back porch, and fired his water gun straight into the window of her first slumber party.

He'd hated her, and she'd hated him, and all had been right with his male-dominated world. Then one summer afternoon everything had changed. That had been the summer he'd turned eleven and spied his dad kissing his fifth-grade music teacher. *Kissing,* of all things.

Beau had been hurt, then he'd been mad, and then he'd glimpsed an actual tongue and he'd been intrigued. For a few seconds. Then he'd been mad again and he'd raced off to gather some chinaberries for his slingshot. He couldn't wait to see how many shots it took to get his dad away from Miss Cline.

He'd been up in Susie's tree gathering berries when she'd wandered outside with her Barbie. He'd meant to shoot off a few practice shots at her, but then her mother had called her back inside. He'd climbed down and been about to stamp the daylights out of her Barbie when he'd realized that it wasn't just any Barbie.

It was a *naked* Barbie.

Just like that, his belief system had done a complete one-eighty. One glance at all those interesting curves and that long blonde hair and those bluer-than-blue eyes, and he'd started to wonder at the possibilities.

Not that he fancied blondes.

Beau loved all women. From brunettes to redheads to platinum blondes, and everything in between. They could be short or tall. Thin or voluptuous. Outgoing or reserved. It didn't matter. They were females and there was just something about the softness of their skin, or the way their eyes twinkled when he let his gaze linger a little too long, or the way their terry cloth robe gaped at the neckline when they leaned over and tossed a condom into the fireplace, or the way their full lips formed the word "suck" . . .

Yep, Beau loved women, all right, and so it only made sense that he would be turned on right now.

Especially when faced with the one woman who'd given him the best five minutes of his life, and a world of hurt thereafter.

Xandra Farrel.

It was her. Right here. Right now. In the flesh.

While he'd recognized her name on the job order weeks

ago, he'd been pretty certain it wasn't *his* Xandra Farrel. After all, Houston was a huge city. There were thousands of Farrels. Undoubtedly one of them was named Xandra, and so he hadn't really thought that it would be her.

At the same time, he'd known there was a chance and so he'd offered to drop off the plans for his assistant so she could take her son to a birthday party. Annabelle usually handled all the residential jobs and assigned them accordingly, but this one was different. This wasn't just a renovation. It was a complete restoration of one of the oldest houses in downtown Houston, and the chance to turn his glorified handyman service into a reputable contracting and construction business. Beau was spearheading this job himself and he wanted things to go perfectly, and so he'd needed to know the truth about the owner before it posed a threat to his concentration.

Right now he didn't have a hammer or a saw in his hands, but come Monday he would, and he would need to be completely, totally focused. He couldn't afford to be caught off guard by a woman. *The* woman.

Aw, hell.

His gaze swept from her pale blonde hair pulled back in a loose ponytail to her toes and back up again. Her soft, terry cloth robe was belted loosely at the waist. The edges parted to reveal one creamy white thigh that tapered down to a shapely calf and trim ankle. Pink-tipped toes rested on the hardwood floor. With each deep breath, her cleavage played peekaboo with him and his chest hitched.

Yep, it was her all right.

While he'd known there was a chance, imagining it might be her and having her right in front of him were two totally different things. His reaction was different from what he'd planned. More potent. More dangerous.

Aw, hell.

"It's nice to see you again, Beau."

Bright, sparkling, familiar green eyes met his and his stomach hollowed out the way it had so long ago when she'd shown up at his daddy's gas station and asked him for an oil change and a date to the Sadie Hawkins dance.

She'd wanted more than a dance, however. She'd wanted him, and he'd wanted her, and it had cost him dearly.

"It's been a long time," he said to her, desperate to re-organize his priorities. It was one thing to get turned on by just any woman, but he couldn't afford to be turned on by *this* woman. He'd learned that the hard way and he wasn't about to repeat the mistake. "Eleven years, isn't it?"

"Eleven years and six months." Her gaze shifted away from his. "Not that I'm keeping track or anything. It's just that the dance was near Christmas and we're starting summer, which makes it six months."

Beau stood there in awkward silence for the next few moments as he tried to calm his pounding heart. He wasn't excited or anxious or the least bit turned on anymore, despite the fact that she looked so good and smelled so sweet and wore nothing but a terry cloth robe with black singe marks . . .

"Are you okay?"

"I'm fine, thanks to you." She held up the throw pillow. "That was quick thinking."

"What can I say? I'm quick." *Do you really need to remind her?* "What were you doing?"

"Killing my ex."

"Come again?"

"My boyfriend and I split up and I was just getting rid

of the last of him. You know, out with the old and in with the new."

"I'm sorry."

"Me, too. It seems like such a shame to waste all that time together. We were together for eight years."

"That's a long time."

"You're telling me."

"So he likes Madonna?"

"What?"

"The pillow." He eyed the box sitting next to her. "Are you getting rid of all this stuff, too?"

"No, no. This is my stuff. I packed it away because he didn't really like Madonna. Or this old robe. Or my CD collection. Or the Dallas Cowboys." At his surprised gaze, she added, "He was a Packers fan."

"Sounds like you guys weren't that great of a match."

"No, no. We were the perfect match. This stuff is all old and people change. It's not really who I am anymore."

"So you like the Packers now?"

She grinned and her face brightened. "Well, I wouldn't go that far."

"So how long have you been here in Houston?"

"Since I graduated from the University of Texas. Mark and I moved here together. He took a job with a brokerage firm—he's a financial analyst—and I came here to work for Lust, Lust, Baby! They make sexual toys and enhancement products. They're the biggest in my industry. I've got a degree in sexology, as well as sales and marketing. I'm a designer."

"A designer for the biggest company in the business. I'm impressed."

"I don't exactly work for them." She frowned. "I came here to work for them, but they didn't offer me the position

I wanted." She shook her head. "Who am I kidding?" Her gaze met his. "They didn't offer me *any* position. They consider their market primarily male-oriented and they didn't think a female designer could add to their current list of products. So I decided to start my own company, geared toward women, and prove that great sex isn't just for men." Another shake of her head. "At least, that's what I started out to prove, but somewhere along the way I lost sight of that." She met his eyes again. "All I wanted was to show them up and get them to hire me to head their design department. That's what I wanted. That's all I've ever wanted." She seemed to think about her words. "That's probably more information than you need, right?"

He grinned. "It's okay. Feel free to talk. I've always been a good listener."

She shook her had. "Enough about me. So you've got your own business, too, I see."

"Ten years and still going strong, but then I'm sure you already know that since you've been meeting with Annabelle." He handed her a business card out of habit and waited for the usual cheesy comments that came when he talked about his business. Everything from "I'd hire a hunk like you any day," to "Can I get fries with that beefcake?"

"Great logo. Did you design it yourself?"

"Actually, a buddy of mine did. His name's Evan."

"Evan Dandridge? With Dandridge Marketing?"

"You know him?"

"I've heard of him. He's talented, but much too pricey for me, I'm afraid."

"That's Evan. He's good and he knows it." He always had, even when they'd shared a dorm room back in college. It had been Evan who'd first came up with the idea for Hire-a-Hunk. Evan had been his roommate and a marketing major, and Beau had been working his way through college. He'd been behind on his tuition payments and this close to calling it quits when Evan had come up with the whole gimmick to give Beau's handyman service a boost.

"You're good-looking," Evan had said. "You should capitalize on it."

"If someone wants their garage renovated, they don't care what the hired help looks like," he'd told Evan.

His friend had smiled. "You'd be surprised."

Beau had been surprised, all right. And swamped with jobs. He'd been forced to hire a fellow frat brother to help. And then another. And another. By the time he'd graduated with an architectural degree, Hire-a-Hunk had been pulling in so much money he would have been forced to take a drastic pay cut to take an entry level architectural position.

He wouldn't have cared. Beau was a low maintenance guy, but his dad had come to depend on the extra income that Beau sent home to help with his younger brothers. Not to mention by the time graduation had rolled around, he had a dozen employees who'd depended on Hire-a-Hunk to survive.

His guys had been loyal over the years and most were still with him. But now they weren't just loyal employees, they were *aging* employees who were entering their comfortable thirties. Qualified men who didn't deserve to lose their jobs just because they'd lost their six-pack abs and traded their high protein yogurt shakes for waffle cones filled with scoops of cookies 'n' cream.

And so Beau needed a new image for his company. He needed to bump things up to the next level, to turn his glorified handyman service into a major renovation team. To turn his trendy Hire-a-Hunk service into the renowned, respected H&H Construction. And to do that, he needed this project.

To restore Xandra's house to its original grandeur would gain the attention of the right people. Namely, the staff at *Texas Monthly*. The magazine hosted a yearly contest to name the up-and-coming restoration company of the year, and Beau was determined to earn that title.

"We're in the process of expanding right now into a full-fledged construction and renovation business. No more of the small time stuff," he went on. "My guys have been loyal over the years and so I want more stability and a larger market share that comes with being more than just a passing fad."

"So you're the man behind Hire-a-Hunk?"

"I'm the man behind and out front and usually smack dab in the middle. Speaking of which"—he handed her the plans—"these are the drawings for the renovations."

"I thought your company's architect was going to drop them by."

"I am the architect."

"You're an *architect*?"

"By default."

At her questioning glance, he shrugged. "I set out to earn a degree in mechanical engineering. But I couldn't afford an architect early on, so I switched some of my classes to learn how to draw plans and read blueprints and before I knew it, I'd earned enough credits for a degree."

"That's great. I mean, sort of. Great that you got a degree, but not that you didn't actually earn it in your area of interest." She smiled and eyed him. "Yeah, I can see you doing the engineering thing."

"How's that?"

"You were always working on cars and fixing things

around the gas station. When I heard about your business, I figured you were handling the physical end of things rather than just the plans."

"Being an architect—a good architect—is a full-service job." He told her the same thing he'd told himself time and time again, whenever the past caught up to him and the regret set in. "I don't just design whatever I'm commissioned to work on, I do hands-on work to make sure those designs are fully implemented. Hire-a-Hunk is a full service contractor. We do most of the work ourselves: electrical, slab, drywall, flooring—we do it all. I'm sure you'll be pleased." The minute the words were out, the image of a girl, her face illuminated by moonlight, pushed into his head. "I mean satisfied." Okay, that wasn't much better than "pleased." "Happy," he rushed on, "with the renovation. Well," he said, turning to pull the folded papers from his briefcase. "Here's a copy of the blueprints for the planned changes and updates, along with a copy of the original plan from the initial builder. Have a look and call me with any questions. My crew will be here first thing Monday morning to start work."

"I don't—"

"We've got the master key you gave to Annabelle, so don't even think that you'll be inconvenienced during any of this. You won't even know we're here. Have a nice day." He turned and started toward the door before she had a chance to open her mouth. At the moment he was holding tight to the possibility that she didn't really remember him—namely, the five minutes they'd spent in the backseat of his daddy's Impala when they should have been at the dance.

Five fast and furious minutes where he'd lost control and totally ruined what should have been one of the hottest sexual experiences of his life. Particularly since he'd been more turned on by Xandra Farrel than he'd ever been with any other woman. Then again, it was that fact that had stirred him up and made him lose control in the first place. He'd blown it. Literally. A few thrusts and he'd exploded, and that had been the end of their encounter. And the beginning of a night spent thinking about her, dreaming about her, and wanting her all over again.

Not that he'd spent the past eleven years wanting her, mind you. Or crying over what had happened. Beau Hollister didn't cry. He'd only cried twice in his entire lifetime. One had been when his mother had passed away. The second time had been less than two weeks ago when he'd had to hand Evan his first mirror since the devastating car accident that had burned half his face.

The incident with Xandra had been totally different. A disaster, as far as he was concerned, but not even close to anything life-threatening. He'd had an off night that had led to an off morning during which he'd bombed the physics exam that would have awarded him a full ride to Texas A&M. While he'd wanted to cry, he'd wanted to smack himself upside the head even more for letting a girl interfere with his lifelong dream.

He'd vowed then and there to never fall into that trap again, and he'd succeeded. While he loved women, he made sure they were temporary women. Those interested in one hot night rather than a morning after. He hadn't let himself get sidetracked since.

He had people who depended on him, like always, and so he wasn't in any hurry to stroll down memory lane with Xandra Farrel.

He didn't want to know if she remembered that night as clearly as he did. If she thought about it. If she regretted it.

She probably *didn't* remember. The whole thing had gone from zero to sixty in about as many seconds. Maybe it had been too fast and she simply remembered the episode as some heavy-duty petting.

The thought bothered him almost as much as it soothed his anxiety. Almost. But Beau needed this job way too much to let his damned male pride get in the way of his future. Her home was the oldest in the area, the most run-down, and the best chance he had to impress *Texas Monthly.* Then it would be bye-bye Hire-a-Hunk and hello H&H Construction. His guys would have the job security they'd earned with their expertise and their loyalty.

And Beau?

He would keep using the degree he'd earned, even if he wasn't all that happy doing it. For Beau, life wasn't about being happy. It was about being responsible. It always had been.

Chapter Five

Beau *Hollister.*

His image rooted in Xandra's head and stayed with her long after the door closed behind him.

In every dream she'd had where she pictured the moment they would meet again and she would get her chance to show him exactly what he'd missed out on by not seeing the hot girl beneath the fat-chick persona, she was always wearing a sexy dress, her hair and makeup firmly in place, her legs freshly shaven.

Instead, she looked like Queen of the Domestic Damned with her ratty bathrobe and unkempt hair, her face free and clear of makeup. There was no mascara to make her eyes look bigger. No lipstick to make her lips look pouty. No blush to take away from her usual pasty complexion.

Nothing to make her look the least bit hot, or make him the least bit regretful.

But Beau . . . Now he'd looked hot. Sure, he looked older, but if anything the changes made him all the more appealing. His tall frame, which had made him seem gangly as a teenager, had filled out. His shoulders were wide, his chest broad, his muscles more solid and well-defined. His stance seemed more confident, too, his gaze lit with a knowledge that said he'd seen and done more than his fair share. His eyes crinkled at the corners when he smiled. The dimple that cut into the side of one stubbled jaw seemed slightly deeper, and she'd had the insane urge to reach up and dip her tongue into the crevice.

Which she would have done in any of her how-do-you-like-me-now? fantasies. But the past few minutes had been more like a yikes-I-look-like-hell nightmare, and so she'd tucked her robe around her unshaven legs, smiled, and tried to look nonchalant rather than caught off-guard.

The story of her life, it seemed, when it came to Beau. She'd done the very same thing the night of the senior Sadie Hawkins dance when they'd gone parking.

She closed her eyes as the images rushed at her. Beau stopping to help her with a flat tire. His kindness giving her the courage to ask him out. The shopping trip to the mall to buy her first pair of high heels and a new outfit to fit the smaller body she'd been working toward her entire senior year. The excitement when she'd pulled off her baggy jeans and sweatshirt and slipped on the black miniskirt and a leopard print tank top. Beau showing up at her door looking so handsome in a plaid shirt and starched Wranglers. Beau looking slightly shell-shocked and stealing glances at her every few minutes during the drive to the school gym. As if he couldn't believe they were actually on a date together. As if he regretted the fact that he'd said yes.

He hadn't been mean or standoffish; he'd just been quiet. Except when he'd asked her to dance. He'd actually looked as if the idea excited him. But then Xandra had turned him down and suggested they go parking, and he'd lapsed back into the awkward silence.

She could still remember the gleam in his eyes and the pull of all those swirling lights. She'd wanted to dance in the worst way, but she'd chickened out because she'd never danced with a boy before. Other than the frantic gyrating she did in front of her mirror in the privacy of her own bedroom, she'd never actually danced, period. And so she'd turned him down and opted for the make-out session.

Which had been the whole point of the entire evening in the first place. It was all about sex. Not slow dancing. Or drinking punch in between the fast dances. Or getting to wear one of those pink carnation corsages she'd seen the other girls carry to school the Monday after.

Sex, she told herself. That's what it had all been about. She'd meant to lose her virginity and have her first sexual experience, and the dance had just been an excuse to ask him out.

Even so, she'd relived the experience in her mind a time or two since, and she'd changed things a bit to reflect what she should have done. Just the way she'd imagined her first encounter with Beau as an adult.

Burning condoms in front of him hadn't been part of the plan. Then again, that was her problem. She was stuck in a rut. Her original plans—namely to secure the job of her dreams and have a family of her own—were thrown by the wayside. She'd lost sight of her path, of herself, she realized as she eyed the singed Madonna pillow he'd used to put out the fire in her lap.

She'd just picked up the pillow to survey the damage when her phone rang again.

"Mom just called me," Skye's frantic voice rushed over the line.

"And?"

"And I didn't answer. She'll ask questions and then I'll have to tell her I'm procreating and—"

"I thought you were just *planning* to procreate?"

"We were, but then Clint tasted my lasagna and it sucked and one thing led to another and . . . You know how it goes."

"You went from sucky lasagna to procreating." Xandra nodded. "Definitely a natural progression."

"It sucked and so I cried and then he tried to comfort me and we started kissing and—"

"Procreation."

"Exactly. Mom's like Big Brother. She'll know. And then she'll give me a hard time, and I'm depressed enough as it is, which is why I called to talk." A heavy sigh floated over the line. "I don't think it worked."

"Why not?"

"Because I didn't feel anything. I mean, I had an orgasm and it felt good, but it always feels good. Great. But it didn't feel *different*."

"Maybe it's not supposed to feel different."

"We're talking about creating human life here. You would think you'd be able to feel something. I mean, Clint's youngest brother's wife said that when she conceived their first child, she just knew it. She felt it. It was like this fantastic moment. Mine was fantastic, but it's always fantastic. I was expecting something different. Like the ultimate orgasm."

"There's no such thing." The minute the words left her mouth, an idea struck. A crazy, far-out concept she should have dismissed without a second thought.

She would have had she not been sitting on the ledge of the fireplace wearing a singed robe, her body still buzzing from the encounter with *Beau Hollister,* of all people, a half dozen packages of surviving condoms littering the floor near her feet.

Her gaze shifted from the condoms to the fiery heat licking at the grate and her mind started to race.

"Not yet, that is."

"You want to make the ultimate *orgasm*?" Albert finished lacing up his tennis shoe, stood, and reached for his racquet.

"I want to make something that gives women the ultimate orgasm."

"Like a vibrator?"

"Maybe." She shook her head as she leaned back against the wall of the court and drank a sip of her bottled water. "Probably not. I need something a little more inventive. Something a woman can actually use while she's having sex with a partner."

"A stimulator."

"Kind of." She closed her eyes and prayed for Albert and his racquet to go away. "Don't look at me like that."

"Like what?"

"Like you expect me to get up and play."

"I do expect you to get up and play." He came over and reached for her hand. "That's why I dragged you here. You need to play. To get your blood flowing. To get your mind off the whole Mark thing."

The kicker was, she'd stopped thinking about Mark hours ago. Instead, she'd been thinking and rethinking her meeting with Beau Hollister.

"Can't I just vegetate a little longer?"

"I guess so, but just so you know, the more sedentary you are, the quicker your arteries are to harden. Then your bones start to creak when you do move. And before you know it, you're popping One-A-Days like they're candy and shopping for orthopedic shoes."

"I guess if I have to get old I should at least go kicking and screaming." She got to her feet and reached for her racquet. Not to mention, she needed a distraction from Beau and all the should-haves racing through her mind.

She should have looked better. And sounded more witty. And thrown herself out the nearest window when she realized it was him.

Shaking away the thoughts, she grabbed the ball and dropped it into a serve.

They spent the next thirty minutes slapping the ball back and forth while Xandra brainstormed various ideas for her ultimate orgasm. All too soon, she'd run out of ideas and she found herself telling Albert all about her unplanned meeting with Beau and the fact that she hadn't shaved her legs in two weeks.

"It gets worse."

"Worse than two weeks of stubble?"

"Unfortunately. He owns the construction company doing the restoration on my house, which I already knew, which was why I picked his company. Not that I expected to see him. I suppose I thought I might see him, but not this soon, not today. But I come to find out he actually does hands-on with his business, which means I get to see him for the next three weeks until all the work is done." She blew out an exasperated breath. "The Big Lady Up High definitely has it out for me."

"Your first sexual experience really took all of five minutes?" Without waiting for an answer, he grinned. "That ought to make you feel good."

"That he was in a hurry to be finished?"

"That's one way to look at it."

"And another?"

"Maybe he was so excited that he couldn't control himself. You're a vivacious woman."

"You didn't know me back then. I mean, when we did it, I wasn't a total tubby. I'd lost twenty of the thirty-five pound goal I'd set for myself. And I actually put on a skirt for the event. But I was still young and awkward and geeky and I knew absolutely nothing about sex." At his raised eyebrows, she added, "I mean, I *knew* everything. But I'd never *done* anything. Doing was a lot different from knowing."

"I don't know if I can remember back that far."

"You were probably more than experienced by the time you turned eighteen."

"I'm not talking about remembering when I was eighteen. I'm talking about remembering the doing. It's been a while."

"How long is a while?"

"Let's just put it this way . . . I'm a traitor. I've tried every product the Lust, Lust, Baby! guys have put out." At her narrowed gaze, he added, "Hey, our products are geared for women. A guy has to do what a guy has to do. Besides, somebody from our company has to keep tabs on what they're up to. It might as well be me."

"And?" she prodded when he lapsed into silence. "What's the latest and the greatest?"

"They've got a vibrating hand that simulates a hand job. The only problem is that it isn't self-lubricating, which means you have to stop every few strokes to add more lotion or oil or whatever you're using."

"They should have put some sort of a secretor into the

palm. Then all you would have to do was add the lubricant to the hand itself."

"We could do it."

"And how would that appeal to our mostly female clientele?"

"We could expand our clientele to include males."

"Then we wouldn't have anything to distinguish us from every Tom, Dick, and Harry sex company out there." She shook her head. "We have to stick to our niche. It's the only way to stand out." Her gaze met his. "So what do you think they're planning for the Sextravaganza?"

"I think it doesn't matter what they're planning. We need to worry about what we're planning, which isn't much at this point."

"It will be by the time I'm done." She wasn't just getting herself back on track personally. She was doing it professionally, as well. She was going to pick up where she'd left off eight years ago, when she'd been all about making things happen rather than letting them happen. That's how she'd snagged Mark in the first place. She'd been determined to find a perfect boyfriend, and she'd done just that. She'd been determined to start her own company and she'd done just that. But those had merely been steps to get her to her true goal—her own family and the position as head designer for the largest sex aid company in the world.

She'd fallen into a major rut and it was time to pull herself out. She was going for the gold this time—a baby of her own and the job of her dreams.

And the first steps to take her the distance? Her Perfect Daddy list and the ultimate orgasm.

The thought sent a surge of determination through her and she picked up her steps on the racquetball court. She slammed the ball and sent Albert running with each return shot, until they were both panting and sweating.

"I'm getting too old for this," he gasped as he missed the last shot and gave up.

Xandra smiled. "I believe that's my line. Men don't get old. They get better."

"Okay, so I'm getting too good for this. Either way, I'm this close to having a heart attack. Let's call it quits and grab some lunch."

"Whatever you say, Gramps."

Albert knotted the towel around his waist when he stepped from the shower later that afternoon and made a solemn promise to himself.

He was not going to look.

He did not have any gray hair *down there*. And even if he did, all the better. For men, gray hair meant maturity and knowledge and experience and—

Christ, he had a gray hair.

He drank in a deep breath as he examined the area in question. Hey, a lot of guys had one gray hair. Some probably even had two. And quite a few more likely had three. It was no big deal that he had . . . *Five*?

Albert closed his eyes and did his best to ignore the sudden hollow feeling in the pit of his stomach.

It didn't matter. A few gray hairs down south, even five, did not change who he was or make him any less of a person. He was a successful guy. A happening guy. He had big blue eyes thanks to good genes and the added oomph of a pair of colored contacts. A great smile thanks to five years with braces and thousands of dollars spent on cosmetic whitening. He had a thick, full head of hair courtesy of the multitude of vitamins he sucked down religiously. He had a nice build, good muscle tone, and an above average package. He also had a great job that brought in a six-figure salary. And a high-rise apartment in the heart of downtown Houston, complete with valet parking and a doorman.

Yep, he was in his prime. At the top of his game. The world was his oyster and all he had to do was reach out, suck it in, and enjoy.

The last thing he needed to worry about was losing his youth or his edge or his whole happening guy status.

It wasn't like he'd found *six* hairs, for crying out loud. Or that life was downhill from here on out. Or that the only thing he had to do on a star-studded Saturday night was have dinner with his parents.

"You're a half hour early," Chuck Sinclair declared when he pulled open the door.

Albert forced a smile for the man who'd nurtured him through colds and made costumes for his school plays and baked him brownies when Becky Dreyer had broken his heart in the sixth grade. "I thought maybe we could visit before dinner."

"What a wonderful idea!" Chuck beamed. He wore khaki slacks, a white button-up shirt, and a red apron that read KISS THE COOK. He had a head full of silvery gray hair—barely visible beneath the white chef's hat he wore—and an equally gray mustache.

If Albert hadn't known better, he would have sworn the man standing in front of him was Chef Boyardee rather than his father, who'd been a personal stylist for a local television network in his younger years. Now he sold real estate part-time and lived for macramé and his Kathie Lee Gifford aerobics video collection.

"And you brought a gift, too," Chuck exclaimed when he saw the bottle of wine in Albert's hand. "For moi?" He all but teared up as he took the white zinfandel. "You're such a sweet, sweet boy. Francis"—the man turned and called over his shoulder—"guess what Albert brought us?"

"A bottle of wine?" came the deep masculine voice from the den.

"How did you know?"

"He always brings wine."

"That's because he knows how much we like wine." Chuck turned back to Albert. "You're so thoughtful, dear. Come in, come in. Your father's watching *Outdoor World,* as usual."

"I heard that," came the deep voice from the other room.

"I hope so. I said it loud enough." At Albert's wide-eyed expression, Chuck added, "We're all about communication now. Our therapist said that we shouldn't suppress our feelings. We should just let it all hang out. If I'm mad because your father leaves his socks in the den, I don't hold it in anymore. I just let it go."

"You guys are seeing a therapist for communication problems?" It wasn't the fact that they were seeing a therapist that bothered Albert—his parents were always seeing a therapist. Albert himself had been a regular at Dr. Cherry Chandler's office until his eighteenth birthday when his parents had decided he was sensitive and well-rounded enough to face the world on his own. That, and the fact that Dr. Chandler stopped seeing individual patients to focus on bringing her message of sensitivity to the vast majority, rather than one convert at a time.

Up until then, however, they'd been concerned with his emotional stability. After all, it wasn't easy being the son of a gay couple. And it was even harder to be the son of the only openly gay couple in suburban Texas.

But Albert had managed just fine thanks to a house full of love and support, and the fact that he'd been an impressive six feet two by the time he'd turned fifteen and a pretty decent football player. Most people were willing to overlook the two men sitting in the stands, wearing GAY IS HERE TO STAY buttons, so long as their son was throwing touchdown passes.

"We don't talk enough. I tend to suppress my needs and wants in the vain hope that your father will be intuitive enough to sense them. But he isn't. I'm convinced he slept through that 'Being a Sensitive Mate' seminar we took summer before last. Why, the only thing he's in tune with is the television."

"But you're okay, right? You and Dad are still solid?"

"Of course, dear. But we're still just people and we need a little help once in a while. That's why we're doing a communications seminar with one of Dr. Chandler's associates at the University of Houston." Chuck motioned to a nearby bookshelf filled with a row of bright red books. Everything from *The Sensitive Housemate* to *The Sensitive Communicator*. "The instructor teaches straight from Dr. Chandler's books and she said our situation is common at this point in the relationship. It's empty-nest syndrome."

"I've been out of the house for over fifteen years."

"It's latent empty-nest syndrome. See, we were so excited at the chance to do our own thing once you left— no offense, dear—that we didn't feel the loss right away. But now that we've settled into a boring routine that involves just the two of us, we're each feeling empty and isolated. The only way to combat that feeling is communication."

"Or a great, big, fat steak," Francis called from the other room. "Is dinner ready yet?"

"Almost, and you know steak is bad for your arteries. We're having spaghetti and veggie balls."

"Whatever. I need to eat."

"You need to turn the TV to something we can all enjoy."

"You like fishing," came the grumble from the other room.

"I like to cook and eat fish. I don't like fishing."

"They flash recipes before they roll the credits. I'll write one down for you."

Chuck smiled. "See? The therapy is working already. I talk and your father really does listen." He shut the door behind Albert and motioned to the open doorway to the left. "I've got bread sticks in the oven. Why don't you go join your father? Maybe you can get him to change that awful channel."

"You're not supposed to criticize the other person's lifestyle," Francis said from the other room.

"I didn't criticize," Chuck replied. "I voiced an opinion."

"Same thing."

"Hardly." Chuck disappeared into the kitchen while Albert headed for the den.

"Hey, Dad," Albert said as he walked in and spotted the large man wearing faded jeans, a Texans sweatshirt, and a FISH TEXAS baseball cap. He was sprawled in a leather recliner, his white-socked feet crossed, a remote control in his hand.

"Hey, son." The man smiled. "How's work?"

"Good."

"Good. And how's . . . Holy moly, would you look at the size of that catfish?" His dad's attention shifted back to the television and Albert spent the next fifteen minutes watching his father watch fishing until Chuck called them to dinner.

"This is pretty good," Francis said as he shoved a bite of food into his mouth and set about devouring the plate of pasta in front of him.

"Very good," Albert agreed, taking a bite, followed by a sip of wine.

"This is so nice," Chuck said as he stretched out his arms and touched both men on either side of him. "I miss the three of us at dinner together. We should do it more often."

"The boy's busy. He's got a life."

"I know that," Chuck said. "I just said it's lonely at the table. That doesn't mean I expect him to give up everything to drive home and eat with us every night. It just means that I miss having more people at the dinner table. Speaking of which, Molly and Margie's oldest daughter is pregnant. They're going to have grandbaby number four. Isn't that wonderful?" Chuck sighed. "What I wouldn't give to have *one* grandbaby, much less four."

"Now, Chuckles. You know what Dr. Chandler said in her last book—a truly sensitive partner is supposed to be considerate of all family members, meaning we're not supposed to let our latent empty-nest syndrome fall back on Albert. He has his own life to lead and our problems are our problems."

"I'm not saying Albert needs to give me a grandchild. It's just that he's getting to that age where most people seriously think about settling down with the right person and having children, so it's only natural that I would start to think about the possibility of grandchildren. Or at least the possibility that Albert will actually bring a date to Molly and Margie's youngest daughter's wedding. She's getting married in three weeks." Chuck turned to him. "Are you seeing anyone right now?" When Albert shook his head, Chuck added, "Is there anyone you're even the least bit interested in that you might ask?" Another shake and Chuck frowned. "Dear, I know it's hard in this day and age to meet the right person, but you have to try. You're not getting any younger. At your age, I was already making cupcakes for your kindergarten parties and your father was coaching Little League. Not that I'm saying you're old. It's just . . . Time is wasting."

"Chuckles," Francis warned.

"Now, now, I'm not doing anything. I'm just giving Albert a little food for thought and drawing his attention to the fact that he could at least bring a date to the wedding."

"I'm sure he has plenty of other things to think about besides a date for some fancy schmancy wedding," Francis said.

He was right. Albert was spearheading the product development of three different new vibrators, not to mention overseeing the manufacture of the company's new spring line. The last thing he needed to think about was a date for Molly and Margie's youngest daughter's wedding. Or how his clock was ticking. Or how the most intimate contact he'd had with a woman in the past six months was earlier that afternoon when he'd tripped over his racquet and stumbled into old Mrs. Witherspoon who'd been manuevering her walker toward the sauna.

Christ, his clock *was* ticking and it was just a matter of time before the alarm sounded.

Time's up!

Chapter Six

What does every woman *really* want?" Xandra stood at the head of the pink marble conference table Monday morning and posed the question to the half dozen members of Wild Woman's corporate team who'd assembled for their weekly meeting.

"A lifetime supply of Godiva chocolates."

"A pair of run-resistant panty hose."

"Another season of *Sex and the City*."

"The starring role on the next *Bachelorette*."

"A Persian cat addicted to peanut butter and a jar of extra creamy Jif."

"Good answers, but I'm talking *every* woman, regardless of race, creed, color, socioeconomic status or"—her gaze shifted to Stacey Bernard, the engineer in charge of product implementation—"lack of a decent social life. A need that crosses all lines of distinction. A desire all women share, whether they're short or tall, blonde, or brunette, whether they're from Podunk, Idaho, or New York City. A longing that spans all cultural and geographic boundaries."

"How about *two* Persians?" Stacey offered.

"Now we know why you're in charge of product implementation, rather than development," Albert said.

"I'm just as creative as you." Stacey glared at Albert.

"In your dreams."

"Believe me, you're not anywhere close to my dreams."

"It's just you and the peanut butter and the Persian."

"At least I have a sex life that consists of something besides my hand."

"Yeah, one that has you at the top of the SPCA's most wanted list."

"Peanut is as happy as a clam—"

"People," Xandra cut in. "Can we please stick to the subject."

"Fruit," Stacey muttered.

"Witch," Albert muttered back.

"I can practically feel the love in this room," Xandra said before giving Stacey a look that she quickly shifted to Albert. "Can we please get back on track?"

"I'm with you, boss," Stacey said.

"Me, too," Albert added.

"Good. Every woman. Serious need. Think people." She eyed the roomful of people and took in the shrugs and exasperated sighs. "An orgasm," she finally declared. "Every woman wants an orgasm, but not just any old kind. One that's intense. Mind-blowing. Life-changing. The *ultimate* orgasm."

"Mine are all like that," Stacey said.

"Says who?" Albert eyed her. "Peanut?"

"Would you just leave Peanut out of this?"

"You brought him up."

"Peanut's a *she,* not a he."

"And you think *I* butter my bread on the opposite side?"

"Forget Peanut," Xandra shouted. "This is about coming up with a product that will guarantee every woman an ultimate orgasm, regardless of how good or bad her partner is. It's about this." Xandra held up the drawing she'd spent all of Sunday working on.

"It looks like a female condom." The comment came from Kimmy Adams.

Kimmy was Xandra's personal assistant. She was blonde and beautiful and always the best dressed employee at Wild Woman. Albert, the only male team leader, wore khakis and a white polo shirt. Stacey wore black slacks and a black blouse covered with a white lab coat. The half dozen others went for comfort, wearing either jeans or capris paired with a casual shirt.

Kimmy, on the other hand, put fashion above everything else. She wore a trendy red skirt with a matching jacket. Red sandals with two inch high heels completed the outfit, along with a set of silver bangle bracelets and a pair of hoop earrings. With the brains to back up her looks—she was an honors graduate from Rice University with a degree in marketing—Kimmy was the epitome of the young, hip professional.

Even more, she looked as if she was comfortable all dressed up, unlike her boss who felt like a stuffed sausage in her pin-striped Liz Claiborne skirt and jacket.

Xandra tugged at the hem of her jacket and drew in a much-needed breath—with her extra ten pounds she was busting at the seams. "It *is* a female condom," she went on. "But it's also much more. It has heat receptors." She pointed to the illustration of the small device she'd seen featured in the most recent issue of *Science Digest*. "Or at least, it will when we're done with it. See, the idea is this:

to take a female condom, fill it with heat receptors, and market it as the new orgasmic enhancement product."

"Why a female condom? Why not the all-familiar male condom?"

"Because male prophylactics are designed to fit a man's penis which, unfortunately, is not always designed to fit his partner. This product will be crafted specifically for a woman's body, to fit comfortably inside and cling to the walls of her vagina. She'll be able to choose from a variety of sizes to guarantee a perfect fit. A man's penis size won't matter at all. This product is all about a woman taking charge of her own pleasure, guaranteeing it. As long as the man can move, it won't matter how expert his lovemaking skills. Which brings us to how it actually works. See"— she pointed to the diagram—"the penis—any penis—generates friction and heat with a steady in-and-out motion. These receptors will trap that heat and send out an electrical pulse. This pulse brings the female condom alive and, in turn, stimulates the adjoining tissue. In essence, it zaps the nerves."

"Sounds painful."

"I suppose it could be if the pulse were fierce enough and the receptors strong enough, but they will be too small to pose a danger, just large enough to convert the trapped heat and stimulate the already sensitive tissue. The faster the movement, the more warmth will be generated, and the more intense the electrical pulse."

"I get it. The faster you go, the more it builds."

"Exactly. It follows the natural process of sexual stimulation, but with a bonus. You get a more intense experience until bam! major sensory overload." She smiled. "An ultimate orgasm."

"Great idea."

"Fabulous."

"Groundbreaking."

"It will be. Once we turn the idea into a reality. I've done the basic design with a detailed description of the receptors and how they should work. We need a finished product that carries the Wild Woman guarantee of sexual satisfaction in three weeks—just in time for the Sextravaganza. It'll be the prime opportunity to introduce it to the public and cause an industry buzz. That means we need a prototype as soon as possible."

Albert glanced up from the design notes. "How about early next week?"

"The end of this week would be better."

"We'll give it our best."

Xandra smiled. "That's all I'm asking." Her glance shifted around the group. "We also need a savvy logo and a packaging concept. If we debut at the Sextravaganza, we need to be ready for a rush of orders. With a lot of hard work, this could turn the industry on its ear." And show the higher-ups over at Lust, Lust, Baby! that they'd made a big mistake when they'd passed on Xandra for their design team.

With the introduction of such a revolutionary product, Wild Woman was sure to triple their net income, which would put them neck and neck with the dominating company's figures reported for last year.

That would get their attention. Martin Browning, CEO for Lust, Lust, Baby!, was sure to regret not snatching her up so long ago. He would make an offer for Wild Woman and bring Xandra and her team into the Lust, Lust fold, with Xandra heading the design division.

And if Martin didn't make an offer to absorb the company and keep her employees? She would hand over controlling interest of Wild Woman to Albert, who had a creative streak of his own, and become just a silent investor. Wild Woman would continue without her as a niche company while she headed the design team for Lust.

"What if it doesn't work?" Stacey asked.

"It'll work," Xandra said. "It has to work." Otherwise, Xandra would have to admit that the gray hair wasn't just a fluke. She really was getting old and slow and senile, and it was all downhill from here.

She ignored the thought, adjourned the meeting, and gathered up her portfolio.

"It's good to see you spent yesterday doing something constructive," Albert said after everyone had left. "You seemed okay on Saturday, but I thought you might fall back into a funk, overdose on Snickers, and have to have your stomach pumped."

"I only ate three, and it didn't make me feel better. Just fat. Which made me think about what a loser I was. Which made me think about what a loser I'd be if I didn't come up with something great. So I started thinking and I came up with something. Speaking of which, designing it is one thing, but making it work is another. Do you think it's possible?"

"It's definitely possible. You really did some great research on this materials sheet." He grinned. "You're a smart woman. And nice. And kind. And fun. And you're in the prime of your life. You're a great catch, and Mark is an idiot. I know you probably don't see that right now, but you will eventually and you'll move on to greener pastures."

"Probably, but I don't have eight years to graze."

"Maybe it won't take eight years. Maybe that perfect someone is out there right beneath your nose. Maybe it won't take eight years to reach your comfort level. Maybe you'll feel comfortable just like that. You'll both like the same things. You'll respect each other. You'll have great sex."

"And maybe my mom will be on next month's cover of *Bride-to-Be*."

"Hey, stranger things have happened." At her pointed stare, he shrugged. "Okay, so maybe nothing that strange has happened in a long time. I'm just saying that maybe finding a life mate isn't going to be as hard as you think."

"I don't think it's going to be hard at all."

"That's the spirit."

"Because I'm not going to try. I don't have the time or the energy. I'm going to focus on this business and this." She waved a notebook at him that she'd ordered off the Internet Saturday night. "It's a procreation planner," she told him when he gave her a puzzled glance. "It outlines everything from how to finance the birth of your baby, to how to increase your chances of conception, to how to influence your baby's sex. Not to mention it has all these lists and charts to fill out to tailor the complete birthing experience to your specific needs. How great is that?"

"You're actually going to have a baby?"

"Not at this moment, but I'm through with just thinking about it. I want a detailed plan. Something solid. A goal with a realistic approach ironed out to meet that goal. Don't you see? I fell into comfort with Mark and Wild Woman, and I forgot all about my dreams."

"You got busy with daily life. We all do it."

"Maybe, but I'm not doing it anymore. If I had been pursuing my ultimate goal, I wouldn't have wasted so much time with Mark. I would have seen early on that his reluctance to set foot in a Chuck E. Cheese meant he wasn't interested in children and *I* would have dumped *him*. I should have dumped him, but I lost sight of what was really important." She held up the book. "This will help me plan for daddy extraordinaire and when the time's right, I'll know exactly what I'm looking for and, hopefully, how to find him." She smiled. "There's an entire list of meet markets for good daddy candidates, not to mention suggestions if you're looking for a daddy with certain interests. For instance, if I want my son to be an expert marksman, I should join a skeet shooting club."

"You hate guns."

"That's irrelevant. If I have a son, he might eventually be drafted and I would certainly want him to know how to defend himself. Not that I've decided to have a son or that he would be eligible for the draft because he could be too young or he could be in college. You're missing the point. I don't know what I want when it comes to a baby. That's the purpose of this planner. To help me focus on my goal."

"I still think you're giving up on a relationship too soon. But I like your determination and your creativity." He glanced at the drawings of her ultimate orgasm idea. "This is really pretty fresh."

"I don't see why. I'm sure women the world over have prayed for something like this more than my grammie prays to win the lottery. More than fresh, it will be a relief for women everywhere. If it comes to fruition." She gave him a pointed look. "That's where you come in. You're a genius, Albert. If anyone can construct an actual product that works, it's you."

"You really think I'm a genius?"

"I wouldn't have hired you otherwise."

"How about we get together for dinner tonight?"

"We might as well. We'll be working late until this gets

out of the developmental phase, so I'll buy for the entire team."

"That's not what I—"

"Linda from Vamp Me Lingerie is on line one," Kimmy's voice came over the intercom. "She said something about doing a joint promotion in their stores," Kimmy went on. "Sylvia from Peterson Plastics—line two—wants to know if you have to have the King Kong in neon blue because the dye is doing something to the plastic and it's coming out more purple. Daniel from Kingsbury Media—on three—wants to know if you've proofed the new catalog layout. Your sister Eve—four—wants to know Mark's new address because she's kicking his ass for hurting you, and I need to know if you want roast beef—it's Boar's Head—or chicken salad—Butterball—from the lunch cart." As well as a love of designer clothes, Kimmy also had a fetish for name brands.

"I'll take line two first and the chicken salad, and maybe some fruit."

"Apple, banana, or grapes?"

"An apple."

"Washington or Granny Smith?"

"Just give me the grapes."

"Dole or Del Monte?"

"The banana. I'll have the banana."

"Chiquita or—"

"You pick. Anything is fine so long as it's from the right food group." She punched the button and reached for line two. "What were you saying about dinner?"

"Nothing. I'll see you tonight."

Albert left Xandra's office, closed the door behind him, and stood in the outer office where Kimmy's desk was situated. Xandra's assistant had obviously gone off in search of lunch, and so no one was around.

He leaned back against the door and tried for a deep, calming breath. It was obviously going to take a lot more than a dinner invite for Xandra to see Albert as her Holy Commitment Man.

He didn't blame her. He'd balked at the idea himself. It had popped into his head late last night as he'd watched Jacqueline Farrel's *Get Sexed Up!* The show was starting a series of episodes called Smart Dating. Dr. Farrel was giving pointers before beginning the first episode with four L.A. women. The cameras would follow along as they ventured on a first date and record every grueling moment. Then Jacqueline would do a live critique on the show and tell the girls what they were doing wrong in their quest for the right partner.

Last night's all-important tip: Be careful not to venture too far into scary territory in search of a significant other. The awesome Holy Commitment threesome is often right beneath your nose. It's someone you already know. Someone you connect with. Someone you spend time with. Someone you like. Someone who already likes you.

You're a genius, Albert.

Xandra was his someone. They both liked racquetball and Snickers bars and they lived and breathed their work. Even more, they respected each other.

Hello? They already had two out of the Holy Commitment Trinity. It was just a matter of adding great sex to the mix and bam!—Holy Commitment Heaven.

Obviously, Xandra hadn't watched the same show and had yet to have the same epiphany. Then again, she rarely watched her mother's show because she heard enough advice during their daily phone calls.

And he knew that because?

Because he knew everything about Xandra. The good, the bad, and the totally ugly—namely the worn University of Texas nightshirt she'd been sleeping in since college. The one with the ragged hem and the hole near the collar. The one she refused to retire because it was comfortable.

He'd seen her in the godawful nightshirt and he *still* liked her. Yep, she was Miss It, all right. The One, as far as he was concerned. The perfect woman.

Unlike present company, he thought, as his gaze collided with a pair of rich brown eyes. Or rather, they would have been rich. Warm even, like hot fudge ready to be poured over a bowl of ice cream. *If* they hadn't belonged to one Stacey Bernard aka Diva of the Damned. She walked toward him, a frown on her face and a glimmer of bloodlust in her eyes.

She was not only snobby and obnoxious, but antagonistic. She'd purposely been getting in his craw since the moment he'd come to Wild Woman.

She'd been here six months prior, which gave her seniority and a chip on her shoulder the size of Texas. They were both mechanical engineers. Both graduates of Texas A&M University. Both the rulers of their world—she as chief of product manufacturing and he as chief of product development. He took Xandra's ideas and made them work. And Stacey took his product and made it cost effective. Once upon a time, however, she'd been in charge of both—development and manufacturing—until it had come to light that she didn't have the creativity to visualize during the developmental phase. Xandra had designed her first vibrator, the King Kong, and Stacey had made it look more like the Mini Monkey, and so Albert had been brought in.

The decision had been strictly business. That's what Xandra had told Stacey. While the woman had made a big show of getting angry, Albert knew she understood. Stacey wasn't his favorite person, but she was smart. A genius when it came to materials. The professional in her understood, yet the woman inside wouldn't let her give up her grudge.

Personality aside, she was attractive in a cool, detached sort of way. The classic professional in her starched white lab coat, her dark hair pulled back into a tight bun, her face void of all makeup except a touch of pink that accented her full lips and made them actually look kissable.

He'd actually entertained a full ten seconds of lust when he'd first met her, but then she'd opened her mouth, revealed the inner bitch, and killed his whole please-ride-me-on-top-of-my-laboratory-counter fantasy. She'd started egging him on and he'd started giving it back to her, and they'd been at each other's throats ever since.

"If I were you, I would stop daydreaming and get to work." She passed him to place several cost sheets on Kimmy's desk.

"Daydreaming is part of my work, but you wouldn't know that because you're not me. Therefore, the whole concept is out of your realm of capability."

"You're a jackass," she threw over her shoulder.

"It takes one to know one."

"Now that's original. What are you? A third-grader? Because you're certainly acting like one."

"As I said, it takes one to know one."

She frowned. "Just get to work. We're on a time limit here, and I don't want to have to backtrack you and replace all of your materials with something more cost effective because you didn't do your homework in the first place."

"The day you backtrack me is the day I strip naked in the middle of the Galleria and sing 'The Yellow Rose of Texas.' "

If he hadn't known better, he would have sworn he saw a small smile tug at the corner of her lips. But then she frowned, and he realized he was suffering from a lack of sleep thanks to *Get Sexed Up!* and his Holy Commitment revelation.

"Just get to work," Stacey growled before stamping off down the hall.

"I intend to." But the work Albert had in mind had little to do with the Sextravaganza project—implementing Xandra's well thought out idea would be a piece of cake, as always—and more to do with the designer herself.

It was high time Xandra Farrel had an epiphany of her own.

"Mark is an asshole," Eve Farrel declared when Xandra finally called her back. "A total rat bastard."

Eve was the middle Farrel daughter. She was also the producer and director for Sugar & Spice Sinema, a company that produced how-to videos to help couples discover and reach their true sexual potential.

"It's about time you came out of hiding," Xandra told her sister as she arranged the lunch Kimmy had left on her desk. "I tried to call all weekend."

"I wasn't hiding. You know I need complete concentration when I'm working. That means no TV, no phone, no Mom. I have to humor my muse. But I am sorry I didn't hear the phone when you called. I'll gladly go after Mark and break both his legs on your behalf if that will make it up to you."

"Thanks, but I'm okay."

"Are you sure? Because that's what older sisters are for. Older, single, *sane* sisters. Skye is in la-la land right now, so she doesn't count. I swear, the more I talk to her, the more I'm starting to think Mom may be right about her being brainwashed. She sounds too happy."

"She's married to the man of her dreams. She *is* happy."

"Yeah, but she's not a normal happy. It's like she's got some freaky smiling disease that she's desperate to spread around. Last month when Clint's team raced at Napa Valley, she invited me to join them for dinner after the race."

"So?"

"So she didn't just invite me. She invited the driver for Clint's new car—some blond, apple-pie looking guy by the name of Linc Adams." Her voice lowered. "She fixed me up. Can you believe that?"

"She's never tried to fix *me* up."

"You've always had Mark."

"But I don't now."

"Give her time to get over this baby crap and I'm sure she'll get around to it."

"I thought you liked babies?"

"I do so long as they're not in the same room with me."

Xandra smiled. "I distinctly remember someone actually volunteering to sit with the Miller twins every Friday night while their parents went to dinner."

"I liked the money, not to mention they paid double. Now don't try to change the subject."

"Which is?"

"You and your emotional well-being. I never understood why you bothered with a man anyway when you've got so many vibrators laying around the house."

"So sayeth the woman who just tattooed a man's name on her ass."

"It's a fake tattoo, for Pete's sake. You know my sole purpose in life is to shock Mom into complete silence."

"It isn't working."

"You can't blame a girl for trying. So Mark is really history? You're not pining away, scarfing Ding Dongs or smoking your way into the Camel Hall of Fame, are you?"

"I'm working on the ultimate orgasm."

"Atta girl. Have great rebound sex and you'll forget about the creep just like that."

"I'm not having sex. I'm talking the ultimate orgasm as in a new Wild Woman product that will help women achieve the ultimate fulfillment despite a dud of a partner."

"Speaking of duds, I hear you ran into Beau Hollister."

"I didn't run into him. I hired him and his company to renovate my house."

"Is he still hot?"

"Scorching."

"Is he still terrible in bed?"

"I wouldn't know. I've only seen him once and it wasn't pretty." She went on to tell Eve about the condom-burning and Beau's sudden appearance.

"It's an unwritten rule of the universe. Look your best and you never run into anyone. Look like hell and you'll see everyone you know."

But rules were made to be broken, as far as Xandra was concerned. From here on out, she intended to be fully prepared for a face-to-face with Beau. No more ratty old bathrobes or puffy, tear-filled eyes or Medusa hair. She was going to show Beau exactly what he'd been missing all these years.

In the meantime . . . She eased the painful pumps from her feet and slid a few buttons free on her blazer as she turned her attention to the stack of accounts receivable Kimmy had placed on her desk.

It was time to get as comfortable as possible and get back to work.

Chapter Seven

"We've got trouble with a capital 'B,'" Annabelle Marshall declared when Beau stopped by the main office of Hire-a-Hunk near lunchtime.

Annabelle was an old college friend, his personal assistant, and the only woman Beau knew who could recite the name and catalog number of every type of wood offered by Home Depot. In a former life, she'd been a Dallas Cowboys' cheerleader. A knee injury and the twenty extra pounds accumulated during recovery had killed her career, and so she'd come to him for a job. She'd started as a receptionist, fielding phone calls and writing the occasional job order, a task that had come easy since she'd worked with her father's construction business while growing up. The man had passed away before she'd entered college and the business liquidated, but the know-how had stayed with her. She'd been a natural for the job.

But as the company had grown, Beau had started to need more than a receptionist. He'd needed someone who was outgoing to meet with clients when he was too busy. Someone with a head for numbers who could price jobs in his absence. Someone who knew how to order supplies. Someone who wasn't intimidated by a roomful of rough-neck men.

Annabelle had been perfect for the new job, not just because of her background with her father's company and her business degree, but because she actually liked rough-necks. So much so that she'd married Warren, Beau's crew chief, a few years back.

It was just after twelve and the room buzzed with life, from the automatic coffeemaker dripping in the far corner, to the computer screen lit with a spreadsheet detailing this week's supply order, to the half dozen men that gathered around Annabelle's desk as she assigned more jobs. The other eight men employed by the company—Warren the crew boss, Tom the electrical expert, Bobby the concrete man and five others whose specialties included everything from drywall to flooring—had been assigned to Xandra's house and were already at the location.

Beau had meant to get out there first thing this morning, but he'd been delayed finishing up the renovation of a doctor's office down in the medical center. Once he left his office, he intended to head out to Xandra's place and get busy.

"The word 'trouble' doesn't start with a 'B,' " he told Annabelle as he took the stack of work orders she handed him, gave them a look-see, and handed them back.

"It does if you're Savannah Sawyer and you write a weekly column for the *Houston Chronicle* called 'Just Us Girls,' otherwise known as 'I'm a Bitter Divorcée Who Likes to Bitch About Men.' " She eyed him. " 'Bitch' being the key word, mind you." While Annabelle could stand up to any man, she had trouble doing the same with women.

Particularly holier-than-thou controlling women who reminded her of her three older sisters and her mother.

"So what does she have to do with us?"

"Savannah Sawyer was the deck refinish job called in last week. The one who wanted the cedar stain that we had to special order."

All of the employees at Hire-a-Hunk had general repair knowledge, but what made them so valuable was that each man had his specialty. Jobs were divided up based on skill and expertise. Bryan was the in-house deck man. A woodworking genius when it came to refinishing, and one of the youngest men at the company. At twenty-six, he still had his six-pack abs even if his hairline was doing a fast retreat toward the back of his head.

"Bryan's taking care of that, isn't he?"

"He was, until ten minutes ago. She called and said that when she hired a hunk, she expected a blond hunk because, in her opinion, brunettes are not hunky at all. Especially balding brunettes. Her ex was a balding brunette and he was a no-good slimy snake. She said to make sure that we sent someone else out this morning because our ad promises full satisfaction and she won't be satisfied with anything less than a blond hunk minus the receding hairline."

His guys were aging and Beau recognized that, but a customer had yet to be so bold as to point it out. "You've got to be kidding."

"Do I look like I'm kidding?" She held up her mug. "I'm on my fifth cup of coffee in as many minutes."

"But you don't drink coffee."

"Exactly." She took another sip. "At the rate I'm going, I'll be over the edge and into Coffee Drinkers Anonymous before you even get started on the Farrel house, much less win that blasted competition and earn this company some much needed respect."

"It's only three weeks until the judging. You can tough it out until then. After that, no one will be calling for a hunk. They'll be contacting H&H Construction and you won't have to worry about the Savannah Sawyers of the world. In the meantime, send Jack." He motioned to the man standing near the water cooler. "He knows enough about flooring to finish the job and he's blond."

"I hate to break it to you, but he's got a beer belly, which pulls him out of the running for hunk of the year."

He grinned. "You really think she'll notice?"

"You really think she won't?"

Beau fought down a wave of anxiety, walked to the coffeemaker, and helped himself to a cup. Pitch black. "Send Jack," he said again. "He's the most capable besides Bryan and the work comes first."

"I know that and you know that. It's Savannah Sawyer who needs to know it." She fingered the stack of work orders, pulled the instructions, and handed them to Jack. "I've got a really bad feeling about her. I wouldn't be at all surprised to see a mention of us in her column."

"As in she's very satisfied with a job well done and she wants to tell the world?"

"As in don't call them because they're just a bunch of beer-belly bubbas."

"Maybe she likes beer bellies." If he'd learned one thing over the years, it was that you couldn't second-guess a woman's taste. Annabelle, who was quite a knockout, had fallen hook, line, and sinker for Warren, despite his own beer belly and receding hairline and his hobby of burping in tune with his favorite song. "You worry too much. When all is said and done, she'll be happy with the job."

Every customer, even the most difficult, ended up being happy because Hire-a-Hunk stood behind their guarantee of satisfaction. They were the best and they proved it in the end with a job well done.

The trouble was, it was getting harder and harder to get the work in the first place. But soon the phone would be ringing off the hook with people who wanted the best, not the best looking, and H&H would have a solid, secure spot in the industry.

Xandra Farrel's house was his ticket to that security. All he had to do was concentrate on the job at hand and forget the woman herself. And the past.

He ignored the sudden image of her that pushed into his head, and walked into the adjoining office. A massive desk took up most of the room, along with a leather chair and a small file cabinet. Leather gasped and groaned as he sank down behind the desk and set his cup to the side. His fingertips brushed the smooth wood and he closed his eyes for a second.

There was nothing as inviting as the feel of smooth wood beneath his hands. That's why he left a lot of the administrative work to Annabelle and did as much hands-on as possible. The average fix-it jobs did little to satisfy him, however, because Beau didn't enjoy fixing things.

He liked to *make* things, to create something from nothing or, as his mother used to say, to create something beautiful from something ugly. He'd taken a half rotted oak tree from his dad's backyard and turned it into a rich piece of furniture. He'd hand-carved not only each leg of this desk, but the scalloped edges, as well.

His apartment in the Woodlands—a suburb of Houston—was filled with everything from chairs to tables to a headboard he'd crafted just last year. He'd even made a hope chest for Annabelle when she'd married Warren.

"Jack, right?" Annabelle's voice sounded from the doorway and he glanced up.

"Stop worrying. This Sawyer woman will be happy. I guarantee it."

"You're the boss."

Unfortunately.

As soon as the thought entered his head, he pushed it back out. He liked being the boss. He enjoyed the freedom that came with running his own company, even if it did bring a world of headaches.

He was his own *boss,* for Christ's sake. Who wouldn't want to be the boss? He came and went as he pleased. He called the shots. He controlled his own destiny.

If only the notion were half as appealing as it used to be.

Beau Hollister was definitely not the same bad boy she'd crawled into the backseat with on that humid November night.

Xandra came to this conclusion as she pulled up near the curb late Monday afternoon and stared through the windshield at the scaffolding that now surrounded her falling-down house. The scaffolding platform extended up to the second floor, where Beau stood in front of her upstairs bedroom window, prying a rotted shutter loose.

Sure, he was still *bad,* as in mesmerizing violet eyes and a wicked smile that could charm any woman right out of her panties—any shy, naive, desperate woman who didn't own one of the most successful sexual aid companies in the country, that is. But the word "boy" didn't even touch the 100 percent prime, grade A, hunk-a-hunk of beefcake *man* standing in front of her.

Her gaze started at the bottom and worked its way up.

Worn denim, the cuffs slightly frayed where they bunched over his dusty brown work boots, molded the long length of his legs. The material clung to his thighs and cupped his crotch. A faded black T-shirt stretched across his broad chest and hinted at the rock-hard definition beneath. A white hard hat perched atop his dark head and shielded the upper half of his face from the fading daylight. His forearms tightened and muscles bulged as he hammered the crowbar beneath the edge of the shutter and pulled. Wood splintered and cracked. His full lips pulled into a determined line as he turned to the opposite side, hammered the bar beneath the edge and pulled again.

Her gaze lingered on the broad outline of his back before making a beeline south.

He had a really great tush. Not too wide or overly round like some of the guys she saw walking the treadmill at her gym. Nor was it too flat or narrow like the guys she saw pumping weights. His was tight and firm and just wide enough to fit his hips and strong thighs.

Then again, he'd always had a great tush. He'd always had a great everything back in high school. He'd been more gangly and thin back then, his body more lean than muscular, but he'd still been a hottie with the same undress-you eyes and teasing grin.

Beau was the boy that every mama forbade their daughter to date, and so no one had *dated* him. The girls had sneaked out with him after football games, or went sniffing around his dad's gas station when they craved what their Polo-wearing, college-bound boyfriends couldn't give them: an exciting taste of the forbidden.

While he hadn't wanted for female company, he'd still been considered a social outcast. Beau and Xandra had had that in common, although her excuse had nothing to do with being working class in a small town full of academic snobs and old money. Rather, she'd been the fat chick, and her mother was the infamous Jacqueline Farrel—a militant, morally defunct nutcase in a community where marriage wasn't a choice, but an expected way of life.

You were born. You grew up. You got married. You squeezed out a couple of kids. You played the doting grandmother once your couple of kids squeezed out a couple of their own. You died. End of story.

A fairy tale as far as Xandra was concerned. She'd grown up with a different mantra all together, and so she hadn't ever fit with the rest of her peers. Beau hadn't fit either, but he'd fit in perfectly with Xandra's plans. She'd needed experience and he'd oozed the stuff, and so she'd asked him to the Sadie Hawkins dance.

A big mistake.

She knew that now, but back then it had felt like the right move. From the moment she'd climbed into his car and suggested they forfeit the dance, right up to the point that he'd killed the engine, leaned over and kissed her.

She could still feel the firm intensity of his full lips, the slow glide of his tongue against the seam of her mouth, the soft thrust as she'd opened up for him . . .

She cleared her throat and forced the image aside.

Sure, it had been a great kiss, followed by a dozen more equally great kisses, but once they'd progressed from kissing to everything else, things had gone downhill. Fast. Which was why it had turned out to be not only a mistake, but a good waste of five minutes. She hadn't come out of it any more knowledgeable about the reality of sex, except to conclude that it *had* to get better or she would just as soon check herself into the nearest convent.

It had gotten better, of course, because she'd gotten better. She was more knowledgeable now. More experienced. And a good twenty pounds lighter. She'd gone from the chubby virgin chick Beau Hollister had been in such a hurry to be done with, to the hip, semisvelte—at least when she squeezed into a tight black skirt like the one she was wearing right now—CEO of a thriving sexual aid company, and she was now worthy of every man's slow, sweet time.

Okay, so maybe not *every* man. Mark had obviously moved on to greener pastures, just like her steady boyfriend during her freshman year in college, and the two blind dates she'd had—thanks to her older sister Eve who'd been determined to help her beef up her sexual résumé—during the summer between high school and college. But Beau didn't have to know any of that.

Nor did he have to know that she would rather watch back-to-back episodes of *Howard Stern* than slide her feet into a pair of four-inch Manolo Blahniks like the ones she was wearing now. And he certainly didn't have to know that she wasn't the least bit comfortable dressed in a sexy business suit, particularly since she'd gained ten pounds and said suit was much tighter than it should have been. Or that she slept in sweat socks and an oversized University of Texas T-shirt. Or that the only reason she dressed herself up like CEO Barbie day after day wasn't because she liked it, but because she had an image to maintain.

But again, Beau didn't have to know any of that.

As far as he was concerned, she looked like a full-blown hottie. She walked like one. She talked like one. Therefore, she was one. And because he'd overlooked all that hottie potential way back when, he would now have to content himself with admiring her hotness from afar.

With that thought in mind, she squared her shoulders, pushed out her well-rounded 34Ds, opened her car door, stepped out, and made her way up the walkway. Wood creaked as she mounted the first porch step. She saw the scaffold tremble as he turned overhead and stared down at her.

"Don't let me interrupt." She didn't glance up as she topped the steps and picked her way past the piles of supplies.

Her heart pounded faster and louder than the drummer for Metallica. A crazy reaction since she had no reason to be nervous. It wasn't like she was still attracted to him, for heaven's sake. Sure, he was good-looking but Xandra wasn't the least bit swayed by looks. She wanted substance. Character. A man who wouldn't be put off by a few extra pounds or a pair of ratty sweatpants.

Hello? Since when do you want anything from a man other than viable sperm?

She didn't. It's just that she wanted her child to grow up with character and substance and so it would only stand to reason that she would want those qualities in a potential father. Yep, character and substance were going at the top of her Perfect Daddy list.

As for the heart pounding . . . That was a purely hormonal reaction due to the fact that she and Mark hadn't had sex in over six months. In her current state of deprivation, she would have gone weak at the knees for any halfway decent-looking man, especially one standing an arm's length away, sweaty and smiling.

Yep, he was smiling.

She swallowed and concentrated on making her way toward the front door.

"Just keep doing what you're doing," she called out.

"Actually, I'm nearly done for the day." Metal creaked as he descended the scaffold ladder. Dusty brown work boots filled her peripheral vision to her right as his feet met the porch. "Just give me a few minutes," he told her, "and I'll clear some of this stuff off to the side and out of your way."

"No need, really. I can make it through—Ugh." Her heel came down on something very slippery and she grappled for one of the scaffold legs. It trembled, providing little reinforcement, and she teetered. But before she followed her briefcase to the ground, a strong hand closed over her upper arm. His fingers burned into her and a delicious heat curled in her stomach.

"You look really good." The words were out before she could stop them. "I, uh, mean the house looks really good." She tore her gaze from his and glanced around. "Great."

He gave her a puzzled look. "We're in the process of stripping it and tearing out the rotting wood."

"I, um, can see that, but for an old house being stripped and torn out, it, uh, looks really great."

Atta girl, Barbie. Wow him with your wit and get him to lust after you intellectually as well as physically.

She licked her lips and gave herself a mental shake. "What I mean is, I'm sure the house is going to look great when everything is done."

He grinned. "You're right about that. The details on this place are ingenious. Once everything is sanded and refinished, the rotted pieces replaced, it's really going to be something."

She heard the words, but they didn't quite penetrate. She was still stuck on his grin. His mouth crooked at the corner and his face softened and his violet eyes sparkled.

Her stomach hollowed out and her fingers trembled and

damned if she didn't have the insane thought that she wanted to kiss him. And touch him. And feel him kiss her. And touch her. And—

"When am I going to get inside?"

"I'm wondering that myself." Boy, was she ever.

"I was thinking tomorrow morning would be a good time. The boys and I can work on the interior in the mornings, so that we'll be out of your way come afternoon."

"You and the boys . . . ?" His words registered and heat flamed her cheeks. "You mean the house."

"What did you mean?"

"I, uh, meant the house, too." She busied herself searching for her house key. "I just wanted to make sure that you meant the house and that we weren't getting our wires crossed with one person thinking one thing and the other thinking something else."

"What *else*?"

"Not that anyone was actually thinking anything else," she rushed on, desperate to ignore his question and the vivid image that it stirred of him leaning over her. "Or that there's anything else to think. Boy, it's getting late. I've got a ton of work to do. You can let yourself in tomorrow morning." She motioned around her as she shoved her key into the lock. "It's going to be great. I can feel it."

Liar. The only thing she felt was hot. And embarrassed. And the insane urge to drop her briefcase, wrap her arms around him, and show him the "what else" she'd been referring to.

Okay, so maybe she'd gained twelve pounds instead of ten and the added weight was making her suit tight enough to constrict blood flow to her brain.

She drew in a deep breath as she unlocked the door. Her chest pressed against the confining buttons and she couldn't seem to get enough air. Yes, that was it. Thankfully, otherwise she would be inclined to think she was actually attracted to Beau Hollister.

"You forgot something."

"Pardon me?" She turned.

"You forgot this." He bent and picked up a glass Pyrex casserole dish, the top covered with aluminum foil. "One of your neighbors dropped it by about fifteen minutes ago. She said to tell you to keep the faith and remember, he's not worth killing your figure for."

"It's my neighborhood watch. They don't want me going off the deep end because my ex left me."

"Aren't neighborhood watches usually more interested in crime?"

"The women handle the emotional well-being of the neighborhood, and the men worry over the physical well-being."

"That explains the old man who keeps walking by here with his pit bull." He motioned to the weathered-looking man with a shock of white hair who stood a few houses up, watering his lawn. His dog barked from the porch.

"That's Mr. Mitchell. I heard he had his flowerbed trampled by a plumber last year and he hasn't been the same since. Just don't make any sudden moves toward my begonias"—she motioned to the small flowerbed off to the side of the house—"and you'll be okay."

He smiled and she smiled.

And then she frowned because her heart skipped when it should have been beating. A calm, steady beat rather than the fast, furious drum of a woman on the edge.

"I *really* have to go."

Chapter Eight

With the casserole dish in hand, Xandra left Beau standing on the front porch and retreated into the secluded safety of her front hallway. The door clicked shut behind her and the dark interior swallowed her up. She tried for another deep breath with little success.

Her heart was pounding and her blood was rushing and she actually felt light-headed . . . It was the suit, all right. A problem she could easily fix.

Add to tomorrow's to-do list: Buy larger suits.

A quick trip to Saks and she would be back to her usual self. No more shortness of breath. No more pounding heart. No more trembling hands. And no more mental road trips into Smutville with Beau Hollister.

He was supposed to lust after her, not the other way around. This was her moment of retribution. Her proverbial bird flip to every guy who'd failed to notice her back in high school. Her moment in the sun.

The thought wasn't as calming as it should have been. She needed something full of preservatives and totally unhealthy for that.

Flipping on the light, she set her briefcase on the floor and the casserole dish on a small antique table that held magazines. She started down the hallway, shedding clothing along the way. The shoes went first. The suit jacket followed. She loosened the button on her skirt and untucked her blouse and . . . Ah, there. *Now* she could breathe.

A few minutes later, she sat on her sofa and powered up her laptop. She loaded the CD-ROM that had come with her procreation planner and readied herself for her first truly proactive step in achieving personal success: the Perfect Daddy list.

She'd vowed to take a step forward both personally and professionally each day from here on out, and so she was going to add at least one daddy must-have to her list every day.

Starting now.

She keyed a few of the general traits that every woman usually wanted in the father of her child.

Handsome.

Intelligent.

Rich.

Nix that. He didn't have to be rich because he wouldn't be providing for her. He just needed the brains and the drive to make himself rich if he wanted.

Determined and capable of monetary success.

The entry stirred an image of Beau standing on the scaffolding, looking so tall, dark, and handsome. And intelligent. And very determined.

And capable of monetary success?

Yes and no. Yes, he'd looked more than capable of monetary success—he had his own business, which came highly recommended. But no, he did not look capable in the daddy sense.

And why not?

Because he was *Beau Hollister,* of all people. The man
responsible for the worst sexual experience of her life, and
no amount of monetary success could overshadow that
fact. Her Perfect Daddy would know his way around the
bedroom. Conceiving her child was going to be a momen-
tous occasion in her life. One she definitely wanted to
enjoy.

Experienced and capable when it came to sex.

She finished keying the next entry, stared at it for a moment, then deleted it and retyped it.

*Experienced and capable when it came to hot, steamy,
thrilling sex.*

There. That definitely put Beau last when it came to potential prospects.

Then again, she had zero possibilities at the moment,
which meant he was the only man on that particular list.

Before she could think too hard about the notion, she
saved her file and turned off the computer. Better to stop
now before she found herself remembering the past and
several key factors leading up to their fast and furious sex
session. Like how she'd actually *enjoyed* Beau's touch.
And his kiss. And the way he'd stroked the side of her neck
with the pad of his thumb just before he'd dipped his head
and licked her pulse beat . . .

She shook away the memory, set her computer aside
and pushed to her feet. In the kitchen, she hit the ON switch
and fluorescent light flooded the newly renovated space. It
was the only room that had had a complete makeover before she'd bought the house thanks to the fact that the previous owner had been a professional chef. Everything was
brand new, but at the same time it retained its old-world
charm. While the appliances were state-of-the-art stainless

steel, the cabinets had been finished with a pine glaze that gave them a worn look. The countertops were done in granite. The floor was the original hardwood resanded and refinished. Wood groaned with each step as she headed for the cabinet where she'd unpacked her groceries the previous night. Her gaze lit on an unopened bag of Doritos and her mouth watered.

The phone rang just as she reached the countertop. She grabbed the receiver that hung on the wall to the left.

"Don't do it," a voice declared.

"Excuse me?"

"Don't touch the chips."

Xandra glanced around her, from the stainless steel refrigerator at one end of the counter, to the matching oven at the other. No stranger lurking in the background. No video camera visible to the naked eye.

Her gaze swiveled back to her hand just an inch shy of the bright red bag.

"Who is this?"

"Katy." The voice went from stalkerlike to sorority-girl sweet. "Katy Templeton from across the street."

Xandra turned toward the window that faced the front of the house. The shades were up, the curtains parted. She saw a woman framed in the window of the house that sat opposite hers. She was pretty in a pink jogging suit, her brown hair pulled back into a ponytail. Identical toddler boys overflowed her arms, one poised on each hip. A phone nestled in the space between her chin and shoulder.

"I know it seems like a good idea to lose yourself in a bag of Four Cheese Doritos and a big bowl of cheese dip and a glass of chocolate milk but, trust me, it's not worth it."

Xandra eyed the single bag sitting next to a four-pack of

toilet paper and this month's issue of *Cosmo*. "I don't have any cheese dip or chocolate milk."

"That's beside the point. I know you're upset now, but no man wants to marry an Anna Nicole Smith when they can have a Tyra Banks. I know. I've been there. David and I broke up twice while we were dating. The first time, I got so freaked that I put on ten pounds. The second time, I put on twenty. But then David—bless his heart—promised me a platinum wedding band and a honeymoon in Bali if I dropped the weight. Talk about incentive."

"You mean your husband wasn't going to marry you if you didn't lose the weight?"

"Not a chance. Who wants to marry a cow? Not David. He's into sales and marketing. His life revolves around image. But that's beside the point."

"Which is?"

"Losing it was so tough because I had really let myself go. We're talking *twenty pounds*. Luckily I was extremely thin to begin with and I could stand to gain a little weight. But you're right there on the edge."

"Excuse me?"

"Don't get me wrong. You look great. But there's a fine line between voluptuous and chubby. So don't do it. Don't destroy yourself."

"It's just a few Doritos."

"*Now.* But then comes the cheese dip and the chocolate milk. Before you know it, you're licking the lid from a pint of Ben & Jerry's because you've inhaled the contents and you're desperate for more. Don't start down that path. Turn the other way now. I left an asparagus and turnip salad for you."

"You're the one responsible for the Pyrex dish."

"Certainly. I'm number two on the phone tree, so I

whipped up my specialty. Asparagus has lots of vitamins to boost your energy and turnips are a cleansing vegetable. Doritos have no nutritional value whatsoever. Swear you won't eat them."

"This is silly."

"Listen, the boys want juice boxes and dinner. I'm here if you need me. Until tomorrow morning, that is. Julie will be taking over then. That's Julie with the beige Ford Expedition, not Julie with the red one. Now swear."

"I'm not going to do any such thing."

"Then I'll just have to keep talking."

"I swear."

A dial tone filled Xandra's ear. She eyed the Doritos for a full minute as guilt churned inside her.

Well, hell. She couldn't very well eat the Doritos when she'd sworn. Even if the swear had been coerced.

She let loose a deep sigh and tried to calm the pitter-patter of her heart. No luck. She turned toward the pantry, pulled open the door, and eyed the contents. A bag of Oreos called to her from the top shelf.

The phone gave a shrill ring just as she pulled the bag free and closed the pantry door.

"Too much sugar," Katy said before Xandra had a chance to say hello. "And sugar turns to fat and fat turns to cellulite and before you know it you're having liposuction. Swear you won't eat the Oreos."

"Okay, okay."

"Say the words."

"I *swear*." Xandra slid the receiver back into place. She thought about walking back down the hall and retrieving the casserole. But asparagus and turnips?

She turned back to the Doritos. Before she could reach forward, the phone rang again.

"Look," she said when she snatched it up. "I'm not trading my Doritos for a platinum wedding band and a honeymoon in Bali."

"Of course you're not, dear," came Jacqueline Farrel's voice. "You're a sane, rational womanist in the prime of her life. Unlike your poor mother who is this close to popping a major vessel and stroking out."

"What's wrong?"

"I'm giving dating advice on my show. The executive producer wants to add an element of realism to *Get Sexed Up!* and the whole idea is making my stomach churn. Then there's your—"

"*Dating* advice?" Xandra cut in. "*You?*"

"Ridiculous, isn't it?" Before Xandra could respond with an enthusiastic "hell, yes!," Jacqueline rushed on, "The whole segment will center around a quartet of women in four different metropolitan cities—we're filming on location, so I'll be in Houston in a few weeks. Cameras will follow the women on an evening out, I'll evaluate the tape, offer comments, and then the women will head back out and try again using my advice."

"I can kind of see it. Dr. Phil has his families and you have your daters."

"They're not daters, dear. They're single, independent, professional women looking for long-term commitment in a vastly shrinking pool of potential partners."

"It sounds interesting."

"It's prostitution, that's what it is. A full-fledged exploitation of the entire man–woman relation ritual in the name of ratings."

"I can see your point."

"Of course you can, dear. You're not the problem. You're never the problem. It's my blasted producer. And then there's your father. Since your sister's enslavement ceremony—"

"It's called a wedding," Xandra cut in.

"Same thing. Anyhow, since the enslavement, your father has become completely obsessed with the whole couple thing. He wants to open a joint checking account."

"When you guys have only been together a measly thirty-seven years?"

"That's what I told him, but he simply will not leave the subject alone. And then there's Skye, who is totally obsessed with this procreation business. Now don't get me wrong, I love babies. I would adore a happy, healthy granddaughter. But your sister is dead-set on having a boy because that man—"

"His name is Clint and he's your son-in-law."

"Whatever, dear. Anyhow, that man wants a boy and so Skye wants to give him one. Sure, boys are nice. Necessary. The world needs them. But to purposely try for one? I tell you, my heart can't take much more."

"I think you worry too—"

"And then there's Eve. Do you know what she's done now?" Before Xandra could take a guess, her mother rushed on, "She got a tattoo. Not that I have anything against tattoos, but this is not a Kama Sutra position or the words to a voodoo sex spell or a female praying mantis devouring her mate or any of the other things I might expect from your sister. It's a man's name and it's tattooed right on her gluteus maximus. I saw it myself when I stopped by for coffee last week on my way to the studio. A *man's* name, for heaven's sake. She's like branded cattle. But I know you don't want to hear any of this."

"I don't mind."

"Of course you don't mind. You're such a sweet, obedient child. And so patient to listen to all of my worries. But enough about me. How's the business doing?"

"Actually, we're doing pretty well. I'm working on this new proj—"

"Of course you're doing well. You're a Farrel, dear. You would think that the apples wouldn't fall far from the tree, but I swear your two sisters were switched at birth. Imagine Skye wanting a boy on purpose . . ." Jacqueline spent the next several minutes going on about everything from boy babies to a new yoga technique she'd just learned to combat stress.

"It really leaves me feeling clear-headed and more focused. It's the only thing that's kept me from giving up the ghost over the past few months with the enslavement and your father and that blasted tattoo."

"That's great, Mom."

"Of course it is, dear. I'll be sure to show it to you when I make it down to tape the Houston Smart Dating segment in two weeks."

Which meant Xandra had two weeks to break the whole Mark thing to her mother. Two weeks to confess that she wasn't the perfect womanist daughter in the perfect womanist relationship, following in her mother's perfect womanist footsteps.

"Not that you need a stress-relieving technique," her mother went on. "Why, you're much too young with too good a head on your shoulders to fall victim to such a thing."

"Actually, I could use a good technique. Since I gave up the smoking, it's been nothing but gum and candy. Anything that will relieve my cravings—"

"Gum is bad for you, dear. And the candy. Just say no."

"It's not that easy—"

"Of course it is. You're my daughter, after all. Strong. Independent. A fearless Farrel without two ungrateful daughters and a stubborn significant other determined to send you to an early grave—they're calling me to the set. Take care, dear."

"Nice talking with you, Mom," she said into the phone as the dial tone echoed in her ear.

Oh, well. It's not like she wanted to really *talk* to her mom; Jacqueline complained and Xandra listened. That's the way it had always been. The way it would always be because Jacqueline Farrel thought her youngest daughter had it all together. No complaints. No worries. Even when she did manage to slide a worry of her own into the conversation, Jacqueline tuned it out, and Xandra let her. Because that's what Xandra always did. She lived for everyone else first, and herself second.

She forced the thought aside. This was her mother, for heaven's sake. The woman who'd given birth to her. The least Xandra could do after eighteen hours of labor, complete with a full two hours of pushing, was play the good daughter and pretend life was perfect.

The sound of a door closing drew her to the window and she glanced out to see Beau load the last of his equipment, climb into the driver's seat, and rev the van's engine. Her gaze locked with his for a split second and her heart gave a double thump.

Perfect?

Yeah, right.

She yanked the shade down, grabbed the bag of Doritos, and ripped it open.

Chapter Nine

Say hello to my little friend." Albert sat on the corner of Xandra's desk and did his best *Scarface* imitation. He pulled a small plastic bag from his pocket and dangled it in front of her.

Xandra's face split into a smile as she took the small baggie that contained what looked like a neon blue female condom. "It's only been two days."

"What can I say? Your research was right on the money. We used the materials you suggested, and lo and behold, the first prototype. We've been calling her Mabel the Love Glove."

"Mabel?"

"Diane, one of our newbies, put in the heat sensors and the name of her sex ed teacher in high school was Mabel Sparks. It's just our working title. You have any ideas?"

"I want something that says 'orgasmic breakthrough.' Providing it *is* an orgasmic breakthrough." Her gaze met his. "You really think it works?"

"We ran it through all of our scientific tests. It passed with flying colors. It withstood the actual simulated sex act and generated an impressive heat reading even under artificial circumstances. With real warm bodies, the heat level will increase. The more heat, the stronger the electrical pulse, the better the orgasm. But there's no danger factor. The material is heat sensitive, but it only warms to a certain temperature, so there's no chance of anyone getting hurt."

"How did you manage that?"

"I took plain latex and blended it with a special synthetic plastic—the same stuff that they use on the space shuttle as a matter of fact. It forms a protective shield, so to speak, and withstands high temperatures without heating or meltdown. I only used a small fraction of the stuff. Enough to make it safe, but not enough to defeat the whole purpose. The result is a blend that's soft and pliable and sensitive, yet durable enough not to break."

"*Guaranteed* not to break?"

"It held up through all of the standard strength tests used for condoms and the like, so I stand behind it."

"Hot sex that's also safe sex." Her smile widened. "This is definitely going to cause a stir." She stared at the contents. "Is it cost effective?"

"About the same as a typical condom. We played around with the idea of doing something permanent rather than disposable, like a diaphragm. But once Mabel heats to her max time, it weakens the material. She can withstand one really good sex session, complete with multiple orgams, but we don't recommend taking her out and saving her for later. Besides, she does double duty as a condom, so disposable is definitely the way to go."

"I'd like at least six trial tests to confirm or disprove the results."

"There are more samples in the works. Those should be

ready by this afternoon. In the meantime, this one is all yours."

Once Albert shut the door, Xandra flipped on her red research light, walked back to her desk and slid into her leather seat. She opened her drawer and unearthed the very first King Kong vibrator she'd designed eight years ago. Wild Woman no longer offered this version, but it still remained Xandra's personal favorite. It had been her first product, and her first vibrator ever.

She turned on her computer and pulled up her notes. Typing in "Trial Test I," she left the keyboard blinking, turned the dimmer switch and killed the bright lights in her office. She slid a popular Nelly CD into her stereo, leaned back in her chair, and closed her eyes as the sexy "Hot in Here" pulsed through the room.

She meant to envision one of her favorite fantasies, but instead of envisioning Brad Pitt or the lead singer from Creed, she saw a tall, dark, and delicious man that looked suspiciously like Beau Hollister.

Funny because he'd never once occupied her sexual fantasies since she'd discovered that, while he was as hot as all the girls thought, he was much too fast on the draw.

Mmm . . . but not this time.

He touched her slow and sweet and in all the right places, and try as she might to tune him out, she couldn't. His hands were so warm and knowing as they moved over her body, stirring her breasts and bringing her nipples alive. His touch moved lower, until he reached the ache between her legs. He worked her into a frenzy then, stroking and plunging until she was breathless and desperate and this close to bursting into flames . . .

The orgasm hit her hard and fast and *electric* . . . Her insides tingled. Sensation spiked through her body, rushing along her nerve endings until she buzzed like a live wire.

Several heart pounding moments later, she pulled herself together, deposited the Mabel sample into the nearest trash can and flipped on the overhead lighting. She turned her attention to the computer screen to key in the test results.

Xandra considered herself an expert when it came to masturbation—after all, she tested all of her own products. But she'd never, in her eight years in the business, felt an orgasm quite that intense just from using a vibrator.

It was the most incredible thing she'd ever felt.

At the same time, it was just a hint of the satisfaction to come once she tried out her invention as it was meant to be used: with a warm male body.

The thought was a lot more depressing than it should have been because it wasn't as if she had a line of warm bodies beating down her door.

So? Just get out there and find one. Problem solved.

She could do that. She was attractive. Intelligent. Sane—at least by today's dating standards. She would simply march out of her office this afternoon and find someone for a little after-hours action.

That's what she told herself as she finished off a pile of paperwork, packed up her briefcase, and headed up to the engineering department. As promised, Albert had a dozen of Mabel's sisters ready and waiting.

After packing the little beauties into her briefcase, she felt armed and ready to find herself a man.

An easy task, she told herself as she left the suite of offices. This was Houston, after all. An overflowing metropolis. There were men everywhere.

A half dozen professional types stuffed into the elevator

as she got in and headed to the ground floor. More suits overflowed the lobby of the Chase bank building, which housed Wild Woman's headquarters. Men of all shapes and sizes bustled along the sidewalk as she made her way to the parking garage one block over.

She spotted a typical Texas cowboy in his Resistol hat and starched Wranglers, and a yuppie wearing Dockers and a polo shirt. A policeman stood near the corner sipping a cup of coffee. A doctor wearing green scrubs shouted into his cell phone and nearly knocked her over. A handful of construction workers whistled from their work site on the opposite side of the street.

Of course, the man in question would have to be between twenty-one and fifty—the average age range of her customer base—which ruled out at least half of the available pool surrounding her. Add a few more gotta-haves based on her own personal preferences—a pleasant scent, nice eyes, and a full set of teeth and she'd all but eliminated a handful.

A handful of strangers.

And the problem is?

Okay, so she'd fantasized a time or two about a one-night stand, but she'd never actually picked up someone just for sex. Not that she had anything against it if both parties were unattached and responsible. But she didn't know how to initiate a one-night stand and, truthfully, the reality wasn't nearly as exciting as her fantasies. Instead, it was downright scary.

She didn't want a nameless, faceless someone who might wear BVDs beneath a conservative navy suit, or polka-dotted boxers beneath his starched policeman's uniform, or an animal print thong beneath his Levis. Not that she had anything against BVDs or boxers or thongs—

okay, so maybe she did draw the line at a man wearing a thong. But the BVDs and the boxers she could deal with, regardless of the design. It was the fact that she didn't *know*. She hadn't a clue what to expect once the door shut and the festivities began.

A woman could find herself in all sorts of bizarre, not to mention downright dangerous, situations should she pick the wrong man to fall into bed with. Why, she might pick up a fetish freak who wore women's panty hose or a black rubber bustier with spikes for nipples. Or maybe a rude, crude obnoxious jerk who farted during sex. Or worse. What if he turned out to be a Jack-the-Ripper wannabe?

The questions haunted her as she climbed into her car and started for the West End historic district downtown from where she lived.

She quickly came to the conclusion that picking up someone was not a possibility. Regardless of how hot or how sexy or how normal someone looked, looks could be deceiving. She'd learned that firsthand a long time ago. Beau had looked every bit the sensual, sexy, perfect man to initiate her into the Sisterhood of Sexually Active Women, but he'd been a complete dud.

Never again.

She turned onto her block and maneuvered into the driveway. Retrieving her briefcase, she clicked the lock and headed up the sidewalk toward her house. A large commercial truck, along with two white vans with the Hire-a-Hunk emblem emblazoned on the sides sat directly in front of her house. A tarp covered her minuscule front yard. A two-story ladder leaned against the far front edge of the house and supported a large man, beer belly pushing against the front of his white T-shirt. He held what looked like a large sander and was stripping the paint off the lattice eave that surrounded the second story of her house. The smell of wood burned her nostrils and the loud whirring filled her ears.

When she was halfway up the front walk, the sound paused and the smell subsided slightly as the man stopped to take a long swig from the soda can sitting near his left foot. He let loose a loud burp and went back to work, having totally killed the Hire-a-Hunk image.

Likewise, the two men who worked at the far corner of the roof looked more like Laurel and Hardy than a pair of hot bods straight out of the Blue Collar Hunks calendar she'd seen a few years back that Beau's company had participated in to help raise money for the Texas Children's Hospital. Xandra could easily understand why Beau felt the need to change that image. It was either that, or hire a new crew, and she had the gut feeling he would never do that.

A surge of warmth went through her, followed by a surge of pure heat when she caught sight of him. He stood just a few feet away on the front steps, his attention focused on the hand railing that followed the five steps up to the porch. He worked at the wood with a piece of sandpaper, rubbing furiously before wiping away the dust.

Yep, she'd learned firsthand that appearances could be deceiving and she had Beau Hollister to thank. He'd looked every bit the sexy, experienced boy who knew what to do and how to do it, and he'd always been nice to her, and so she'd picked him to take her virginity. But he'd been all wrong. A tactless, awkward dud.

Except for the kiss.

The first kiss had been pretty incredible, but then he'd started fumbling with his hands and they'd gotten down to the actual act. Before she'd even had a chance to close her eyes and enjoy the moment, it had been over. She hadn't even come close to an orgasm. If only she'd had Mabel back then, maybe things would have been different.

The thought stuck in her brain as Beau leaned over. His T-shirt slid up, revealing a few tanned inches of his back. She glimpsed the waistband of his underwear.

White cotton briefs—the same type he'd worn back in high school. Probably even the same brand. He leaned over a little more and she caught a glimpse of the colorful tag. Fruit of the Loom, all right. The same brand he'd worn that moonlit Friday night when she'd seen him shove them down. She also knew a few more key things about him— namely that he wasn't a serial killer and he didn't fart during sex. He also smelled pretty good, had incredible violet eyes and all his teeth.

Hello warm body.

The truth hit her as she paused on the bottom step and stared up at the man who stood on the top step.

She couldn't have conjured a more perfect subject. He represented the ultimate test for her product. He was hot and sexy and heterosexual, and he was terrible in the sack. If she could have an ultimate orgasm with Beau Hollister, of all people, then she would have proof beyond a doubt that she'd stumbled onto a winner with her new product.

She mounted the steps and her heart hammered in anticipation.

Not of the actual act, mind you, or because to get to that act she would surely feel his lips on hers again. But because she was standing on the brink of a major breakthrough.

She was one step shy when the wood creaked and he turned. Violet eyes collided with hers. Something sparked in the vivid depths, as if he could read the intention in her gaze.

"We're just finishing up here," he told her.

"Don't rush on my account."

"I would like to finish this banister before tomorrow morning."

"Have at it. I'm just going to go inside and do some work. Maybe fix a little dinner."

"I think that's already taken care of." He motioned inside. "It's in the kitchen."

"Did it smell funny?"

"Actually, it looked funny. Very green. It didn't really smell like anything."

"I guess I'd better go check it out." She smiled and walked past him. It wasn't as if she could just come out and say "Hey, you were so bad that I think you would be the perfect test subject to try out this new product. If I can enjoy myself with you, then I'm in business."

She wanted to have sex with him, which meant she needed him in an *up* mood—literally—and such a proposition would surely kill his ego and his erection.

No, she would have to be a bit more subtle. Be flirty and open and maybe a little forward, and let things progress from there.

Inside, she closed the kitchen blinds and gave a little wave to Katy who smiled from across the way before she turned to the Pyrex dish sitting on her table. She took one look at the green contents before depositing it into the refrigerator.

She would figure it out later. First things first, she needed to change into something casual but sexy and think of an excuse to get Beau Hollister off her front porch and into her house before he packed up his supplies and left.

She headed upstairs into her closet and retrieved the only casual item she owned—she lived in sweats, overalls and oversized T-shirts—that even came close to being sexy. It was a pair of blue jean shorts that she'd bought for the company picnic last year. When it came to work, she tried to keep up her sexy, vibrant image, and so she'd purchased the shorts, worn them for the event, and forgotten about them. Until now.

Ten minutes later, she was flat on her back, pulling frantically at the zipper of the shorts.

Funny, but they hadn't seemed that tight when she'd bought them. She shimmied and wiggled and tugged until her fingers were raw and the zipper finally closed. Another deep breath and she managed to suck in her tummy enough to slide the button closed.

She'd done it.

She struggled to her feet, ignored the urge to find the nearest pair of scissors and cut the waistband enough to breathe and retrieved the white cotton tank top she'd bought to go with the shorts.

Not a good choice since the fitted cotton showed her tummy bulge, which looked even more prominent with the tight shorts pushing everything north. She stood in front of her closet and debated a little longer before settling on an oversized T-shirt that she knotted at the waist.

A few minutes later, she gathered her courage, and pulled open the front door.

"Hey Beau!" she called out. He was standing beside his van, reaching for the door handle. "The light in the upstairs closet is messed up. I've replaced the bulb and flipped the switch and nothing. Do you think you could take a look before you leave?"

He gave her a wary glance and she had the sudden

thought that he was going to haul open the door, climb behind the wheel, and leave her to fix her own problems.

"It would really help me out if you could take a look."

Beau eyed her a few more seconds before shrugging. His hand fell away from the door handle and he turned toward the rear of the van. "Let me get my small toolbox."

A few minutes later, he tested the light himself before heading down to the basement and the breaker box. Xandra followed close behind.

"The breaker tripped," he told her after a quick look.

"Really?" She stared past him to the black switch she'd flipped before requesting his help.

He flipped the switch back into position. "Problem solved."

"*This* problem, but I've still got a few others. There's the light in the fridge—it doesn't work. And the garbage disposal. And the toilet."

Twenty minutes later, they'd dealt with the first two and were headed up the stairs to the bathroom, and Beau didn't seem any closer to kissing her than when he'd first walked in.

Despite her sexy shorts and the fact that she'd flirted with him. Or at least, she'd tried to flirt.

"So what's the problem?" His voice drew her from her thoughts. "Is it stopped up?"

She watched him as he peered into the toilet bowl. "Maybe. Or maybe I'm just not flushing it right."

"Either you're flushing or you're not." His gaze shifted to her. "There's no 'right' involved."

"It's definitely stopped up." Thanks to the roll of toilet paper she'd flushed earlier. "I tried the plunger, but it's not working."

"Sometimes there's not enough power in an ordinary plunger. You need a snake."

"A snake?" *Now* they were getting somewhere.

"It's a piece of pipe. I think I've got one out in my van. I'll be right back." He started downstairs and she watched him go, damning herself for not making a move when she'd been so close to him.

But she'd actually been nervous. Crazy because sex didn't make Xandra Farrel nervous. She should be excited. Ready to go. Eager.

Then again, this wasn't the ordinary, get-ready-for-a-good-orgasm kind of sex. It was the did-I-just-miss-something? kind. Or it had been that night so long ago.

No wonder she was more nervous than excited.

"Here it is," he said ten minutes later when he topped the stairs and walked to where she waited in the bathroom doorway. "This should work." He held up a long, winding silver pipe as he started inside.

"Wait," she cried as he moved past her.

"What's wrong?" He stopped and turned toward her.

"Nothing." And then she threw her arms around his neck and kissed him.

Chapter Ten

Beau wasn't sure what freaked him out the most:

The fact that Xandra Farrel was *kissing* him.

Or the fact that *Xandra Farrel* was kissing him.

Her soft, full lips covered his. Her hands came up to clutch at his shoulders. She canted her head and licked the seam of his mouth.

Instinct kicked in and he opened up before he could think better of it. Her tongue dipped inside and touched his, and his initial panic faded in a wave of hunger. He'd been on the wagon for too many months now, contenting himself with a few fantasies in the dead of night when the stress and worry overwhelmed him. But it wasn't enough to satisfy him completely. He needed something more, something real.

This.

The snake slid from his hand and clattered to the floor. He leaned into her, pressing her up against the bathroom wall. His hands slid around her waist. His fingers pressed into the lush curve of her bottom, drinking in the warmth of her body that seeped through the thin material of her shorts. The tile of the wall was cool against the back of his hands, but it did little to soothe the heat that rushed through him.

A soft moan vibrated from her mouth as she curled her hands up around his neck, her fingers insistent at the base of his skull. Her legs shifted slightly apart, cradling the hard-on that throbbed beneath the fly of his jeans.

Suddenly he didn't need to focus nearly as much as he needed to explore the cavern of her mouth and tangle his tongue with hers and see if she tasted half as sweet as he remembered.

As hot.

As wet.

He pulled her even closer and deepened the kiss, drinking her in like a man starved for water after a heavy duty workout. But he couldn't get enough of her. She wasn't close enough and so he held her tighter. He couldn't taste enough and so he kissed her even deeper, longer. His heart pounded and his nerves buzzed and his fingers itched to slip beneath the waistband of her shorts and feel her flesh against his own.

"God, you taste so good. I want to eat you up," he gasped against her lips.

His mouth covered hers again as his hands slid around to plunge beneath the hem of her shirt. He cupped her lace-covered breasts. Her nipple jutted through in one spot and rasped the center of his palm.

She moaned into his mouth and her body arched. Her hard, hot nipple pressed forward, greedy for more.

Sex.

The wild and wicked kind that made him want to take her right now up against the bathroom wall. No time to shed their clothes. Just her with her shorts tossed aside and him with his pants down around his ankles and water rushing from the toilet—

The thought stalled as the sound of splashing water pierced the haze of lust that surrounded him.

He tore his lips from hers and his eyes popped open.

"What's wrong—" she started, but the words died as her gaze followed his.

Water flowed over the sides of the toilet and spread across the tile floor.

He let go of her and reached for the silver knob behind the toilet base. Turning off the water, he retrieved the snake and turned his full attention to the toilet.

Not her.

Or the fact that she still leaned against the wall, her chest jutted forward as if his hands were still warm on her breasts, his palm feeling up her nipple. Her eyes were still at half mast, as if she were slightly dazed by the intensity of what had just happened.

Surprised even.

He ignored the thought and fed the snake down the toilet drain. A few minutes later, he'd fished out a sopping wet roll of toilet paper.

A full roll.

So much for the surprised look. It was just an act, like everything else. The past few moments rushed at him. The determined look in her eyes as he'd reached the bathroom threshold. The way she'd hauled him close and touched her lips to his without so much as a thought for the stopped-up plumbing.

"Do you normally use an entire roll of toilet paper when you make a trip to the bathroom?"

She pushed away from the wall and gave him an innocent look. "Why, it must have fallen in."

"That or someone stuffed it in."

"You mean like sabotage?" She shrugged and avoided his gaze when he turned accusing eyes on her. "I guess maybe it's possible, but what reason would someone have for wanting to mess up my plumbing?" When he started to answer, she held up her hands. "All right, all right. I confess. I've never been a very good liar." Her gaze met his. "I wanted to get you inside the house. I wanted to kiss you."

"And the breaker switch?"

"I threw it myself."

"And the light in the refrigerator?"

"I unscrewed the bulb."

"And the garbage disposal? Don't tell me you shoved your stocking down there on purpose."

"Are you kidding? Those are from Saks and damned hard to come by in that color. That's why I was hand washing them in the sink. It must have slid down the disposal when I pulled the plug to let the soap out. Thanks again for getting it to work."

"You're welcome." He eyed her. "I think."

"What's that supposed to mean?"

"That I don't have a problem fixing things. I do have a problem kissing you."

"You didn't seem to have much of a problem."

"The problem isn't the kissing itself, but the kissing of *you*. You're a client."

"And?"

"And I don't mix business with pleasure."

She smiled. "So leave your tool belt at the door, I'll stop breaking things, and we can get back to the pleasure part."

"It's not that simple. I'm committed."

The smile faded. "Don't tell me you're married?"

He shook his head. "Not that kind of committed."

"A girlfriend?"

"No."

One eyebrow slid up. "A boyfriend?"

"Hell no. I'm committed to my business. I'm in the middle of a touchy transition. I don't want to do anything that might mess that up. I'm not in the market for a relationship."

Relief washed her features. "Neither am I. This isn't about a relationship. It's about sex."

"Right."

"I'm serious. I don't want a relationship. I mean, I wouldn't mind having one eventually, if it met all three requirements of the Holy Commitment Trinity, but that's not what this is about. It's about you and me and sex."

"Yeah, sure."

"I'm serious. I would never, ever even think of you as relationship potential. I settled for two out of three before and ended up wasting eight years of my life. I'm not going that route again, which means you're completely out of the running because you've already got one strike against you."

"What strike?"

"You're really bad in—" she started before catching her bottom lip. "You're really *bad* around the house, as in good. I, however, am a total klutz when it comes to home improvement. We're totally mismatched, which kills us on requirement number one—common interests. So the only thing I would be remotely interested in with you is sex. No strings, no awkward morning after."

"There's no such thing." He grabbed his toolbox and headed for the door before he did something really stupid. Like take her up on her offer, press her up against the nearest wall, and give her another kiss like the one they'd just shared. And more . . .

A memory pushed into his head and he saw her face illuminated by the green dashboard lights. Her full, kiss-swollen lips. Her disappointed gaze.

He shook away the image. His refusal had nothing to do with that night and everything to do with the fact that he had a job to do.

It's been a long time. You're not a kid anymore. Who's to say she'll get to you the way she did back then?

But she was already getting to him. Just looking at her turned him on. Hearing her voice sent a wash of desire through him. Smelling her sweet scent made his gut clench and his insides ache. Touching her had his hands tingling.

Even after all this time, he still wanted her in a bad way. The way he'd wanted her that night when he'd slid inside her and she'd crawled into his head and screwed things up for him but good.

He needed to concentrate on completing this project to the best of his ability. It wasn't just his livelihood on the line here. It was about his men. They were loyal, dedicated, and good. They deserved the security that came with working for a solid company rather than a fad.

He wasn't going to let anyone distract him from his goal. Especially Xandra Farrel.

Not ever again.

"There's no such thing as just sex. Not for a woman." Okay, it sounded chauvinistic, but he was grasping here. He couldn't very well tell her that she turned him inside out. That would be like handing her a gun and telling her to shoot him. "You're all after one thing when it comes to men."

She wiggled her eyebrows. "Some great tongue action?"

He frowned and did his best to ignore the lacy thong hanging on the hook behind her bathroom door. "Emotional intimacy. You don't just want to get busy. You want to get close. To cuddle. To talk." He made a big show of shuddering. "No thank you. There's no such thing as temporary with any woman, especially one that gets under your skin and into your head and stays there no matter how much you try to push her out." So much for not handing her the sun. "We're not going at it," he rushed on, "so you can just stop all this. Keep your short-shorts and your sexy T-shirt and your lace thong to yourself."

"What lace thong?"

He pointed to the scrap hanging on the silver hook. "Your red lace thong."

"Oh, I don't actually wear that." She cleared her throat. "Um, what I mean is, I don't just wear it. I practically live in it, except when I've got on one of my many others that are just as skimpy. And just as sexy." She snatched up the thong and stuffed it into her pocket. "Look, I don't want a relationship any more than you do. I'm all about the physical."

"Says you."

"I'm serious. I'm a good-time girl. I'm all about having a good time right now."

"While you want to have a good time right now, you'll be seeing the house and the kids and the SUV come morning."

"For your information, I already have my own house and my own plan for children which, I can assure you, doesn't involve you, and I hate SUVs. I'm a BMW convertible kind of girl all the way. I really don't think of you like that. This isn't about commitment."

Damned if the comment didn't bug him a hell of a lot more than it should have. "Sure."

"Look, I ought to know what I want when it comes to men and it's definitely not you. At least not in the long-term sense. As for right now . . ." She smiled and his heart skipped a beat. "Why don't *you* kiss *me*?"

"I don't think that would be a good idea."

"No, it would be a great idea. You're a really good kisser." Her eyes twinkled with challenge. "Unless you're afraid."

"Afraid of what?"

"That you'll want more than a kiss, just the way I want more."

"I don't want more."

"Prove it. Kiss me. Just kiss me."

"That's not a good idea."

"Because you're not as immune to the whole idea as you want to be. You do want me."

"Maybe I do and maybe I don't. It's not about that. It's about the fact that you want something more than sex."

"But if I didn't, you would do it, right?" She came up behind him. "If you were one hundred percent convinced that I didn't want a relationship with you—that I'm telling the truth—then we could have sex, right?"

"Sure," he heard himself say. "And we could do it laying on top of the ten million dollars I'm going to win in tonight's lottery. And after that we could go outside and do it in the snow."

"It doesn't snow in Houston, Texas."

"Now you're catching on." His gaze collided with hers and he saw a flash of disappointment that made his chest ache and softened his voice. "Look, it's nothing personal. I just can't do this with you."

"You mean you *won't* do it with me." The disappointment faded into hurt and damned if he didn't have the sudden urge to reach out and pull her into his arms until the look disappeared.

Hurt? Why would she be the least bit hurt? He was the one who'd suffered the last time. He'd lost his scholarship because of her and had spent his college days working his ass off when he could have had a free ride.

"I can't, and I won't. You and me and sex . . ." He shook his head. "It's just not going to happen."

"Maybe not now," her voice followed him out. "But there's always tomorrow."

Xandra watched Beau climb into his company van, rev the engine, and pull away from the curb. The hardwood floor was cool beneath her feet as she walked over to the sofa and powered up her laptop. She opened up her Perfect Daddy list and stared at the three entries she'd made.

She tried to think of another trait, but the only thing on her mind was Beau. And the way he'd kissed her. And touched her. And worked her into a frenzy.

Her heart still pounded and her skin still tingled and her nipples pressed tight against her bra.

She shifted in her seat, but it didn't ease the feeling between her legs. He'd turned her on. Beau Hollister had really and truly turned her on in a major way.

And then he'd stopped.

"Stubborn," she muttered as her mind rushed back through the encounter not once, but twice.

Before she could stop herself, she closed the Perfect file and opened a new one. Her fingers flew across the keyboard as she typed *The Imperfect Daddy list.*

While she wasn't sure what she wanted in a perfect daddy, she knew good and well after her encounter with Beau what she *didn't* want.

She spaced down and added her first entry.

Good-looking.

Okay, so she'd used that for number one on the other list, but the concept was totally different this time. An Imperfect Daddy was one who was good-looking in a bad way, because his hot, sexy looks made a woman want him even though said woman knew he wasn't the right man for procreation. Because of number two on the list: *too damned stubborn.* And number three: *too suspicious.* Imagine him thinking she wanted a *relationship,* of all things, and just because she was a woman. Which brought her to number four: *chauvinistic.* Not to mention five: *gullible.*

She reached into her pocket and retrieved the red thong. A party favor she'd saved from Skye's bachelorette party. If he'd been the least bit perceptive, he would have noticed the thing was a miniature version of a real one, not to mention there was the happy couple's name stamped in gold foil on the front, along with the wedding date.

Then again, it was a good thing he hadn't noticed that because the thong fit with the whole sexy image she wanted to portray.

She backspaced and deleted number five before closing the file and powering down the computer. Then she headed into the kitchen and stood in the open refrigerator doorway. Unfortunately the cold did little to cool her hot body. She would have to crawl inside the damned thing for that. She popped open a Diet Coke and took several long drinks before setting the can back inside and closing the door. Then she headed upstairs to trade her tight shorts for a pair of sweats, stretched out on her bed, and turned toward the drawer of vibrators she kept in her nightstand.

But for the first time, even one of her favorites—the Clitty Kitty—didn't ease the frustration swirling inside her. She had an orgasm, as usual, but when she came back down from the all-too brief high, there was no lingering feeling of satisfaction, no relaxed muscles, no faint humming in her ears.

Nothing but Beau with his intense, hungry eyes and his purposeful lips, and an impatience that kept her tossing and turning all night long.

Chapter Eleven

No, no, *no*," Jacqueline Farrel pleaded as she stared at the video footage of her first batch of L.A. daters—single, successful, professional young women in search of viable matches for Holy Commitment Heaven. The footage had been filmed earlier that night as the women had embarked on their search, starting at a loud, crowded bar called the Crazy Chicken on Sunset Boulevard.

Jacqueline watched helplessly as a tall redhead—Jeanine—committed one of the seven deadly sins when it came to men and relationships.

"You never, ever, let a man buy you the first drink. You might as well nail yourself to the cross and wait to be crucified."

Always pay your own way, she scribbled in the number-one slot of her tip sheet. *When a man pays, he expects something in return.*

But if a woman pays, it establishes her strength and independence from the get-go. Otherwise, a man is liable to think he can manipulate her. That he can buy her a drink and she'll gladly give him her phone number. That he can splurge on dinner and she'll serve herself up as the dessert.

No self-respecting woman should ever let a man buy her anything that isn't related to a very special occasion— such as a birthday or Christmas. Even then, it should be something very modest so that the woman isn't made to feel indebted or guilty.

She'd just finished jotting down the advice when the doorbell rang.

The doorbell? It was midnight, for heaven's sake.

Jacqueline retrieved the mace she kept in her purse and walked to the front door. Her fingers tightened around the small cannister as she peered through the peephole to find an eye peering back at her.

She jumped back, her heart racing, and knocked over a small umbrella stand. She was about to bolt for the phone and dial 911 when she heard the deep, vibrant laughter coming from the other side of the door.

"Honey, it's me. Open up."

"My name," Jacqueline said as she set her mace aside, turned the deadbolt and hauled open the door, "is *not* honey."

"Don't sell yourself short." Donovan Martin, a suitcase in one hand and his briefcase in the other, stood in the doorway. "You're certainly sweet enough." He planted a kiss on her lips. When she didn't kiss him back, he leaned back and eyed her. "Aren't you glad to see me?"

"Shouldn't you be at home preparing tomorrow's lesson on the mating habits of South American monkeys?"

"I've taken a small leave of absence. My teacher's aide is handling the lectures for the next two weeks." He smiled and for a split second, her heart actually stalled. The reaction still surprised her, even after thirty-seven years and three daughters.

It surprised her *because* of the thirty-seven years and three daughters. In the beginning, she'd written off the feeling as a young woman's lusty response to an attractive young man.

And now?

An old woman's lusty response to an attractive old man. Even at sixty-two, Donovan was a sight with his tall, lean build, his salt-and-pepper hair and his brilliant green eyes. He was still as handsome as ever, more so because he had the maturity to go with his looks. And she still wanted him as much as ever.

At least she did when her schedule allowed and they met for their monthly appointment. He would fly to her or she would fly to him and they would forget everything save their hunger for one another.

But this was different. They weren't at some hotel during a scheduled visit. This was her apartment and it was the middle of the night and he hadn't so much as called to announce his visit. As if he expected her to drop everything to accommodate him.

The way her mother used to accommodate her own father when he returned from one of his sales trips. Ruella Farrel had always been waiting with open arms, and what had her devotion gotten her? An earful of complaining about everything she did wrong, a stern lecture about a woman's duty, and the occasional fat lip.

"We need to spend more time together," Donovan said.

"I think we spend plenty of time together."

"Well, I don't." He stepped forward and she had no choice but to step back. He set his suitcase inside the doorway and shut the door.

"I can't spend time with you right now. I'm working."

He grinned. "No problem. I'll take a shower while you finish up, then we can have something to eat. I'm starved."

"But I'm not even close to being finished. I have several hours of tape to study."

"I'll wait." He kissed her then, just a soft press of his firm lips against her open mouth and damned if she didn't have the sudden urge to toss her notebook aside, kill the video, and join him in the shower.

The thought faded in a rush of panic as she shook her head. "This simply won't do. I need to concentrate."

"Does that mean you see me as a distraction?" Hope gleamed in his eyes.

Her mouth drew into a tight line. "It means," she bit out, "that I need complete quiet and solitude when I'm working. I don't need to hear the shower running, and I don't need you puttering around the kitchen, distracting me."

"Don't give it another thought. I ordered at the twenty-four-hour deli around the corner." He gave her another kiss. "I got you a corned beef on rye." His eyes twinkled. "Your favorite."

"Maybe I'm not hungry."

"You can save it for later. Look," he told her, his large hands closing over her shoulders, "I just want us to spend a little quality time together. I miss you."

"I miss you, too, but—"

The shrill wail of the doorbell disrupted her words.

"That's the deli. Why don't you answer the door while I jump in the shower?" Before she could reply, he snatched up his suitcase and started down the hallway for the bedroom.

Frustration welled inside her and she had the sudden urge to rush after him. But judging from the stern set of his shoulders, she wasn't about to turn him around let alone steer him back out the door.

"How much do I owe you?" Jacqueline asked when she opened the door to the teenage boy holding two large brown sacks.

"Not a thing. Mr. Martin already paid when he ordered." He handed her the sacks. "He even took care of the tip." And then he turned and left her standing in the open doorway, her own words echoing in her ears.

When a man pays for something, he expects something in return.

"Jacqueline?" Donovan's voice drifted from down the hallway. "Can you bring me a towel?"

The question echoed through her head, stirring a rush of memories from her past. Of her father demanding this and ordering that. Of her mother crying herself to sleep at night because she'd tried so hard and her efforts still hadn't been good enough. Her father had been mean and manipulative and physically abusive and the day he'd died had been the best day of her mother's life.

"For your information," she said as she pushed open the bathroom door a few seconds later and ripped the shower curtain aside to glare at her very naked significant other, "my freedom cannot be bought with a corned beef sandwich."

"I would never dream of buying your freedom with a measly sandwich." He grinned and peered into the bag. "That's what this extra-thick slice of cheesecake is for."

"Very funny." She did her best to ignore the way the muscles in his arms rippled as he pulled the white box from the bag and held it out to her. Water drip-dropped down his tanned skin and she swallowed. Hard.

"Strawberry glaze on the side," he added, pushing the box into her hands. "Just the way you like it."

"I'm not hungry." She set the box on the nearby vanity and folded her arms over her chest. "I'm busy. You can't just barge in and disrupt my life."

"I'm not barging and I'm not disrupting. I'm simply taking a shower and then I'm eating and then I'm going to bed." He handed her the bag and winked. "You can go back to doing what you were doing. I won't disturb you." At her doubtful expression, he added, "Cross my heart, hope to die, stick a womanist needle in my eye."

She eyed him for a long moment before giving in to the grin that tugged at her lips. Okay, so maybe his presence wouldn't be that unsettling to her routine, and she *had* established boundaries—namely that her work came first and he came second. It was sort of nice knowing he missed her. Not that she *needed* him to miss her, or that the knowledge fulfilled some sort of empty void inside her, or anything ludicrous like that.

It was just nice to know, and she was making much more of his sudden appearance than need be. He wasn't moving in, for heaven's sake, or making excessive demands or disrupting her routine in any way, shape, or form. He was simply paying a visit. Keeping her company. Spending time with her, with her full consent, of course.

But before she consented, she intended to finish studying her tape and documenting her advice and preparing fully for tomorrow's taping, and she wasn't giving Donovan a second thought.

"Try not to use all the hot water," she said as she pulled the curtain closed. She made it two steps before his voice stopped her.

"Don't forget the towel, honey. Oh, and it would be

really nice if you could help me with my back. I can't quite reach."

So much for boundaries.

Xandra Farrel had a plan.

After a sleepless night spent thinking and rethinking about what had happened that evening—namely Beau Hollister's pronouncement that he didn't want a clingy female following him around—Xandra had come up with an idea to get him off her front porch and into her bed. Judging by his stubborn expression, she knew nothing short of a polygraph was likely to convince him of her sincerity when it came to the relationship issue. Which meant she had to approach him from a different angle.

A sexier angle.

He'd obviously been turned on, just not to the point of surrender. Which meant that all Xandra had to do was turn him on even more, until he reached the point where he could no longer think. Just feel. Then to sex or not to sex would no longer be a choice.

She had a plan, all right, and it involved the full-blown seduction of Beau Hollister.

Okay, so maybe it was more of an outcome than an actual plan. She knew what she wanted to do, but she wasn't the least bit sure of how to get there. While Xandra knew sex better than most women, she wasn't nearly as competent in the seduction department. Other than the night with Beau when she'd been barely seventeen, she'd never had to seduce a man. Mark had been the one who'd pursued her early on in their relationship. He'd taken the initiative when it came to sex and everything else in their lives. Later on, she'd never had to do anything more than kiss him to make her intentions clear.

But this was a different situation altogether.

Soft, cool fingers brushed her thigh and drew her from her thoughts. She opened her eyes to see the woman who stood beside the table.

"Relax, sweetie. Otherwise, it's going to sting."

Xandra stared down the length of her towel-clad body to the exposed thigh and pelvic area. Her fingers dug into the sides of the table as the hot wax was applied to her bikini line and lower. Much lower.

While she didn't know nearly as much as she needed to when it came to seducing a man, she did have enough sense to know that making herself as physically attractive as possible was a good first step. That meant cutting out all the sugary substitutes for her smoking habit and finding something healthier to put into her mouth. The extra ten pounds she'd gained would melt away before she knew it. In the meantime, she had an unwanted gray hair to get rid of.

"You've done this before, right?" Xandra asked.

"Too many times to count," replied the young woman who was wearing a white peasant blouse and pants. With long brown hair, a name tag that read GIGI, and a wide, upbeat smile, she looked more like a cheerleader than the chief skin specialist at Savoy's, an elite salon and spa located in the heart of Houston's upscale Galleria area.

"Too many, as in a thousand?"

"Give or take a few hundred."

"Which is it? Give or take?"

Gigi smiled as she reached for a cloth strip and applied it over the hot wax. "Just take a deep breath and find your happy place."

Xandra clenched her teeth against the warm sensation

tingling along her pubic area. It might have actually been enjoyable if she didn't know what was to come.

Not that she actually knew, but she could just imagine how much it was going to hurt.

Forget sting. Taking off Band-Aids stung. This was going to be more along the lines of full-fledged, grit-your-teeth-to-keep-from-screaming *hurt*.

"You're not in your happy place." Gigi smoothed the fabric strip over the wax, rubbing this way and that.

"I'm not likely to be until I get out of here."

"I didn't mean literally. Happy is a state of mind. All you have to do is visualize." More methodical rubbing. "A white sand beach. A field full of daisies. A clearance sale at the Gap. Just pick one, close your eyes and go there."

"I'd rather see what you're doing."

"Watching takes away the element of surprise, which takes away the element of—"

"Ouch!" Xandra squealed as the woman ripped off the fabric strip. Pain splintered through her, pulsing along her nerve endings and making her head spin.

"Gotcha," Gigi declared, her voice much too high-pitched and pleasant for a woman who was this close to meeting her maker.

"You got me, all right. And just as soon as my eyes stop watering, I'm going to grab a few handfuls of that shiny brown hair and see how you like it."

Gigi laughed and smoothed another strip near her opposite thigh. "You're vocalizing your tension. That's good. If you keep it pent up, you'll stay tense and being tense just makes it—"

"—sting," Xandra finished for her. "Yeah, I know."

"But if you're relaxed or focused on something else, it's much better. See, you were focused on the sound of my voice, rather than what I was doing, so you weren't expecting a surprise and—"

"Holy cripes!"

"Gotcha again." She held up the strip dotted with hair. "We got 'em. All five of them."

"Five of what?"

"Five gray hairs."

"But I don't have five."

The woman's forehead wrinkled as she stared at the strip and then down at Xandra. She smiled. "You're right. There aren't five. There are six—wait. Make that seven." She turned and reached for the wax spatula.

Seven? "You're not doing it again, are you?"

"You wanted a neat Brazilian wax, no gray hair."

"Which means you're not doing it again." Because no way did she have *seven* of the godawful things. No way. No how. *No.*

"There, there." The woman smiled and dabbed the wax. "Just go to your happy place."

Xandra drew in a deep breath, closed her eyes, and damned Father Nature.

That's right, *Father* Nature, because no woman would doom another to gray hair and Brazilian waxes and unnaturally cheerful spa consultants named Gigi.

Chapter Twelve

Seduce Beau Hollister into having sex.

Later that afternoon, after waddling back to her office and munching a full bag of carrot sticks, Xandra was still sore, hungry and clueless. She stared at the first entry on her daily to-do list and tried to come up with a solid approach to the task. While she knew what she wanted to accomplish, she had no clue how to go about getting it done.

Sex was her business. Her passion. And so she knew everything when it came to giving and receiving pleasure, from the hottest foreplay techniques to the most popular cuddling positions during the postorgasmic bliss phase.

But seduction? That was a different matter altogether.

She knew she had to keep her approach very low-key and nonthreatening. She had to be sexy, yet sweet.

Inviting.

Alluring.

Romantic.

The notion was about as familiar to the daughter of the country's leading womanist as the dreaded "L" word itself. Xandra spent the next few hours doing an Internet search and printing out any and everything she could find on the subject of seduction. By the time five o'clock rolled around, she'd come up with a substantial list that included everything from surprising someone with a bed covered with rose petals, to a steamy bubble bath, to a massage by candlelight.

The problem? She would have to get Beau into her house to accomplish any of those things and she had a feeling *that* was going to be the real killer. He was sure to be skeptical after yesterday, not to mention she'd used up most of her good excuses for needing a man in her house.

Which meant she really needed to be subtle.

Which meant she was in deep trouble because Xandra wasn't much for subtlety. She was raised by a woman with a loud voice and an attitude when it came to everything. Jacqueline Farrel lived by the steadfast rule that women had been quiet for much too long. It was time to shake things up. To wake people up—namely men.

A woman is like a sleeping lion. She looks so soft and cuddly with her eyes closed and her face buried in her paws, but she is really a strong, ferocious creature to be dealt with. Men, of course, don't realize this until we lift our heads and prove it. So roar, sisters. Roar!

Jacqueline had raised her daughters accordingly, to be lions in every aspect of life, from the bedroom to the boardroom. Xandra wasn't accustomed to beating around the bush. She went after what she wanted like Cujo after a great big piece of steak.

In this instance, Beau was her T-bone.

The thought consumed her for the next few minutes, until Kimmy walked in looking as perfect as ever in a fitted champagne-colored jacket and skirt. A pink blouse added a splash of color to the outfit, along with matching four-inch stiletto heels that would have done Barbie proud.

"Great bracelet," Xandra said as the woman set a stack of folders down on the corner of her desk, along with the latest issue of *Cosmo* which featured a full color ad for Wild Woman. Silver hearts inlaid with tiny diamonds dangled from her wrist.

Kimmy smiled. "I'll pass on the compliment to Lawrence. We went on our first date a few nights ago and he surprised me with this yesterday." She beamed and touched a matching earring. "And these. They're Brighton. Just his way of saying thanks."

The men Kimmy hooked up with all had the same way of saying thanks after a date, be it jewelry or a scarf or a pair of shoes.

Xandra had wanted to ask many times exactly what they were thanking her assistant for, especially since their show of appreciation usually cost a pretty penny—Kimmy had a weakness for top-of-the-line stuff—but Xandra had always been too afraid. The young woman was like a daughter to her, and nobody but nobody wanted to think of their pure, naive daughter doing *it,* much less doing *it* well enough to warrant a big show of gratitude.

Daughter?

Okay, so make that her younger, impressionable, wholesome, well dressed kid sister. Either way, the idea was the same. She didn't want to blow her image of Kimmy.

Then again, she was desperate at the moment.

"When you ask a man into your apartment," she asked Kimmy, "what do you say? To get him inside for a little, you know, fooling around."

"Well," the young woman said as she set aside the finished catalog for next season and perched on the edge of

Xandra's desk. "It depends to what degree we're going to fool around. Sex or making out or both. If I wanted sex, I would probably say 'Would you like to have a bite to eat and get naked?' At Xandra's questioning glance, she added, "I like to cook for my men. Anyhow, if I wanted to just make out, I would probably say something like, 'Would you like to have a bite to eat and make out?' If I wanted both, I'd probably say 'Would you like to have a bite to eat, get naked, and make out?' I find that being up front usually works best."

Yeah, right.

Xandra forced her attention to the *Cosmo* issue that was sitting on her desk. "This looks good."

"It's great, and what's even better is that Tyra Banks is on the cover and she's wearing this black Armani dress that's really banging." Kimmy sighed. "And she's carrying a Fendi bag. And wearing this gorgeous shade of red lipstick. Sephora's new Blazing Berries. I just bought a tube yesterday. And the silver eye shadow. Christian Dior. And the blush. M.A.C.'s Cherry Jubilee."

"Do I pay you that much money?"

"Hardly, but that's why God invented financial analyst boyfriends."

Xandra arched an eyebrow. "As in plural?"

"I don't do singular. They're too complicated. That way if one breaks your heart, you've got the other for backup. And for that extra pair of Manolo Blahniks. Shoes make the whole heartbreak thing a lot less painful."

"Don't you think it's a little inappropriate to take such expensive gifts from men?"

"Maybe." Kimmy shrugged. "I don't really think about it. It's not like I ask for anything, or even expect anything. The men in my life are simply in tune to my likes and dislikes and I make them happy, so they want to make me happy in return. I don't see anything wrong with that, do you?"

Xandra saw all kinds of things wrong with it for herself. Then again, none of the men she'd ever slept with—three including Beau and their five-minute marathon—had ever been so wowed they'd wanted to say thanks for anything she'd done in the sack.

She opened her mouth to ask exactly what Kimmy did, and how she did it, that earned her such expensive gratitude, but then she forced her lips together. The whole image thing again.

Xandra turned her attention to the copy for the new *Cosmo* ad scheduled to run in the next edition. "Tell the agency that this is a go."

"Will do." Kimmy slid a folder overflowing with documents in front of her. "This is your to-sign stack. And when you're done, Albert's in the conference room. He said he really needs to speak with you."

"About the new project?"

"I don't know. He just said to ask you to stop in on your way out." She glanced at the empty carrot bag on Xandra's desk. "I've got more carrots in the break room if you're still hungry."

"I'm starved."

Kimmy smiled. "I'll get them before I head home." She wiggled her eyebrows. "I'm going out with Mike the mechanic tonight."

"I thought you only did financial analysts?"

"I'm roughing it tonight. Besides, after all those smooth, manicured hands it's nice to feel a few calluses." She gave a little shiver before turning her attention back to the carrots. "So do you want them sliced or whole?"

"Either."

"Del Monte or sun-drenched Floridian?"

Okay, so even her carrot sticks had a brand name.

"Your choice."

"I prefer Del Monte. They've got a fresher taste."

"Sounds good to me." Xandra watched Kimmy leave before closing her portfolio and turning her attention to the cost analysis her accountant had e-mailed her.

She stared at the blur of numbers and her stomach heaved. She hated the financial end of the business. She much preferred sketching a new design or researching materials or brainstorming packaging concepts. Which was why Wild Woman had started out as a temporary entity. A means to an end. The way for her to gain the attention of the big boys in the sex business, and prove to them that she was the best.

She was almost there. A few more weeks she'd have a perfected Mabel and she could kiss the cost analysis sheets good-bye forever.

In the meantime . . . She tamped down her churning stomach and concentrated on a particular row of numbers.

Forty-five minutes and a full package of carrots later, she approved the analysis, e-mailed her response, packed up her briefcase, and headed down the hallway. She was about to step into the elevator when she remembered Albert.

"I'm so sorry," she blurted as she pushed open the door to the conference room where her team met for their weekly brainstorming sessions. "I got so busy that I almost forgot you . . ." Her words faded as she stared at the gigantic conference table.

Gone was the brass replica of her very first vibrator design. The marble top had been covered by a white linen tablecloth. A gold candelabra fitted with five slim white tapers stood at the center. The candles cast a play of light over the table, which was laden with every chocolate dessert imaginable.

There was decadent fudge cake. Scrumptious chocolate cream puffs. Rich chocolate brownies. Chocolate bonbons. Chocolate-covered strawberries. Chocolate mousse. Chocolate truffles. *Chocolate.*

The scent spiraled around her and slid into her nostrils. Her taste buds panted and every nerve in her body jumped to life. Her heart raced and her blood rushed almost as fiercely as it had the night before when Beau had been this close and she'd been that close.

She licked her lips.

"Do you like it?" The voice came from her right and she turned to see Albert standing just inside the doorway, an expectant look on his face.

"Are you kidding? I've had the neighborhood weight watch babysitting me for nearly a week. I can't even remember what a good piece of chocolate tastes like."

"I know how much you love it, and while I know you're freaked out about the whole ten-pound weight gain, you're also under a lot of stress. Depriving yourself isn't the answer because then you'll just want more and when you finally give in to the craving, you'll be out of control. This way you can indulge while you're in control."

It made sense.

"Besides, ten pounds is nothing."

"Ten pounds is definitely something." But at least it wasn't twenty pounds. And just because she might treat herself to a few bites didn't mean she'd totally shucked the idea of switching to a healthier craving substitute. It wasn't as if she were going to pop a brownie every time she wanted a smoke. This was a one-time thing. A treat for the past forty-five minutes she'd spent in cost-analysis hell. Some much-needed satisfaction after a sleepless night spent tossing and turning and thinking about Beau Hollister and how good he'd tasted.

She reached for a chocolate brownie. Sweetness exploded on her tongue and she groaned as she sank down into a chair. Okay, it wasn't Beau but it ran a pretty close second.

"Try these." He held out the platter of cream puffs.

"Wonderful," she said in between bites. To hell with Beau. "Too good for words." She sampled each of the decadent desserts, relishing the sweet taste of sugar and rich cocoa, before reaching for the glass of wine he'd poured for her.

"If you liked that," Albert told her, "wait until you get a mouthful of this." He rounded the table to a small sideboard he'd set up. A few moments later, she heard the sizzle of fire and he turned back to her with a flaming plate. "The evening wouldn't be complete without the ultimate dessert. A rich, moist chocolate flambé."

A few seconds later, the flames died down enough for her to spoon the dark, velvety cream into her mouth. She closed her eyes as the luscious taste sent a buzz along her nerve endings. "Why am I wasting my time with Mabel? *This* is the ultimate orgasm." She savored another bite. "You're such a lifesaver. I needed this in the worst way."

"I knew that." The seriousness in his voice drew her attention. "I know you."

She eyed him. "What are you talking about?"

"Since the dinner invite didn't work—"

"What dinner invite?"

"After the first planning session for Mabel, I suggested we have dinner."

"You always suggest we have dinner when the team works late. People have to eat, after all."

"I meant dinner, as in just you and me. Alone. Together. *Us*."

"Oh."

"But since you didn't get it, I thought I would bypass the whole five-course thing I had planned and go straight to the good stuff. I thought we could have a little dessert. And then maybe a little *dessert*."

"You and me and *dessert*?"

A strange awareness crept up her spine as her gaze swept the room again, from the flickering candles, the immaculate white tablecloth and silver dishes, to the slow sweet evocative ballad by INXS pouring from a nearby CD player. It had been one of her favorite songs back in high school because of its powerful lyrics about worlds colliding and how nothing could ever tear two people apart.

Funny, but she hadn't noticed the song before. She'd been too overwhelmed by the sight and smell of chocolate. But there it was, filling her ears and easing the dull throbbing of her temples the way the chocolate soothed her hunger.

"You like chocolate," Albert went on, "and so do I. You like music and so do I."

"I like Aerosmith. And Nickelback. And Beyoncé. And anything I can dance to."

"Which includes this."

"I never dance to this. I just listen to it. I like eighties music, too."

"That's beside the point," Albert told her.

"Which is?"

"We like a lot of the same things, Xandra. We both love *Science Digest*. We both get off on watching the New Invention channel. Not to mention, we both love the *Jerry Springer* show—"

"I just like to make fun. I don't actually enjoy it."

"Right. Anyway, what I'm trying to say is that we like the same things and we think the same way. *And* you're the smartest woman I know. You're attractive and you've got a great business sense. You're a whiz with numbers."

"I hate numbers. They make me nauseous."

"It doesn't matter. You're good with them anyway, and so am I."

"Since when do you mess with any numbers?"

"I've never once had a bounced check and I can mentally tally my groceries and the seven percent sales tax before I get to the checkout stand."

"And you're pointing out all of this because?"

"Do you like me?"

She frowned. "Of course I like you. You're one of my best friends."

"Exactly. I'm one of your best friends because of all the things I just mentioned. Plus I'm creative and so are you."

"You're very creative."

"And I'm smart."

"You are. You're one of the smartest men I know. And you're sweet, too."

"I knew it."

"Knew what?"

"We're two for two with the Holy Commitment Trinity. We share the same interests. We both respect each other."

"There's three points to the Holy Commitment Trinity, not two."

"I know. The great sex part. That's what this is about." He turned toward the table. "Seducing your taste buds is the first step to seducing the rest of you. I feed your deprived senses and you turn to putty in my hands. At least that's how it's supposed to work according to *The Sensitive Seductress*, which Chuck swears by."

"What does Chuck have to do with this?"

"He's on this grandchildren kick, and since you're worrying over the whole baby thing, it got me to thinking that we could kill two birds with one stone—satisfy the grandbaby craving and utilize your eggs before they lose their potency."

"I really appreciate the offer, Albert, but I don't think . . ." Her words faded as several things registered at once. Music. Chocolate. Grandbabies. Babies. *Dessert.*

"You're seducing me," she blurted. "Ohmigod, you're actually trying to seduce me. You are, aren't you?"

"I think that's obvious."

"But it wasn't." Her smile widened as the truth stopped her cold. "I didn't have a clue. Until *after* I'd eaten some of everything on the table."

"I don't know if I'm following you."

"Don't you see? I was suckered into consuming a load of chocolate before I realized what this was all about. It was so subtle that I just didn't get it. So alluring. So *romantic.*" She spooned another bite of chocolate cream into her mouth before getting to her feet. "You're a genius, Albert."

He smiled. "Really?"

"Definitely." She grabbed a brownie and kissed his cheek. "I'll see you tomorrow."

"You're leaving? But what about killing two birds with one stone? I thought maybe we could start now."

"I really appreciate all of this, but I just don't think we make a Holy Commitment match."

"Not now, but if we do *it* a few times, who knows?"

"There's just no chemistry between us."

"Maybe there could be if you gave it a chance."

"We spend so much time together, if things were going to spark, they already would have. I just don't think of you like that." She touched his shoulder and his gaze met hers. "Can you honestly say you think of me like that?"

He wanted to say yes. She could see it in his eyes. But in all the time they'd known each other, they'd always been open and honest. "You really don't feel *any* chemistry?"

She shook her head. "Not really." She eyed him. "Are you mad at me?"

"Yes. No." He shook his head. "I'm not mad. Disappointed, maybe. But not mad. I still think you're being hasty. We're perfect for each other in every other aspect. If we hook up, you wouldn't have to waste your time finding someone. And I wouldn't have to waste my time, either. We would have each other."

"We already have each other. We're best friends." She eyed him. "We are still best friends, right? Even if I don't help you and Chuck out with the grandbaby dilemma?"

"We'll always be friends."

"Good." She smiled. "Then can I borrow your blowtorch?"

Chapter Thirteen

For a woman who'd been rejected less than twenty-four hours ago, Xandra looked extremely happy.

Too happy in Beau's opinion.

She even said hello to him as she came up the front steps and picked her way past the construction clutter.

"Mary Caskell," he said when she bent down to pick up the zucchini and mushroom quiche sitting on her doorstep. "From three houses down." He pointed. "She said to tell you to call if you need to talk. Or if you're tempted to eat."

Her smile faltered for a few heartbeats as she glanced in the direction he pointed. She cast another quick look over her shoulder as if someone might be watching her before turning her attention back to the door.

"Thanks." The smile returned as she opened her door and set both her briefcase and the dish just inside. Then she headed back to the car to retrieve a very large cardboard box.

"Let me help you." He set his sander aside and caught her halfway up the walk.

"That's okay. I've got it."

"It looks heavy." He reached for the box, but she held it out of reach.

"Believe me, it's not."

"Look, I don't mind giving you a hand."

"I don't want a hand." She gave him a wide berth as she headed up the front steps. "Thanks anyway."

"Look, maybe we need to talk about yesterday."

"Have you reconsidered?"

"No, but I just want you to understand why."

"Women want commitment and you're afraid I might turn into a stalker. That's it, isn't it?"

"Well, yeah."

She smiled again. "It's okay. I understand."

"Really?"

"Completely. A man has to look out for his best interests and it isn't like you really know me. I mean, you did know me, but I could have changed. Morphed into some crazed woman who has sex, then ends up boiling your pet rabbit."

"I don't have a rabbit. I've got a Lab named Lola, and I doubt she'd fit into a pot."

"Where there's a will, there's a way. The point is, you have to be careful. I understand that."

"Good. I just wanted to make sure things were clear between us."

"Crystal." She turned to the house before pivoting back to face him. "But I do need to talk to you about the plans for the renovation."

"Is there a problem?"

"Not really. I just didn't see any mention of the den."

"We're doing the standard repair and replacement on all the weathered wood."

"But I was thinking that the room looked sort of blah

and since you're an architect, maybe you could suggest something to give it some pizzazz."

"This is a restoration project. We're not renovating."

"Just some suggestions. Maybe different flooring or new paint colors or some interesting trim or something to spice it up. After all, you're the expert."

"I'm still pretty busy right now." He turned to see Warren load the last of the tools into the back of one of their trucks. The man waved and said "I'll see you tomorrow," before climbing into the truck.

Her gaze followed his. "Looks like your guys are finished for the day."

"Yeah, well I'm not."

"That's okay. Just knock when you're done." She disappeared before he could tell her any of the number of reasons why he couldn't help her out.

Sure, he'd all but finished sanding the remaining pieces of trim outlining the porch—a day ahead of schedule. But he still had to head back to the office to check the status on the other jobs in progress and go over the requested supplies for tomorrow's schedule. After that, he was due at the hospital to see Evan. Then it was home to feed and water Lola. His youngest brother, Jake, would be calling later tonight. Jake always called on Tuesday. Hank on Wednesay. Mac on Thursday. That's the way it had always been since the three had gone off to college years back, then out into the real world.

Beau had responsibilities, and they didn't include playing personal architect to Xandra Farrel.

"If I were you," he told her a little while later after knocking on the door and following her into the den, "I would consider adding some bookshelves and turning this end of the den into an office."

While he had responsibilities, he *was* a full day ahead of schedule, which meant he had the time. And she had commissioned him to do the restoration on her house, which meant he was being compensated for his expertise. On top of that, he couldn't help but get the feeling that she was up to something, and he was curious.

"Bookshelves?"

"A freestanding bookshelf custom-made to fit this space." Beau stared at the massive wall and his brain started to work. "Something in oak with detail to match the frieze work on the ceiling molding would be nice." When she arched an eyebrow at him, he added, "I make furniture. Bookshelves, desks, chairs, tables—everything. It's a hobby. So if you want my opinion, I don't think I would alter the structure. Instead, I would fill the space with something that complements the detail that's already here."

She nodded and stared around her. "I can see something like that." She turned and motioned toward the open doorway. "What about the dining room?"

"What about it?"

"It's so blah, too," she said as she walked toward the room.

He followed her, only to regret every step once he reached the entryway. She was up to something, all right.

Up to her neck in chocolate.

His gaze swept the table and the numerous dishes filled with all sorts of chocolate goodies. A candelabra flickered in the center, reflecting off the silver dishes. An old eighties tune drifted from the CD player.

"It's chocolate," she announced, a smile on her face.

"I can see that. What's it for?"

"I, um, was hungry and I thought you might be hungry and so here it is. Pick your poison. I like the brownies myself. They just melt in your mouth." She took a bite, her white teeth sinking into the dark treat, and his groin tightened with the beginnings of a massive hard-on. "Try one." She held it out to him.

He shook his head. "I'll pass."

"It's okay. There's plenty. Sit down and have something and we'll, um, talk about that corner."

"The corner?" His gaze swiveled to the far part of the room and the empty area.

"It needs something, don't you think?" She took another bite and eyed the space.

"Maybe a built-in curio cabinet. Or a china hutch."

"Good suggestions. Let me just soak this in and try to picture it." She made a big show of eyeing the wall. "In the meantime, you might as well help yourself."

"I couldn't. I might spoil my dinner."

"I insist."

"I don't really like chocolate."

Her gaze swiveled then and collided with his. She stared at him as if he'd just confessed to kicking her favorite animal.

"But it's *chocolate.*"

"I can see that." He shrugged. "I'm just not really into chocolate." Or he hadn't been until he'd seen her take a bite of the brownie. Now he had the sudden urge to stretch her out on the table and lick the crumbs from her lips. "Too rich."

"That's the point. It's dessert." She planted her hands on her hips. "You do eat dessert, don't you?"

"Not really. I worked out a lot in college and followed a pretty strict diet to keep up my strength and my energy. I did it at first so that I could handle working and going to school. But then it took on a twofold purpose thanks to the nature of my business. Customers want to hire a hunk of a guy, not a hunk of fat. I usually just do the basics—meat and vegetables and fruit."

"So you never splurge with dessert? *Ever*?"

"Once in a while."

"With what?"

"Popcorn balls." At her disbelieving look, he added, "They taste good. Not too salty. Not too sweet." He shrugged. "And they feel good." At her questioning glance, he added, "My mom used to make them every year for my birthday until she died. I would stand next to her and scoop out a handful of stuff while she was mixing it up. She would frown at me and tell me to scat, but I knew she wanted to smile. That's one of my few memories of her. Not that that has anything to do with this. I appreciate the offer, but I'll have to pass. This is all too much for me."

"But I've got mousse," she told him when he started to turn. "That's a little lighter. And flambé. You have to at least try the flambé." She reached for a small blowtorch and turned the gas knob.

"I wouldn't turn that so high if I were you. I've seen blowtorches take out a pair of eyebrows just like that."

"This isn't a blowtorch. It's a kitchen torch. Chefs use them and they're not nearly as dangerous as the ones you and your guys use." She flicked the lighter and held it up. "They only emit a very small, controlled flame."

A loud *whoosh* punctuated her sentence as fire ballooned from the mouth of the torch and rushed toward the wall. The edge of the curtain ignited and a flame erupted.

Beau pushed Xandra out of the way in that next instant, grabbed the tablecloth and yanked it from the table. Dishes clattered to the floor as he slapped at the flames. After a few frantic seconds, the fire died. Black paint curled around the edges of the window seal and the smell of smoke filled the room.

"Are you okay?" he asked as he turned back to her.

"My face feels weird." Her gaze met his, her green eyes lit with worry. "Hot."

If Beau had half a brain, he would have turned and walked the other way right then. The fire was out. No real harm had been done. Nothing that a few weeks and a can of Solarcaine couldn't cure. But he'd never been able to think clearly where Xandra was concerned. So instead of walking the other way, he stepped toward her.

Stepping, not touching or comforting or any of the other things he wanted to do at the moment. "You just had a flame rush at you. It stands to reason."

"*Tingling* and hot. Like something's wrong." She reached up, but her fingers stalled midway up her cheeks. Her eyes brightened. "They're gone, aren't they?"

"Sort of."

"Meaning?"

"Have you ever seen a dog's eyebrows?"

"Dogs don't have eyebrows. They're furry all over and they just have one or two hairs sticking out on their brow bone—Ohmigod." She closed her eyes for a moment and a tear slid from the corner of her eye.

Beau had the sudden urge to reach out and wipe the moisture away. Instead, he balled his fingers and did the next best thing.

"Look on the bright side," he told her. Her eyes opened, her gaze fueled with hope, and he said the only thing he could think of to make her feel better. "Think of the money you'll save on waxing."

*   *   *

Xandra eyed her reflection in her small compact and touched up her eyebrows for the countless time that morning.

While she'd singed off most of the hair, she did still have the basic shape left, thankfully. It was just a matter of filling in the bald spots.

At least that's what she told herself.

She snapped the compact closed and retrieved her purse. It wasn't even lunchtime, but she was calling it quits in the name of research.

Most women would probably give up when faced with three hundred dollars' worth of fire and smoke damage and a man who hated chocolate *and* a pair of singed brows, but Xandra wasn't most women.

When she'd fallen off the wagon during her senior year dieting mission, she'd simply picked herself up, traded the homemade pancakes her grammie made for breakfast every morning for two cups of black coffee, and gotten right back on track.

When she'd designed her first vibrator only to have it short-circuit just shy of the Big O, she'd blinked back the tears of disappointment, finished herself off with a few hand techniques, and turned back to the drawing board to find a more durable plastic that wouldn't crack during the most intense masturbation session.

Likewise, she hadn't thrown in the towel when she'd found her first gray hair last weekend. Sure, she'd whined to Albert and thrown a pity party, but then she'd outlined a step-by-step solution to her problem. A painful solution that still made her wince when she walked, but an effective one nonetheless.

Seducing Beau was no different from any other difficult task she'd faced in her life. She simply had to come up with a list of possible fixes and try them one by one until she hit pay dirt.

Fix number one had involved finally hitting up Kimmy for the secret to her successful social life.

"A cookbook?" Xandra asked when Kimmy smiled and handed her what she considered to be the single girl's answer to snagging any and every man.

"Haven't you heard that the way to a man's heart is through his stomach?"

"I don't want to get to his heart. I want to go about four inches lower." Xandra shook her head and eyed the book. "A cookbook? You haven't discovered some new sexual position? Or come up with a one-of-a-kind blow-job technique? You don't have some sort of anomaly that makes your vagina vibrate at will?"

"Don't I wish." Kimmy shrugged and gave the book an affectionate hug. "This is it. My complete arsenal when it comes to men and sex. That Cherry Chandler really knows her stuff."

"That's what Albert said."

"You can't go wrong with a *New York Times* best seller— Say, is there something different about you?"

"Nothing I know of." Xandra busied herself flipping pages. "Why?"

"I don't know . . . Your eyes just look different. I thought maybe you were using a new eye shadow."

"No, no. Say, this is a really detailed cookbook."

"This isn't just a cookbook. It's a step-by-step guide to seduction. All of the recipes include foods that have proven aphrodisiac qualities. You make one of these for a guy and he'll be putty in your hands." At Xandra's smile, Kimmy added, "Sorry, wrong image. Let me put it this way, he'll be so turned on, he won't be able to keep his hands off you."

"I just hope this is going to be enough. I mean, I would sell my soul for a piece of homemade lasagna and some tiramisu, but what if this guy isn't as easy?"

"All men are easy when it comes to food. It's just a case of finding the right food."

"Okay," Xandra said. "I'll give it a try."

"On one condition," Kimmy eyed the Mabel samples sitting on the corner of Xandra's desk, "you let me have a few of those."

"I thought you had a long line of satisfied men at your beck and call?"

"I'm satisfying them, but that doesn't mean they're satisfying me. They're all nice and devoted and they try really, really hard, but sometimes my orgasm just isn't that great. Mabel might be just the boost I need."

"Two samples."

"Four."

"Three."

"You're on."

By the time Xandra arrived home from work just after lunchtime, she was armed and ready, packing two overflowing grocery bags and an idea sure to lure Beau right out of his clothes and into her bed. Or at least off her front porch and into her kitchen.

Hey, a girl had to start somewhere.

"Should I keep the fire extinguisher handy?" Beau asked as she mounted the stairs. "Just in case I need to rescue another wall?"

"My walls are safe tonight because the only fire I'll be lighting is the one on my stove." *Liar.* "But if you're interested in self-preservation, you might want to keep it close by."

"Look—" he started.

"Got to get to work," she cut in as she breezed past him. "Happy painting." She disappeared into the house and set about putting her plan into motion.

That had been the trouble last night. She hadn't really had a solid, well-thought out plan. Just a germ of an idea sparked by Albert and his chocolate seduction. That's why the evening with Beau had completely backfired.

Literally.

Her gaze swiveled toward the dining room and the charred spot on the Sheetrock. Her nose wrinkled at the burnt aroma that lingered in the air.

First things first, she doused the dining room with Lysol after depositing her stuff in the kitchen. A few minutes later, she sat at the kitchen table, opened her leather briefcase and extracted the key to tonight's success. The one thing that kept Kimmy's dating card filled with devoted men and her closet overflowing with Prada suits and Manolo Blahniks—Cherry Chandler's best-selling *Seductive Foods*.

She turned to the first recipe and retrieved a large mixing bowl from an overhead cabinet. She'd ruled out the Chocolate Love Balls—Xandra wasn't any more interested in love than Beau was in chocolate. Instead, she'd come up with a menu that focused solely on stirring his libido.

Starting with melt-in-your-mouth Buns of Seduction.

After mixing and kneading a bowlful of dough, she divided it into twelve round shapes, arranged them on a lightly buttered and floured baking tray, and left them to rise while she proceeded to the second recipe.

Four hours later, she'd finished six dishes, all fairly healthful and completely free of chocolate.

She'd made a passion fruit and yogurt salad consisting of peaches, fresh figs, cherries, bananas, and mangoes—almost all of which contained significant amounts of phenylethylamine, the pleasure-inducing hormone released during sex. The main dish consisted of black pepper steak seasoned with cumin and coriander—spices rumored to boost the libido. She'd also made a variation of paella, a Spanish rice dish made with lobster tail, white fish, oysters, and mussels—ingredients with a reputation for supporting and enhancing the libido—just in case Beau wasn't a beef eater. Dessert consisted of vanilla ice cream sprinkled with cinnamon, nutmeg, cloves, and ginger—also to rev the libido. To round out the meal, she had the Buns of Seduction complete with honey butter and a beverage made with spring water, ginseng, lime, honey, and yohimbe, the bark from a tall evergreen tree medically proven to increase blood flow to the erogenous zones and, by constricting the veins, help keep it there.

She smiled.

Beau didn't stand a chance.

Chapter Fourteen

She was up to something.

Beau knew it even before she waltzed out onto the porch, told him to say "Ahhh," and popped a piece of bread into his mouth.

The way she was looking at him, her eyes glittering with determination and desire, was lethal to a bad boy desperately trying to be good. As if she meant to tempt him beyond reason.

As if.

She could tempt away, but he wasn't giving in. He was a man on a mission, his brain completely focused on finishing this project in time for the competition deadline. To top everything off, he had to replace the charred Sheetrock in her dining room, which meant even more work.

Besides, he didn't just suspect she was up to something anymore. He knew with dead certainty. His gut told him as much. And then, of course, he'd overheard the truth when he'd been finishing up the staircase inside the house earlier that day. The phone had rung and her answering machine had picked up. He'd been minding his own business when a man's voice had filled the air.

"Hey, Xandra. It's Albert. I missed you at work and so I just wanted to call and find out how last night went. Did you get a chance to test out the new product? I tell you, it's a stroke of genius testing your product on the five-minute man. If you can have a good orgasm with him, then we'll *know* we're on the right track."

He'd realized then that Xandra didn't just want sex from him. She wanted *bad* sex.

He'd been embarrassed at first. Then angry. Then really, really pissed.

Now he was more amused than pissed.

As much as he would like to prove her wrong and shoot his five-minute reputation to hell and back, he couldn't afford any distractions right now.

He had to resist, and he knew just how to do it. If she was going to pull out all the stops to turn him on, then he was just going to have to shift into overdrive and go the extra mile to turn her off.

That's what he told himself, but then his brain switched to neutral as the taste of warm bread and sweet honey melted in his mouth. His stomach grumbled and his heart kick-started as he savored the mouthful for a few delectable chews before it disappeared and he was left wanting more.

"You like?"

He shrugged. "It's bland."

"Bland, huh?"

"And stale. Very stale." He made a big show of clutching at his throat, as if swallowing had taken superhuman effort.

"It wasn't that bad."

"You weren't the one being tortured."

Xandra frowned. Beau could tell she wanted to tell him where to get off and how far south he could go. He wanted her to. At least then she would be busy putting him in his place rather than seducing him.

"So it's bland and stale, huh?" she finally said through clenched teeth. "I suppose I could spice it up a little and make sure I walk faster so the next batch doesn't get as much time to age between the oven and your mouth." She disappeared inside and he grinned.

Mission accomplished.

But all too soon, Xandra returned with another bite. This one was even better than the first and his brain short-circuited for a few moments while the flavor overloaded his taste buds.

"Better?"

"Not bad." She smiled and his heart revved. "I mean not *too* bad, as in it's still bad but marginally better than the first. Your first time in the kitchen?"

"For your information, I'm an experienced hand in the kitchen." At his surprised expression, she added, "Yes, I know how to cook. I don't get the chance too often since I'm busy at work, but I do know my way around, and there's more where that came from if you're interested."

No. The refusal was there, along with an insult that would surely put another frown on her face, but damned if either made it from his brain to his mouth. As much as he wanted to offend her, as much as she deserved it after trying to manipulate him, he still felt like a heel when he did or said something that wiped the smile off her face.

He liked seeing her smile.

"More?" she prodded, drawing him back to the question at hand. "I've got plenty."

His stomach grumbled its own response. He'd worked clean through lunch on the staircase inside the house, determined to be done and out before she came home. He'd finished in record time, and now he was hungry.

For food, that is, and she obviously had plenty. He set his sander aside and followed her inside.

Plenty didn't begin to describe the spread laid out on her coffee table in the living room—the dining room was obviously off-limits thanks to the previous night's fire. "You normally cook this much?"

"I'm, uh, planning a dinner party and I thought I would try my hand at a few new dishes."

Beau ignored the warning bells going off in his head. Leather groaned as he sank to the edge of her couch. She filled a plate and handed it to him.

It tasted even better than it looked.

He lifted a forkful of the rice dish into his mouth. "This is really good," he said in between bites. "I never pictured you as the cooking type. Not with your mother being such a feminist."

"She's a *womanist*. There's a difference. Feminists tend to tamp down their softer side for fear that it makes them appear weak. Womanists embrace that softer side because they see it as a strength. My mother encouraged me and my sisters to explore all things feminine and feel good about them. My oldest sister, Skye, loves to shop. My sister, Eve, likes to garden, though the last thing I saw growing in her window box looked sort of scary." At his questioning glance, she added, "Eve's a little different. She's very artsy and creative, and she likes to piss our mother off. She's the rebel of our family."

Xandra smiled again, and his stomach hollowed out. He

shook away the sensation and blurted, "She's a nutball," before taking a long gulp of the beverage she handed him.

Her full lips pulled into a tight line. "I prefer the term 'quirky.'"

"Whatever floats your boat, but it still means the same thing: 'nutball.'"

"Try the steak," Xandra ground out, shoving a fork into Beau's mouth before he said another word. It was one thing to know that he was a dud in bed, and another to realize that he was rude and insensitive on top of that.

Add to Imperfect Daddy list: A man who uses the word 'nutball' when referring to her relatives.

"Not bad," he said after swallowing the mouthful. Before she could cut another, he reached past her. His arm grazed hers and heat tingled through her body on its way to every major erogenous zone. "It could be better, but I'll need another bite before I can make a definite suggestion on what it's lacking."

Warmth spread through her. A crazy reaction because this wasn't about how well she cooked. It was about saturating his taste buds and making him hungry for more than what was on the plate.

Beau popped another bite of steak into his mouth, and chewed with a thoughtful look on his face. "It needs something."

"Maybe you need something," Xandra replied, her patience wearing thin.

"What's that supposed to mean?"

"You know you like it. Just admit it."

"Maybe I do, maybe I don't. What does it matter if I like it? You didn't do any of this for me. It's for your dinner party. Right?" Challenge gleamed in his eyes.

"Right." As she watched him enjoy another bite, her

own stomach grumbled. She cut another piece of meat, but his hand closed over hers as soon as she forked it. He took it from her and held it up to her mouth.

"So dig in. You know you want it."

Boy, did she ever.

As soon as the notion struck, she forced it aside. This wasn't about really and truly wanting him. How could she really and truly want something when she knew it wasn't going to be all that? No, this was all in the name of research and the anticipation rippling through her body stemmed strictly from the notion that she was about to validate her ultimate design.

That coupled with the fact that it had been over six months since she and Mark had had sex, even the bad kind. It was no wonder her body was reacting with such fervor.

She ignored the urge to close her lips around the bite of steak. She was already turned on enough. She didn't need any aphrodisiacs adding to her already volatile condition.

"My sisters hate to cook," she blurted, eager to do something with her mouth. "I'm the only one who really took to it. Every night during high school, I helped my grammie in the kitchen. By the time senior year rolled around, I was doing it all. Appetizer through dessert." She smiled. "When I went away to college, that was the one thing I missed the most. A hot plate in a dorm room isn't really conducive to a full-course meal."

"But you make up for it now." He slid the bite into his own mouth and chewed.

"I'm so busy with Wild Woman that I usually get home too late. Though that didn't stop me at first. I just got tired of eating alone. My ex said it was more convenient for him to catch something at the tofu bar at his gym after he finished his workout. He wasn't much for sit down dinners."

"Did you love him?" His gaze burned into hers as he waited for an answer to the blunt question and a strange tingling swept up her spine.

"No." Oddly enough, the admission didn't come with the expected regret. "I don't do romantic love."

He arched an eyebrow. "Is that so?"

"Love is not a key ingredient to a lasting relationship. I'm sure it's nice, if it exists, but it's not mandatory."

"*If* it exists?" He eyed her. "You're telling me you've never been in love with anyone? You've never met a man who makes your knees weak? You've never felt the butterflies in your stomach or the damp palms? You've never had your heart beat so fast that you're scared it's going to jump out of your chest?" His disbelieving gaze held hers. "*Never?*"

Once, a traitorous voice whispered. *A long, long time ago . . .*

She shook her head. "That's lust, not love. So what about you? Do you cook?"

He looked as if he wanted to ask her more personal questions, but then he shrugged. "Not too much now. My schedule is pretty tight. But I used to cook when I was back in high school. I did dinner while my kid brothers set the table and cleaned up."

"Every night?"

Beau nodded as the past rushed at him. "Family tradition. My dad always made us sit down every night at the dinner table when we got home from the gas station." He smiled as he remembered his dad telling everybody to wash up "or else." "It was because of my mother. She was always big on doing the whole dinner table thing and when she passed away, he kept it up. I think he figured she was up there looking down at him and so he had to keep things going or else she'd get pissed off at him."

"My grandmother made us sit down with her every night, too. It didn't matter who had a date or who had homework or who had to watch the newest *X-Files* episode." At his raised eyebrows, she added, "The nutball."

He grinned. "This really isn't half bad." He took a bite of salad. "What's in this?"

"It's got cherries and bananas and mangoes. They're all really high in—" She caught the last word as if she'd been about to tell him some big secret. "They're, um, very high on the fruit chain."

"There's a fruit chain?"

"Um, yeah. It's a variation of the whole food chain idea."

"And what would be at the top of the fruit chain?"

"The biggest fruit, like a watermelon and then a pineapple, and then you've got your coconuts and the whole melon family before you get to the apples and oranges and the like . . . Boy, it's kind of hot in here."

"You know, it really is." Beau took a long gulp of the beverage she handed him, but the slightly sweet liquid did little to quench his thirst. Instead, he found himself even more thirsty. And hungry.

The notion stuck in his head as she popped a cherry into her mouth. Her straight, white teeth sank into the fleshy red pulp and his stomach hollowed out. Juice spurted and slicked her lips and he told himself he was going to hand her a napkin. *You'll hand her the napkin and get the hell out.* But thinking it and doing it were two very different things and instead he leaned forward.

Her eyes hooded as he reached his destination. He

flicked his tongue along her plump bottom lip, tasting the sweet mixture of warm female and ripe fruit. Another flick and he caught her bottom lip between his teeth and nibbled just enough to make her gasp.

He kissed her then, claiming her lips in a hot, wet, thorough kiss that made his heart pound and his groin throb. He plunged his fingers into her hair and canted her head to the side just enough to deepen the kiss.

Soon she was feeding him kisses rather than fruit. She moved against him, her hands exploring until she found the hem of his shirt.

His breath hitched as her fingers touched the bare flesh of his abdomen. She worked her way up then, ruffling her hands through his chest hair, as if learning the outline of each and every muscle.

Need rushed through his body, stringing him so tight his only thought was to push her down on the sofa and plunge into her sweet heat.

He half turned, urging her down, following her. He tore his mouth from hers to taste the soft skin of her neck. He licked the hollow between her breasts before pulling back to unfasten her buttons and open the front closure of her bra. Her breasts spilled out, her nipples ripe and red and ready for his mouth.

Dipping his head, he drew one swollen tip into his mouth and suckled her. Long and hard and . . . sweet. So damned sweet. He'd missed this their first time because he'd been so hot to be inside her. He'd ached so bad.

The thought jarred him from the lust clouding his brain and he stopped long enough to take a drink of air.

His heart hammered as the past rushed at him. He'd not only ached so bad for her, but he'd been so bad that she'd picked him to test her newest product.

"What's wrong?" she asked as he sat upright and took another deep breath. And another.

"Beau?" Her hand touched his shoulder and he turned to look at her.

A big mistake because she looked so damned delicious with her blonde hair all mussed and her lips pink and swollen from his kisses. Her silk blouse hung open. The edges of her lace bra dangled to the side. Her soft, full breasts trembled with each breath and her red nipples glittered from the wet heat of his mouth. And suddenly he didn't care half as much about his pride as he did about kissing her again.

"What's wrong?" she asked again.

"I, um, feel funny."

"What is it?"

You was on the tip of his tongue, but he managed to bite it back. And then he did the only thing that he could think of when faced with so much temptation and a woman who wanted him only for bad sex.

He burped. "I think it was the food. It's not sitting too well with me. There must be something wrong with it."

His insult didn't seem to register because she said, "Oh, no you didn't. You didn't just burp."

He forced another for good measure.

"I don't believe this," she said. "You burped. We were kissing and then you just stopped and burped."

"I wouldn't eat any more of this if I were you. Something's bad." He got to his feet. "Wow, would you look at the time? I'm late."

"For what?"

"Dinner."

"But we're having dinner."

"I hate to break it to you, but that's not really dinner. It's a disaster. Besides, I'm already meeting someone else for dinner."

"You've got a *date*?"

"A date?" *Hell, no.* "Yes. I'd keep practicing for the dinner party if I were you. I'm sure you'll get it right." He patted her on the shoulder. "Have a good night."

"That's what I was trying to do," she grumbled as he headed for the door. "Before the burp, that is."

"I see you started the party without me," Beau said when he walked into the hospital room where his long-time friend sat at a small table.

Evan no longer wore the bandages that had concealed the right half of his face since the accident. The newly grafted skin was healing nicely, the bright pink patches the only reminder of that night and the fact that he'd been driving drunk. He'd wrapped his Beamer around a telephone pole and had been the only victim in the accident. Thankfully. While Evan wasn't the most responsible guy, he did have a heart. Beau knew his friend wouldn't have been able to live with himself if he had hurt anyone else.

The accident had been only a partial wake-up call, however. While Evan had sworn off the booze, he still hadn't traded in the other vices of his fast and furious lifestyle. Judging by the deck of cards and the pile of bills sitting next to it, Beau knew his friend still had a hankering for high stakes cards.

"Actually, you're just in time. Desiree, here, promised to do a table dance." Evan eyed the blonde nurse who'd followed Beau inside and was now unfolding the blood pressure cuff hooked to a nearby wall.

"Now, now. You know I don't dance when I'm on duty."

She winked as she walked over to him, hooked the cuff around his arm, and started to pump.

Beau set a Domino's pizza box on the nightstand and unearthed a six-pack of Coke and several packages of chocolate doughnuts from the paper sack he'd picked up at the grocery store down the street.

The room was dark except for the white fluorescent light humming at the head of the bed. The rest of the room sat in shadows. The curtains were open, the Houston skyline barely visible past the concrete edge of the adjoining building. It was a far cry from the high-rise apartment where Evan lived during the week and partied away the weekends.

"Don't you have anything better to do on a Saturday night?" Evan asked as Beau pulled up a chair.

"Better than a few Cokes, a pizza with the works, and beating you at poker? You forget who you're talking to."

"The guy voted most likely to study himself to death."

"The one and only."

Evan shook his head, took a can of Coke, and popped the tab. "I thought you were crazy the first year we roomed together, did you know that?"

"I knew you were crazy. Playing strip Monopoly and quarters the night before a calculus final? I still can't believe you passed that test."

"I aced it, friend. What can I say? I was a genius."

"You were lucky. You're still lucky," Beau said. "You're looking good."

"Yeah," he touched his face, "and you're still playing it safe."

"How's that?"

"Sitting here with me when you could be out with some hot babe is definitely playing it safe. Your dad's been dead over three years now. Your brothers are all grown up. You don't have to pay for braces or buy graduation pictures or put anyone through college. You don't have to work from dawn to dusk to keep a falling down gas station from actually falling down. You don't have to put food on anyone else's table or pay their electric bills anymore. You don't have to fork over nursing home expenses or pay medical bills. You've done all that, bud. That and more. You can think about yourself now."

"I've still got a business to run. People depend on me. I can't let them down." Which was why he couldn't fall into bed with Xandra Farrel.

Sex with her wasn't just sex. It was intense sex. The kind that followed a man home long after it was over and filled his head with all sorts of crazy thoughts like maybe, just maybe, he'd found The One. The kind that shook him so much he couldn't concentrate on the most important day of his life. The kind that messed with his head and screwed up his future.

He wasn't having sex with her again.

No matter how good she tasted.

"Man, you need to live a little."

Beau licked his lips and tried to ignore the sweetness that lingered on his tongue. "You live enough for the both of us."

"Not anymore." A strange look crossed his face and Beau had the feeling that Evan wanted to say something. But then Beau's cell phone rang, effectively killing any more conversation.

"Beau Hollister," he said when he punched the button.

"She hated Jack," Annabelle's voice filled his ear. "She hated him and she's threatening to report us to the Better

Business Bureau for false advertising if we don't satisfy her."

"Who?"

"Savannah Sawyer. The lady who writes the newspaper column."

"The trouble with a capital 'B'?"

"That's the one. Jack was there for two days and did most of the work. I thought you might actually turn out to be right about her caring more about the work than the worker. But then she called and threatened me. And you. And she made me promise to send her somebody really hot. Somebody without a beer belly who has blond hair and looks like Matthew McConaughey."

"We don't have anyone working for us who looks like him."

"I know. What are we going to do? This is terrible. This is worse than the *Titanic*. I'm this close to trading my caffeine addiction for something really major. I can't deal with this stress. I'm sending Tom."

"Tom doesn't know the first thing about decks. He's an electrician."

"He's all we've got."

"He doesn't even have blond hair."

"I'll hand him a bottle of bleach. He's hot. That'll make her happy."

"Calm down. Send Jason. He's blond and he's in fairly good shape and he at least knows about stripping and varnishing." Jason was the resident painter and the closest thing he could come up with to finish the Sawyer job.

"I don't think he's going to work. He's married and hunky guys aren't supposed to be married."

"She doesn't know that."

"She'll know. His matching socks will be a dead give-away."

"Just send him and relax. Everything is going to be okay." That's what he told her, but damned if he didn't have the crazy urge to tell her to make Jason wear mismatched socks.

He shook the thought away, stabbed the OFF button and slid the phone into his pocket.

"No rest for the weary, huh?"

He shrugged. "What can I say? I'm the boss."

"You don't seem too happy about the fact."

"I'm happy." His temples throbbed from an oncoming headache. "Dammit, I'm *very* happy."

"Sure you are." Evan gave him a knowing look. "And with this new face I'm the next contestant for *The Bachelor*."

Beau frowned. "Are we going to play cards or what?"

Chapter Fifteen

I'm a complete and total loser," Xandra told her sister Eve the next morning as she sat at her desk and stared at the untouched samples of Mabel.

"No, you're not. You're only failing at the seduction stuff, which makes you only part loser."

"You're making me feel so much better."

"You're missing the point."

"Which is?"

"The other part of you—the nonloser side—has it going on in a major way. You're single and successful and totally hot. If I were a guy, I'd do you in a heartbeat."

"Really?"

"You bet."

"You're the best sister in the world."

"And you're letting this guy get to you. So he's not falling for all this seduction crap? Find another guinea pig."

But Xandra didn't want to find anyone else. Her mind rushed back to the previous night and the way he'd licked the fruit juice from her lips.

She licked her own lips. "I'll just have to think of something besides food to fire him up."

"I know this witch down on Hollywood Boulevard who could probably put a lust hex on him if you can get a lock of his pubic hair."

"If I could get close enough to get a lock of his pubic hair, then I wouldn't need a lust hex."

"Good point."

"I need something that doesn't scream 'I want you,' because after last night I have a feeling he's going to be a little standoffish." She could still see the flash of fear in his eyes. As if he'd woken up and realized he'd had a bad dream.

Or maybe a really, really good one.

The notion struck just as his voice played in her head.

There's no such thing as temporary with any woman, especially one that gets under your skin and into your head and stays there no matter how much you try to push her out.

Had he been referring to her?

Right. He hadn't so much as glanced at her from that night on. She'd interpreted his sudden coldness as fear that she might actually ruin his reputation. But maybe the fear had been rooted in something else.

Maybe he'd actually wanted her *again*. Not hard and fast and *bum!* But slow and sweet and *yum.*

Before she could dwell on the idea, Eve's voice pulled her from her thoughts.

"Why don't you bop him on the head with his hammer when he has his back turned, drag him inside, and have your way with him?"

"I'm talking subtle, not homicide. Besides, that would never work."

"Of course it would. It's the classic rape fantasy, just with reversed roles. I did it in one of my instructional videos, *Bring Your Most Erotic Thoughts to Life*. The actress used one of those Nerf bats, bashed him on the head and dragged him into her bedroom for a little forceful fun. It was fantastic."

"But it wasn't real. This is life, not fantasy. There's a big difference." She knew that better than anyone. In her fantasies, Beau Hollister was more than willing. He was eager. And hot. And he rocked her world with enough skill and finesse to give her the best orgasm of her life. She sighed. "There has to be some way to get to him. Something that makes him butter in my hands. Everybody has a weak spot. Yours is flowers."

"What can I say? I'm easy. Hey, maybe Beau likes flowers."

"I seriously doubt that."

"You never know. This guy I dated last year loved daisies. He liked to throw them all over the bed and roll around on the petals. Then again, he was bisexual, so I think that was his softer side coming out. Maybe Beau is gay?"

"He's not gay."

"How do you know?"

"Because . . . Because he's not. He's got a great body and a killer smile."

"So?"

"So he's got all that, and he looks great in a T-shirt and he carries a toolbox, for heaven's sake."

"That's not a good indicator. What's he got in the toolbox?"

"What do you mean?"

"His tools. Are they color-coordinated or in alphabetical

order or arranged according to size? If they're grouped in any other way other than basic function, I'd be willing to bet my next video that he's as fruity as Grandma's Christmas cake."

Xandra thought about the large metal toolbox sitting on her front porch, the lid closed, hiding whatever was inside. "That *would* explain why he turned me down."

"That's right. Turning down a hot, straightforward, got-it-goin'-on woman like you for sex? That's proof enough if you ask me."

"Maybe." And maybe he simply wasn't attracted to her anymore now than he'd been way back when, when he'd been in such a hurry to be rid of her.

Xandra pushed aside the crazy thought. His poor, frenzied performance had nothing to do with her and everything to do with the fact that he simply wasn't half as good as his reputation. End of story.

"So what's next on the lust-him-up list?"

"I don't know."

"So look at the list."

"I don't actually have a list for this. I thought I would make it up as I go."

"*You* without a list? The CEO of Lifesavers must be one happy man. If you're flying solo, you must be eating the damned things like candy."

"They *are* candy, not that you would realize that since you live on black coffee and beef jerky."

"That's only when I'm in the middle of a project. I need my protein."

"You need to sit down with a box of Godiva and live a little."

"Chocolate kills my complexion and frankly, it just doesn't do much for me."

"I hate you."

"Only because you're an obsessive-compulsive nut and I'm not. I'm a type-B personality. I go with the flow, roll with the punches. I don't get stressed out."

"Then that wasn't you who offered to break both Mark's legs for leaving me?"

"I don't get stressed," she repeated again, "I get even. There's a big difference. I don't get my thong twisted over a man. What's the point? There's so many of them and they're all the same. They're like ants. They're focused on only two things—eating and multiplying—and anything that gets in the way gets annihilated."

"So Dad's an ant?"

"Dad's not an ant. He's different. He's much higher on the food chain. He's . . . *Dad.*"

"Good point. What about Clint? Skye obviously doesn't think he's an ant, and I know for a fact that the only biting he does is in the bedroom, and that's only when she begs."

"I'm reserving judgment on him to see what happens. He may be one of the few who've actually evolved from the hunter-and-gatherer phase. He may actually be"—her voice lowered a notch—"*human.*"

"I should hope so. I'd hate to think what their kids would look like otherwise." An image hit her of a small boy with bug eyes and tentacles.

Add to Imperfect Daddy list right below last night's burping entry: A man who hunts, gathers, and bites.

The thought stirred an image of Beau biting into the juicy piece of mango from last night's fruit salad. The sweet nectar dribbling down his chin. His lips slick and delectable.

Her stomach grumbled and her mouth watered and she opened her mouth to ask more about Eve's hammer suggestion. After all, one well-aimed hit *would* bring him to his knees.

Before she could say anything, Kimmy rushed into the room, shouting, "You're a goddess. A diva. The Christian Dior of the sex industry!"

"I'll talk to you later," Xandra told her sister before sliding the receiver into its cradle.

"A one hundred percent, grade-A, certified carnal genius!"

Xandra noted the light in Kimmy's eyes and the glow of her face. "Either Mabel came through or you're wearing one of those makeup foundations with the light crystals."

"Actually, it's both. Sephora's got this new color called Beige Bliss—oh, never mind. I mean, it's a great color, but the real big deal right now is Miss Mabel and her magic current." She shook her head. "I've never felt anything like it. It was like my entire body was humming. A slow steady humming that got louder and louder until bam! I burst into song."

"That's a really great metaphor."

"No, I mean it. I actually started to sing. It felt so fierce that a moan, even a wail wasn't nearly good enough to release all that energy. I sang 'That's the Way I Like It' by KC and the Sunshine Band so loud, in such a high pitch that my next-door neighbor, Mrs. Jackson—she's the old lady with the seven talking parrots—called the landlord and complained that I was having a wild party with a live band." Her smiled widened. "As of this morning, the only thing coming from her apartment was a squawking rendition of 'That's the Way I Like It'—those birds can imitate anything." She shook her head and sank down into the large cushioned chair opposite Xandra's desk. "You did it. You really did it. Or rather, Mabel did it, but it's because you thought of her in the first place. She's going to blow everyone away at the Sextravaganza."

"I hope so. But we can't make that determination based on one performance."

"Three," Kimmy cut in. "I used all three samples."

"Really?"

"And it was even better each time."

Xandra turned to her computer and keyed a few notes on Mabel's testing page. "Still, it was with the same man and during one sex session."

"One hell of a sex session."

"Even so, there are other factors that can contribute to positive results."

"Not with Dennis. We've done it five times—four pairs of Gucci shoes and a Fendi bag—and it's never been this good."

"That's definitely a positive sign, but we'll need more evidence."

Kimmy held out her hand. "No problem. I've got a date with Harold the ho-hum—an entire collection of Sephora lipsticks and Anne Klein pumps. If I can sing disco with Harold, then Mabel isn't just a godsend to women. She's the Messiah herself."

"Maybe." If only Xandra knew firsthand. Unfortunately, her own testing attempts had failed miserably thanks to one stubborn man.

She ignored the urge to hand over the entire collection of samples. At the rate she was going, she wouldn't be using them herself. At the same time, she couldn't forget the way his lips had felt against hers and the feeling fed the small thread of determination inside her.

She handed Kimmy a sample. The woman made a face

and Xandra handed over another. And another before Kimmy smiled.

"Three is my lucky number. Of course, I could always try for four." Her eyes danced.

"We'll save number four for a different session. The goal of objective testing is to use the product with as many different subjects in as many different environments as possible, and document the results. If they're the same, then the positive findings can be attributed to the one constant—Mabel. If not, then the findings are inconclusive."

"They'll be conclusive. So conclusive that I might not be able to make it into work tomorrow."

Xandra smiled. "A day to recuperate?"

"To shop. I have a feeling I'll be so grateful, I'll be the one out buying something for someone."

"I bet Harold would love that."

"Not for Harold. For you. You're a goddess and I owe you in a major way." She slid the samples into her pocket and set the folder she'd been carrying down on Xandra's desk. "And on a more serious note, some guy from Lust, Lust, Baby! called and left a message. He said something about the Sextravaganza."

"What about it?"

Kimmy shrugged. "Maybe they've heard rumors about Mabel and want to hand us the trophy now because there's absolutely no way they can compete."

"In my wildest dreams. More like they want to talk us out of our booth location. They're always in the front row, smack dab in the middle, but I put our application in early this year. Not to mention, Albert knows the woman who does the table setups and she agreed to slip us into the spot in return for a year's worth of free female condoms."

"I bet she'd give us the spot for life in return for a few Mabel samples."

Xandra grinned and watched as Kimmy went through the morning agenda. The young woman looked excited, but not from the stack of work in her hands. Rather, the pink in her cheeks and the light in her eyes came from the fact that she was a woman well-satisfied.

As proud as Xandra was that Mabel was the one responsible for the look, she couldn't help but want a satisfied look of her own.

She couldn't remember the last time she'd looked so satisfied and . . . excited. She and Mark had had comfort, not excitement. Except for the first few months of their relationship, and it had been more wonder than excitement. She'd been in awe that he'd taken an interest in her, and wowed by the fact that he kept coming back date after date after date. She realized now that he hadn't been excited so much as he'd been comfortable. Safe. Xandra hadn't made him feel like the odd virgin he'd been. She'd been clumsy herself and so they'd made a good match.

Xandra and Mark had made sense, not excitement. And while she knew, Holy Commitment–wise, she needed to aim for sense, she couldn't help but want excitement even more.

She wanted to feel the hunger. The pounding heart. The sweaty palms. The butterflies in her stomach—all of the things that Beau Hollister associated with love. Feelings that had nothing to do with such a romantic notion and everything to do with the full-blown lust he made her feel during the presex phase.

Hello? This isn't about presex with Beau. It's about having bad sex with him. Really bad sex. It's about turning that really bad sex into really good sex via Mabel.

She held tight to the thought and focused on Kimmy's words.

". . . ad copy for the new *Cosmo* layout is waiting in an attachment on your computer. They need changes yesterday. And that's it. I've got bagels and cream cheese—Philadelphia—or apples—Granny Smith."

She had a sudden vision of Beau as he'd looked yesterday morning munching popcorn and humming on her front porch. "Any popcorn?"

"Orville Redenbacher or Jiffy Pop?"

"Surprise me."

Xandra spent the rest of her morning munching on popcorn, working and trying not to fret over her lack of seduction ideas. She was trying too hard. She needed to relax, to concentrate on the business aspect of Wild Woman in order to free her creativity. However much she disliked numbers, she had to admit that she came up with her best ideas while examining the hated balance sheets.

Something brilliant would hit her. It always did.

Chapter Sixteen

Five o'clock came and went and the only thing that hit Xandra was an enormous, inflatable penis.

It bopped her in the face when she pushed open the door to product development in search of Albert.

"I'm so sorry, Miss Farrel." The apology came from a young, twenty-something redhead who rushed forward and gathered up the bobbing penis. He wore the standard white lab coat that most of the newbies sported when they first started with the company. After a few weeks with Albert and his team, most of them gave up the clinical look in favor of casual civilian wear.

With Coke bottle glasses, a tightly drawn mouth, and a tight tie that made his neck bulge just above his starched shirt collar, he looked much too uptight to loosen up in just a few weeks. Maybe a few years.

"I thought you were Mr. Sinclair," he rushed on. "My first assignment other than helping out here in the lab was to come up with something hip and creative for Wild Woman. I know he gives the same assignment to all the new people, to see if they've got what it takes to make it in product development." The man pushed his glasses back up. "I do. I've got it. I mean, I've got him." He indicated the inflatable shape that stood at least six feet tall and towered over him by a good twelve inches. "This is Paulie. He's a blow-up punching penis I came up with."

"A punching penis?"

"You punch him. If you're stressed out or mad at your partner," the man went on, "you just take a whack at Paulie."

Xandra glanced from Albert's new protégé, to the rubber penis, and back. She gave Albert free rein in the engineering department—meaning he could hire whomever he wanted, male or female, as long as he hired the most qualified—and rarely doubted his judgment. Until now.

Overall, he usually hired women, but there was the occasional man who applied and, sometimes, beat out his female counterparts. But this guy seemed about as clueless when it came to women as he was when it came to clothes.

"I can't say that I see how a punching penis plays into our mission statement. Wild Woman is all about a woman's pleasure."

"So is Paulie. He's soft and flexible, especially designed to take a licking without giving one back. Believe me, when a woman is really pissed and she takes a swing at this, she'll feel a lot of pleasure. And satisfaction. Especially if she's envisioning whoever has her so upset. Maybe her partner or her boss or a low-down, two-timing SOB by the name of Bobby Dupree who promised her he would call." At Xandra's questioning look, he added, "He's this loser who's dating my sister. Or he was."

Mmm. She could sort of see Paulie fitting into the whole pleasure scenario. After Beau left her high and dry last night, she could have used a few whacks at Paulie to work out her frustration. "He's sort of like a giant, penis-shaped stress ball."

"Exactly." The young man smiled. "It's very functional, not to mention I have a feeling it will make a huge contribution to society in general."

"Really? And how's that?"

"Women can turn their aggression on an inanimate object rather than their poor, defenseless younger brother. If only Lorena Bobbitt had had a Paulie of her own. Life might be totally different now."

Xandra nodded. "I don't know if I would go that far, but it does have possibilities."

"You really think so?" He beamed and pushed his glasses back up. "I just knew you would like it. Mr. Sinclair, too. I hope. He hasn't actually seen it yet."

"Where is he?"

"He's usually working late. That's why I thought you were him. But maybe he went home. He hasn't exactly been himself the past few days. Sort of uptight and preoccupied."

"I know the feeling." Albert wanted her and she wanted Beau. Life was much too complicated.

Especially since she was there to ask for Albert's help with seducing Beau.

The blowtorch had gotten Beau inside the house. The seductive food had gotten her some fantastic kisses and a little exciting foreplay. Albert definitely scored an "A+" in the seduction department and so it made him the perfect person to help her.

At the same time, she dreaded having another talk with him. Another I-like-you-but talk. She didn't want to hurt him and risk losing their friendship. At the same time, she simply wasn't turned on.

She headed back up to the fifth floor. She had fifteen minutes to come up with something solid to use on Beau this evening. Maybe she'd do the whole romantic bubble bath idea. Surely if she screamed bloody murder, he would come running into the bathroom to check on her and she could trip him. That would actually get him into the tub, albeit headfirst. She could improvise from there . . .

Her thoughts ground to a halt as a strange flicker of light caught her eye as she passed the conference room. She turned to see the orange glow licking at the bottom of the door.

She'd had enough experience with fire in the past forty-eight hours to send a shiver of apprehension up her spine. She touched the doorknob. It was cold. The door was cold and . . .

The door creaked inward and she stepped into the room. Where a bevy of chocolate desserts had covered the conference table, there was nothing but a white sheet draped over it now. Candles flickered from every corner of the room. A small warming dish bubbled from the sideboard, a steamy, arousing scent drifted across the room.

Her nostrils flared as the scents of cinnamon, ginger, and clove mingled and filled her head and sent a rush of heat through her body.

"Welcome to Albert's All-Over Body Spa." The deep voice drew her attention to the corner of the room where her friend was standing. He was wearing a white T-shirt and white slacks. He had a robe draped over one arm and a determined I'm-doing-this-come-hell-or-high-water look on his face. As if he were about to eat cauliflower for the first time.

"Albert, we need to talk."

"No talking. You've been talking all day. You look tired. Drained. You need to relax and I have just the thing."

He walked toward her and the scent filling the air grew stronger. She inhaled and a strange sense of peace rushed through her body.

"Just smell," he told her, drinking in a deep breath to demonstrate. "Fill your head with the aroma."

"What is it?"

"Essential oils. The basis for aromatherapy. The different oils give off different scents, which trigger various effects within us, or so sayeth Cherry Chandler. Some oils produce a calming effect. Some are energizing, some arousing. Do you feel aroused?"

The last word rooted in her brain and a warning signal sounded. She opened her mouth to tell him she wasn't, nor would she ever be, *aroused*. But then he came around her, placed his hands on her shoulders and started to knead them. Her thoughts fled as her muscles screamed with delight.

"That feels so good."

"I learned it during the touch part of sensitivity training. You move your fingers like this and it hits certain tension points in your partner. It releases their stress and tunes you into their most vulnerable areas."

"It feels like butterfly wings tapping."

"Exactly." The pressure increased and her temples throbbed. "You're really tense."

"I've had a trying day," she blurted, the familiar, friendly sound of his voice lulling her to spill her guts the way it always did. And making her forget that he wasn't just her friend anymore. That he wanted to be more. That despite their lack of chemical attraction, he thought . . .

Her doubts fled as fast as her stress, and her mouth kept moving of its own accord.

"And then there's this Beau situation. I haven't used even one of the Mabel samples. We're going on two weeks and I'm no closer to having great sex than I was when I started. Mind you, we had some really hot kisses and even some above-the-waist action. But then it stopped and—"

"Don't talk. Don't think. Just feel. Tonight's about feeling. And smelling. You can still smell it, can't you?"

She took another drink of the air and the scent skirted her nerve endings. "Did you mix that up yourself?"

"Following Cherry Chandler's own personal recipe for seductive success."

She gave in to the lulling sensation a full minute more before she tried to gather her wits. "Albert," she forced her eyes open and tried to ignore his magic fingers, "we really need to talk."

"Don't say anything. You're just supposed to feel, re-member?" He kneaded harder and her eyes closed again. "This feels good, doesn't it?"

"Wonderful."

"Just wait until I get you undressed and on the table. I've got pure grape seed and coconut oils, and sweet al-mond oil, all fortified with other essential oils—sandal-wood, jasmine, and cinnamon—guaranteed to seduce the muscles."

"That really feels . . . Did you say 'seduce'?" She forced one eye open.

"Guaranteed. You'll be putty by the time I'm done."

He wasn't whistling "Dixie" either. At the rate she was melting, a few more minutes and she would rip off her clothes, climb onto the table, and beg for more, regardless of the fact that it would give him entirely the wrong impression—namely that she was attracted to him.

She wasn't the least bit attracted, yet here she was, her nerves humming, her body wanting more.

"You're a genius," she declared as she turned and planted a kiss on his cheek. "A seductive genius!"

"I am?" He forced a grin. "I mean, yes, I am. I knew you would come around." He stepped back. "I just didn't figure it would be this soon. I thought for sure I would have to do the full body massage."

"I have to get home." She grabbed two of the bottles from the edge of the table. "Mind if I take these to go? Thanks so much. Look, I know you went to a lot of trouble and I truly appreciate it, but we can't do this."

"We can't." He nodded. "I mean, we can't? Why not?"

"It just doesn't feel right. You're like my brother."

"But I'm not your brother. You don't even have a brother."

"If I did, you would be him. We're good together, but as friends." She eyed the bubbling incense burner. "What did you say was in that?"

"Take it."

"Really?"

"Take it before I argue with you." He eyed her. "I *am* going to argue with you. We're perfect for each other. I know it seems kind of awkward now."

"Very awkward."

"Downright weird," he readily agreed. "But we can get past that. We can get to a comfortable place where things feel right. You'll see."

But the only thing she wanted to see at the moment was whether or not Beau was working late tonight. If he wasn't, she would have to hold off until tomorrow. But if so, tonight was definitely the night.

A few careful ministrations from Albert and she'd all

but melted. Her muscles had screamed for more and she didn't actually do any physical labor for a living. A man wielding a hammer and other more sizable tools would definitely be an easy target for a bone-melting, libido-inspiring massage.

One touch and Beau Hollister would be begging for more.

Albert watched Xandra leave before blowing out the few candles she'd left and tossing his seductive tools into a cardboard box.

So much for seducing Xandra through her sense of smell and her sense of touch. He'd gone for a double whammy again—two senses at once—but he was no closer to convincing her of their great sex potential than he'd been with the chocolate and music.

"It's not going to work." The woman's familiar voice sounded as if she were reading his thoughts.

He glanced up to see Stacey Bernard standing in the doorway. She didn't just look bland in her beige slacks and ho-hum white blouse, she ate bland, as well. She spooned nonfat plain yogurt from the container in her hand and took a bite.

"I don't recall asking your opinion."

"You clearly need all the help you can get because you're not getting anywhere on your own. Obviously she isn't the least bit moved by the sensitive side of a man. She's not going to go out with you. And why you would even want to go out with her, I don't know. Dating is a waste of time. It's pointless. Sure, you get out of the house and have a little fun, but then you break up and it's back to watching Oxygen on Saturday nights."

"And cuddling up with your cat."

She glared. "My cat is none of your concern."

"And my social life is none of yours."

"You mean your lack of a social life."

"Are you always so gloomy?"

"I'm not gloomy. I'm practical."

"Says who?"

"Whoever conducted the latest divorce study. Statistics show that three out of every four marriages end in divorce. So what's the point of dating in the first place? If you're just going to wind up being one of the statistics?"

"Maybe you'll be the one that actually makes it."

"It's a long shot."

"My parents have been together for forty years."

"Yeah, well mine were together for all of six months. Then my mother split and married again. Then she split and married again. Then she split and married *again*. Don't look at me like that," she added when his gaze went from surprised to sympathetic. "I didn't have a rough life or anything like that. I had it great because with each split, my mom took half. By the time she hit husband number four, we were set for life. I had a full-time nanny, designer clothes, a few credit cards for my own personal use, and a new BMW when I turned sixteen."

"I always wanted a BMW."

"Really?"

"A silver one."

"I had a silver one." She smiled. "I never would have figured you for a silver BMW type."

"I wasn't. I was just a wannabe. In actuality, I was a beat-up Ford pickup type—half blue, half rust—that my dad, Francis, picked up at a garage sale." He grinned at the memory. "It was pretty bad, but it did have a killer stereo system—my birthday present from Chuck, my mom."

"Your parents really *are* gay." She looked surprised.

"I thought you already knew that. You're always making comments."

"Because it gets you so worked up. I thought it made you mad because you were some homophobe. I never really thought . . ." She grinned. "I'm sorry. You must think I'm pretty shallow."

"I do. I think you're pretty and shallow." He wasn't sure why he said it, except that the darkness was doing something to him. That, combined with the potent scent of all those essential oils still in the air, muddied his thoughts. Without pure oxygen to keep a clear head, he was having a hard time remembering that Stacey Bernard was the enemy.

Standing there in the doorway, with the candlelight playing across her features, she seemed almost soft. Vulnerable.

"You're just setting yourself up for disappointment," she told him, eyeing the box and its contents.

"What do you care?"

"My concern is completely self-motivated. You're a colleague and I have a responsibility to this company. If you get your heart broken, then you'll be grumpy. The turnover rate in your department will go through the roof, which will mean additional personnel costs, which affects the per product cost and makes my job of making said cost reasonable and affordable for this company very difficult."

"And here I thought you might have grown tired of spending your free time with Peanut and were wanting to test the waters with an actual man."

"What is that supposed to mean?"

"That you need to get out. Go on a real date. Have some

fun with an attractive, good-looking guy who needs to get out more himself."

"Meaning you?"

"Meaning I would love to show you a good time—we're coworkers on the same team, after all, and so we should support one another. You pick the time and place, and I'll be there, in exchange for a small favor." What the hell was he doing?

Getting a date, that's what.

The situation with Xandra wasn't progressing and, in reality, he didn't want it to progress. They were just friends and he wasn't the least bit turned on by her and, well, the clock *was* still ticking.

"You really want to go out with me?" Stacey asked him.

"Why not?"

"Maybe because you hate me."

"I don't hate you. I just think you need to loosen up and have some fun."

"I have plenty of fun," she said the words, but then seemed to think better of them. "Okay, so maybe I used to have more fun."

A grin touched her lips and softened her features, making Albert remember his initial attraction to her in the first place. He felt it in the tightening in his groin.

"I did used to belong to a bowling club. Every Saturday night I would go to Rock-n-Bowl and drink beer, eat pizza, and have a really good time. It's been forever since I did that." She eyed him. "Okay, I'll help you out if you take me bowling. But you'd better not want anything weird or perverted in return."

"That hurts." He came this close to making another cat comment, but thought better of it. Marsha's daughter's wedding was just a few days away and he'd promised to bring a date. While this was more like a business arrangement than a date, Chuckles didn't have to know that.

"So what do you have in mind?" she asked. "A movie? Dinner? Dancing? A football game?"

He smiled. "A really good slice of wedding cake."

Chapter Seventeen

Y ou're not begging," Xandra told Beau when she made her proposition later that evening. She stood on her front porch and watched him pack up his supplies.

"Why would I beg?"

"Because building furniture is your hobby, and I'm offering you the chance to make a little money at it." She beamed. "You can start right now. Just get inside and get to work."

"Inside, huh?" Beau gave her a knowing look, but she didn't seem the least bit clued in to the fact that he knew her game.

Instead, she nodded and gave him a wide-eyed look that screamed innocence. "For however long it takes you to build something to fill up that empty space in my den. Maybe that bookshelf you suggested."

"Maybe. But before we decide on something, you'd better tell me what sort of budget you have for something like this." His gaze locked with hers. "Hopefully it's pretty sizable because handcrafted furniture doesn't come cheap."

"What do you mean by 'pretty sizable'?"

He wanted to tell her that he would do it for free, but since the bookshelves were obviously part of some bigger scheme to get him inside her house, and, ultimately, inside her, he didn't want to make it any easier. Besides, he'd already put in a day's work and then some and he had a headache just this side of hellacious. He wasn't in the mood to be too charitable. "Besides the fact that you're commissioning a handcrafted, one-of-a-kind piece, you're also asking me to work overtime, and that doesn't come cheap."

"Of course, I'll expect to pay extra. Time and a half."

"Actually, I pay all my guys double time. They're the best, after all."

"Double?"

He saw the gleam in her eyes and he knew the business side of her wanted to argue.

"Okay, double," she said at last. "I guess it's only fair if that's what you pay your men."

"Actually, I charge triple. I'm the boss, after all."

"Triple? That's ridiculous."

"I've got overhead."

"What kind of overhead?"

"Materials."

"Wood and varnish? I'll pick some up at Home Depot for you."

"And of course, there's my know-how. That doesn't come cheap."

"I wasn't thinking cheap. But I wasn't thinking triple, either. I think double is more than fair."

"It's triple or nothing."

"Double and a half."

"I guess I could be satisfied with that." *Fat chance.* The

only thing that could come close to satisfying Beau at the moment was another taste of her sweet lips.

He cleared his suddenly dry throat and tore his gaze from her mouth. "I might as well get started tonight," he said as he leaned down to gather up the tools scattered across her porch. "I'll take the measurements and see how much wood I'll need."

"Sounds perfect." The word sounded more like a purr and he turned to see the gleam in her eyes before she shut the door and retreated back inside. Forget the small hope that she truly admired his handiwork. It was a ploy, pure and simple, to get him into the house.

As much as the thought aggravated him, it excited him, as well. He couldn't help but admire her determination, and wonder what she was going to come up with next to get him out of his clothes and into her sweet body.

He forced a frown and tried to remember the all-important fact that he didn't like being manipulated. But a visual popped into his head: Xandra naked in the moonlight, her nipples ripe, her lips parted, her legs open and waiting and . . .

He shoved a hand through his hair and busied himself clearing away the mess on her front porch. A full fifteen minutes later, after retrieving his tape measure and notebook from the van, he knocked on her door.

She let him in and led him down the hall toward the den. She'd shed her killer high heels and her suit jacket. She wore just the red skirt and a sleeveless white shell that looked more like a camisole than any sort of decent blouse. It was thin and skimpy and he could easily see the lacy imprint of her bra beneath the material. And the faint shadow of her nipples. Her very ripe nipples . . .

Aw, hell.

He turned toward the empty space where he intended to put the bookshelves. He meant to push her out of his head so that he could concentrate on the task at hand, but she stayed hot on his heels, following him the few feet over to the area. She bumped into him when he came to a sudden halt, the side of her soft breast pressing into his arm.

"I'd be glad to hold the end of the tape measure," she offered when he all but jumped and whirled at the contact.

"No, um, thanks." What the hell was wrong with him? He knew what she was up to. Nothing should startle him. *Keep the faith, buddy, and just hurry the hell up.*

He unhooked the tape measure and tried to avoid looking at her as she stood there, watching him, but it was no use. She was too close and she smelled too good.

Her lips were full and parted and the second he glanced up, she licked them. Just a flick of her tongue along the bottom fullness, but it was enough to hollow out his stomach and send a wash of heat through him.

He tugged at the neck of his T-shirt. "It's hot in here."

"You're hot?" When he nodded, she smiled and his skin prickled.

"Not hot as in *hot*," he rushed on. "This has nothing to do with you or the fact that you look really nice in red." Why the hell had he said that? *Because it's true,* a voice whispered. She not only looked nice, she looked sexy. Voluptuous. Ripe. But, hell's bells, he wasn't supposed to tell her that. "This isn't about you and me and sex." Or the fact that he wanted it really, really bad.

"Sex? Who said anything about sex?" When he gave her a get-real look, she shrugged. "Okay, so I said something about sex. But that was last week. I haven't even mentioned the word tonight. There are lots of things that can cause a body's temperature to rise besides the notion of two bodies intertwined, pleasuring one another"—her voice grew softer, more breathless—"teasing each other, tasting and savoring and . . ." She blew out a breath of her own. "Whew, I think I'm getting a little hot myself."

Beau stared at her, into the bright depths of her eyes and barely resisted the urge to press his lips to hers. He'd made that mistake last night and he wasn't going there again.

Because if he did, he knew there would be no stopping. No turning back. If he kissed her again, they were headed straight to Sex City. No detours. No red lights. Not even a STOP sign.

Beau forced his attention to the empty space while she watched. He pulled out a pad and pencil and went about taking the required measurements. He trailed his hand over a nearby wall, feeling the straight lines and imagining how they would look with hand-carved wood attached to them, filling up the emptiness and making the space seem warm and cozy rather than stark and empty.

"You really like doing this sort of thing, don't you?" Xandra asked as she came up behind him.

The hair on the back of his neck ruffled and electricity sizzled along his nerve endings. He did his damnedest to ignore the sensation. His lips drew into a thin line. "It's my job."

"Actually, it's not," she pointed out. "Your job is to renovate what's already there, maybe rebuild a few things here and there. But I'm talking about the whole design process. About making something out of nothing. That's what you really like. It's your passion."

"I suppose so, but it's more than that. It's my connection to the past. To my mother."

"Did she make furniture?"

"She was more into refinishing, but the idea is the same.

I make something out of nothing, and she made something beautiful out of nothing special."

"Antiques?"

He nodded. "We had a house full of them. Most came from garage sales and rummage shops. They were usually the worst of the worst, either falling down or so scarred that it was hard to imagine how the piece had once looked. But my mom could. She would strip off the old paint and varnish, sand away the scuffs and scratches and refinish the wood, and make it look brand spanking new. My dad called her Doc because he said she could doctor up anything."

"It must have been really tough on you when she got sick."

He didn't want to talk to her. Hell, the last thing he needed to was sit and stroll down memory lane with Xandra Farrel of all people.

Then again, talking was a welcome diversion to the alternative—namely kissing and touching and stroking one damnable female hell-bent on seduction.

That, and the fact that there was something oddly compelling about her voice. As if she wanted to listen to him as much as she wanted to have sex with him.

Yeah, right.

Despite the doubt, he opened his mouth and the words came out, "One minute she was this happy, healthy woman and the next, she was gone. I think she suspected she was sick for a long time, but she was afraid to go to the doctor. She kept going about her business, pretending like nothing was wrong until she dropped twenty pounds in a month and my dad checked her into the hospital for a full checkup. She died less than six weeks later." He shook his head and blinked back the moisture that sprang to his eyes.

He busied himself jotting down another measurement before sliding the tape measure along the floor to get the width. The damned thing bunched up until Xandra hunkered down, grabbed the end, and held it in place while Beau pulled in the opposite direction.

"I remember her. She ran the cash register whenever my grammie stopped at the station for gas."

"She was always doing something." He jotted down another measurement. "She got so mad at the doctor because he made her stay in the hospital. She was right in the middle of restoring this dresser she'd picked up at a church rummage sale. The thought of it sitting around half done bothered the hell out of her."

His hand faltered on his pencil as a memory rushed at him. Of his mother and the way she would hug him when he ran into her hospital room. All too soon, she would push him away, wipe her eyes, and talk about all the things she still needed to do to that dresser.

"I think it gave her something to focus on, so that she didn't have to think about the fact that she was dying."

"What happened to the dresser?" Xandra asked.

He pocketed the notepad and pencil and got to his feet. "I refinished it for her."

"How old were you?"

"I was seven when she died. Twelve when I finished the dresser." At her raised eyebrows, he added, "I'd never refinished a piece of furniture in my life and so I had to take it slow and learn along the way. Not to mention, I had to help my dad with my brothers and the gas station."

"I can't imagine having so much responsibility at such a young age."

"Responsibility is my middle name." The words came out more sharp than he intended given the fact that he'd come to terms with carrying so much weight a long time ago. He shrugged, his voice softer as he added, "I thought it would lighten up a little when my dad passed away and my brothers graduated from college. But now I've got the guys at Hire-a-Hunk to worry over." He gathered the tape measure up, dropped it into his toolbox, and reached for his ruler and wood-marking pencil. Placing the straight edge up against the wall, he marked a few spots where he wanted to put the main anchors for the shelf.

He put his full concentration into the task for the next few minutes, eager to get his mind back on his work and off his past and the fact that talking about it hadn't stirred nearly the hurt it usually did. Which was why he always avoided the subject.

Until now. Until Xandra.

"I can't imagine what it must be like to lose a parent," she said, breaking the silence and drawing his attention. "I still have both of mine. Not that I see them that much. They're both involved in their careers."

"Your mother seems very driven." He marked a few more points and stepped back to eyeball the space.

"She is. She feels she has a responsibility to women everywhere to enlighten them when it comes to men. Namely, that men are the inferior sex and we women can't let them dominate."

"Is that what you believe?"

"I believe that women are very strong emotionally. They have to be to survive in a man's world."

"That's not what I asked you. I asked you if you think men are the inferior sex?"

"I think men and women are a lot more equal than my mother believes. I think men are stronger in some aspects, but at the same time, so are women. I think they balance each other out." She shrugged. "Not that it matters."

"You're entitled to your own opinions, even if they differ from your mother's."

"It's easier to keep my mouth shut."

"Easier, or safer?"

"I'm not afraid. I just don't like to argue with her and she's sure to blow a gasket if I announce that I don't buy into the doctrine she's been preaching her entire life. I can hear it now: 'No daughter of mine would dare think such a thing.'"

"Meaning you wouldn't be her daughter anymore."

"That's crazy. I'll always be her daughter."

"I know that," he told her. "I was just wondering if you did."

"I—" She caught her lip as if to hold back the rest of what she was going to say. "I, um, forgot something in the other room. Will you excuse me?"

"No problem. I'm almost done."

"So soon?" Her voice carried from the other room.

"This is the preliminary phase," he called out. "There's not much I can do without the materials." He made several more marks and a few lines before turning to his pad. He drew a quick sketch of the image that danced in his head. "All done," he announced a few minutes later. "I'll just let myself out." He gathered up his toolbox.

She popped her head around the corner, a box of matches in her hand. "But you can't leave yet."

"I have to order supplies. I can't do any actual work without them."

"But I was almost ready," she blurted before she seemed to think better of it. "I mean, I was almost ready to, um, heat up some leftovers from last night." She gave him a hopeful look. "I've got plenty if you want to join me."

I'd love to. "I'm afraid I can't." He rubbed his stomach and made a face. "I still haven't recovered from those awful rolls. And that salad. And that fish and rice." Her gaze narrowed and he knew he'd crept up a few notches on her obnoxious scale. "I was up all night, if you know what I mean. And all day. The Porta Potti out front hasn't seen so much action since Warren ate a half dozen chili dogs to win a lunchtime bet." He fanned the air. "I wouldn't go out there if I were you."

"I wasn't planning on it."

"Good." He winked, gathered his tools, and turned to leave. "Sleep tight."

"Yeah, right."

Chapter Eighteen

Xandra listened as Beau's van pulled away from the curb. Disappointment washed through her. She tossed her matches next to the candles she'd borrowed from Albert, loosened the button on her skirt, and collapsed on the couch with her laptop.

After powering up the screen, she opened a file and keyed in another entry on her ever-growing Imperfect Daddy list.

She had the insane urge to key in *See Beau Hollister* since he was the inspiration for the list of traits she didn't want in the future father of her child, but she'd vowed to be detailed and specific, and so she broke down his bad qualities and added them one by one.

Ungrateful when presented with a home-cooked meal.

Bad-mannered because he insults said home-cooked meal.

Tasteless because he doesn't melt in your arms thanks to said home-cooked meal.

Shocking because he openly discusses bodily functions that result from said home-cooked meal.

Uses a Porta Potti and probably doesn't even think about wiping the seat.

After adding the offensive traits, she opened her Perfect Daddy list and keyed in her must-haves.

Grateful for all home-cooked meals.

Compliments all home-cooked meals.

Will do anything for a bite of home-cooking.

Doesn't discuss bodily functions.

Uses a Porta Potti only under dire circumstances and carries his own disposable seat covers.

She closed both files, leaned back on the sofa and closed her eyes. Not that she could sleep, mind you. Instead, she spent the next half hour daydreaming about tomorrow and the success she was going to have once Beau stepped into her house to work on the bookshelves. Forget talking to him and working her way up to the moment of action. She was getting straight to the point tomorrow night, straight to the seduction, and to hell with subtlety.

That's what she told herself. But when she closed her eyes and pictured the scene, she didn't see them in bed doing the deed. Instead, she pictured them curled up in bed surrounded by candlelight. She had her head on his shoulder and he had his arm around her and they were talking—

Her eyes snapped open and she bolted to her feet. They were not going to talk tomorrow night. They were going to do it and she wasn't going to jinx it by thinking otherwise.

Come tomorrow night, Beau would be off her mind and into her bed. Or at least in her den where there was a nice, soft couch and plenty of room.

Beau was in Xandra's den by six o'clock the next night.

He moved about the room and set up his work space while Xandra watched from the sofa. She still wore the hot-pink miniskirt and matching long-sleeve blouse she'd worn to work that morning. She'd kicked off her shoes, as usual, and sat with her legs folded and her feet tucked under her.

"Don't you have any Wild Woman stuff you have to do?"

"I do, but I would hate to be an ungracious host and leave you all to your lonesome."

"I'm not a guest. I'm an employee."

"In that case, I think I need to stay and supervise."

He ignored the strange flutter in his heart when she smiled again. He spread out a drop cloth, then busied himself by unfolding his table saw and popping the legs into place. He unpacked his tools, plugged everything in and reached for a piece of unfinished cedar he'd picked up that morning.

He was about to power up the saw when he noticed movement out of the corner of his eyes. He turned just as she sprang from the couch.

"I'll be right back," she told him.

"Take your time." He watched her disappear and then he turned his attention to the cedar. He powered up the table saw, pulled his safety glasses into place, and started cutting. The next half hour passed in a loud, dusty blur as he cut the wood for the basic frame.

He'd just started to hammer the sides together when he heard her voice somewhere behind him.

"Boy, it smells funny in here." The strike of a match sizzled in the air. Soon the sweet scent of vanilla and cinnamon and something he couldn't quite name overpowered the sharp smell of wood and filled his head.

He half turned to see her place what looked like a pot-pourri dish on a burner that sat on her coffee table. "I'll just put this right here to freshen up this place."

He had half a mind to tell her that no amount of pot-pourri in the world could kill the smell of freshly cut cedar, but then he decided to let her figure it out for herself.

Ten minutes later he caught movement from the corner of his eye again and turned to see her wrinkle her nose.

"It doesn't smell the same way it did the other night."

"What did you say?"

"I, um, said it doesn't smell the same way it did at the store."

"It's the sawdust." He opened a nearby window before retrieving his nail gun and popping a nail into the ends of the wood until he had the basic frame together.

"No," she said after a few minutes. "I don't think it's the sawdust. I think maybe I need a double dose." She added more of the colorful stuff to the pot. "There. I can smell that. Can you smell it?" She turned a hopeful gaze on him.

"I don't smell a thing," he lied.

Her gaze narrowed. "Surely you can smell this. The aroma's so thick I'm practically choking on it."

"I'm afraid between the sawdust and the red beans and rice I had for lunch, I'm not smelling much of anything else."

"Red beans and rice . . . Oh, no. You didn't."

He made a big pretense of waving at the air surrounding him. "Sorry, but when a man's got an urge, a man's got an urge."

She wrinkled her nose and victory sang through him. This was it. She was going to tell him off once and for all and that would be the end of Xandra the Seductress.

"I can't believe"—she blew out an exasperated breath—"that anyone would have the nerve to . . ." She caught her bottom lip. "I mean, eating red beans and rice really takes a lot of nerve, especially when you know what it's bound to lead to. You've got guts."

"Ugh, thanks."

"But I don't think it's just you. I ate some of that cauliflower casserole my neighbor dropped off earlier and I haven't been the same since." He saw the challenge that gleamed in her eyes and he knew she didn't totally buy his excuse. "It's way too musty in here." She moved the simmering bowl of incense to an end table closer to his work space. "There. That should make the working conditions bearable." She stepped back and just stood there.

"You might want to retreat a little. I feel another one coming on." He scrunched up his face and the challenge in her eyes faded into worry. "Yeah. It's going to blow anytime now." That sent her back a safe distance to the sofa and he barely stifled a grin.

A sliver of guilt worked its way through him, but he tamped it down. He hated being so crude, but a man had to do what a man had to do to preserve his sanity against a sexy-as-hell woman like Xandra Farrel.

He reached for the shelves and fit them into place in the main frame. He'd never been much for incense or candles. Sure, he'd prayed for them a time or two after Warren finished a particularly spicy lunch, but he'd never needed any for himself, at least not in front of anyone, despite his earlier claim.

His nostrils flared and the scent filled his head and his heartbeat kicked up a notch. He had to admit, it smelled better than cedar dust.

Spicy. Exotic. Cleansing, even.

He drank in another deep breath and another, and oddly his muscles started to relax.

"It's looking good." Her voice came from directly behind him and he stiffened.

"It's getting there. This is just the basic structure, of course. I've got to do all the detail work and then the stain and finish." He hunkered down and tried to fit the shelf he'd just cut into its spot, but he hadn't shaved quite enough wood. But maybe if he pushed just a little . . . Maybe even a little harder . . .

His muscles bunched as he put on more pressure. Wood creaked and cracked and the edge of the shelf splintered.

"You're much too tense," she said a heartbeat before she touched him. Warm fingertips closed over his shoulders, her touch heating him through the thin material of his T-shirt. "You need to relax."

"You don't have to do that," he said, setting the ruined shelf aside. But she was already kneading and massaging and as much as he hated to admit it, it felt really good.

"I want to. You've done so much work on the house and now you're building the bookshelf. It's just a little massage. It's the least I can do."

He wanted to remind her that she was paying good money for him to do all of those things, but then she might stop. He also wanted to shout another warning for her take cover before the Big Kahuna blew again, but that would definitely make her stop.

It *was* just a little massage. She was barely touching him, and he certainly wasn't touching her. And, most importantly, he wasn't kissing her and as long as he kept it that way, there was no harm in getting a little closer to her. Especially when he could make another red-beans-and-rice excuse at any time to put a damper on things.

He meant to keep his eyes open, but then she kneaded harder and his eyelids drifted closed. She continued working on him and his muscles screamed with relief for the next few minutes.

"You're loosening up, but you're still too tense. Come on over here and sit down." She urged him to his feet and steered him toward the sofa.

He sank down onto the soft leather as she came around to stand behind him. Her fingers grasped his neck, pushing and drumming and working out the tension that held him so stiff and made his head hurt.

"There. That feels good, doesn't it?"

"Very," he managed.

"It would feel even better if this T-shirt weren't in the way." Her arms came down and she tugged at the hem of his T-shirt.

He had half a mind to resist her, but the other half wanted the T-shirt off. Now.

He leaned forward and let her peel the shirt up and over his head.

"There. Now I can really work the kinks out." Her bare hands touched him, her fingertips burning into his shoulders, and heat flooded his body. His blood rushed and another warning sounded in his head.

It's just a massage.

Her words played over in his head and eased his sudden panic. He closed his eyes and focused on the relief swamping his overworked muscles. For the next fifteen minutes, her soft hands pushed and pulled and worked at his shoulders and upper arms until he forgot all about lunch and bodily noises and the need to keep a safe distance from her. He forgot everything, except her hands and the way they played over his body.

"You really don't have to do this," he said again.

"But you want me to, don't you? Be honest."

"Yes," he said, despite the warning that sounded in his brain. Her voice held a note of desperation, as if she needed to know her true effect on him, and he couldn't resist alleviating her worry.

"Then you'll like this even more." Her hands disappeared for a moment before he felt them close around the back of his neck. They were warm and slick and scented with oil. They slid across his skin, spreading the oil and massaging it in. His skin tingled and his nostrils flared with the fragrant, intoxicating scent.

"What is that?"

"A mixture of base oil and essential oils."

"What's an essential oil?"

"It's a very powerful oil that promotes vigor and lust."

She said the last word directly into his ear. A heartbeat later he felt the warm rush of her breath and the soft flick of her tongue along his earlobe. The sensation was subtle, but it sent a delicious ripple through his body that landed smack dab in his lap.

"Relax," she breathed when his entire body stiffened in reaction to his growing erection. "Just smell and feel." Her hands slicked down his chest, spreading the oil onto his muscles and swirling the hair on his chest. Her palms rasped against his nipples and his breath caught. "It feels good, doesn't it?" She didn't wait for his answer. She came around him then and knelt before him. Her hands went to his chest again and he watched as her red-tipped nails flicked his nipples, tugged and pulled until they were rock-hard nubs. Then her hands moved lower, down his abdomen. She toyed at his belly button a moment before following the dark funnel of hair to where it disappeared beneath his jeans.

Her glistening fingertips plucked at the button of his

jeans and the opening slid free. She grasped his zipper, but it wouldn't tug down over the substantial bulge in his pants.

He meant to button his pants, but when his hands reached the rough denim, he found himself easing his zipper down.

She caught the edge of his underwear and tugged it down until the dark head of his erection sprang forward. Her fingertips touched the smooth ridge and swirled around it.

He wanted to close his eyes and savor the sensation. At the same time, he couldn't look away. Her skin was such a stark contrast against his own, her milky white fingertips so soft and slick against the ripe purple head of his penis.

She pulled his underwear lower and stroked him, tracing the veins that bulged along his length until he sucked in his breath and every muscle in his body went tight.

He touched her then, one hand on her shoulder while the other cupped her cheek and forced her gaze up to meet his. He had the insane urge to tell her exactly how much he wanted her. How crazy he was to be inside her. How he'd been thinking about her, fantasizing about her for so long, and now she was real, and it was almost too good to be true.

Instead, he murmured, "I thought the whole point of this was to relax me. I'm as hard as a rock."

"Maybe that isn't so bad." She smiled and got to her feet. Her hands kept touching him, stroking and stirring and the sensation was so pleasurable he couldn't help but close his eyes.

He felt the soft brush of her hair as she leaned down. Her warm breath caressed his lips. "Kiss me."

Her soft command penetrated the haze of lust that

clouded his brain and he opened his eyes. He stared into her green gaze and saw his own need mirrored there.

A feeling of déjà vu washed over him and he remembered that night in the moonlight. She'd stared up at him just the way she was staring at him now. He hadn't just been the one to slip inside her that night. She'd slipped inside him, too, with that look. Right into his head and under his skin, and that had been that.

The end of his scholarship, his future, or at least the one he'd mapped out for himself back then. He could have gone to college for free and saved a load of money, but he'd blown it. He'd traded the security of a scholarship for a few lust-filled moments that she hadn't even enjoyed.

Mr. Five-Minute Man.

His mouth drew into a tight line. "I won't."

"Okay, then I'll kiss you," she said, but he was already pushing her away and reaching for the zipper on his pants.

"It's late. I really have to go."

She leaned back and eyed him. "Another dinner date?"

He wanted to nod. That's all he had to do to confirm the suspicions he saw swimming in her gaze—namely, that he'd run out on her last night because of another woman, and that he was doing the same thing tonight.

"An early breakfast meeting," he blurted the truth. "I've got kolaches and doughnuts with my subcontractors in the morning and I have to finish several work orders before then." With considerable effort, he pulled up his zipper and got to his feet. He reached for his shirt and pulled it over his head. "Thanks for the massage."

And then he walked away because he considered himself a man who learned from his mistakes—and falling for Xandra Farrel in the backseat of his dad's Impala had been his biggest.

One he wasn't about to repeat, no matter how much he suddenly wanted to.

She wasn't going to cry.

Not from sexual frustration. And especially not because her feelings were hurt by Beau's rejection.

This was purely sex, and sex was her business. She didn't let her feelings get in the way when it came to getting ahead. She would simply beef up her offensive and launch another attack.

He wanted her. She knew that. She'd seen it in his eyes, in his very prominent arousal. She'd felt it in the tremble of his fingers when he'd held her shoulders and touched her cheek.

He wanted her, all right. He just didn't want to want her. He thought she was after a relationship rather than sex.

Fat chance. She wasn't settling for less than her Holy Commitment Man from here on out, and Beau with his hair trigger in the sack and his love of tools and ho-hum attitude when it came to chocolate was as far removed as a man could get.

Xandra liked long, slow, thorough lovemaking. Her favorite tool was a Palm Pilot. And she'd had more than one fantasy about a box of Godiva truffles.

Relationship nirvana with Beau Hollister was completely out of the question.

If only he realized as much, then they could stop this game. As it was, she would simply have to move on to yet another seduction attempt.

Just as soon as Albert made his next move.

Xandra went in to work early the next morning, eager to get as much work out of the way as possible before Albert tried to seduce her and she, in turn, rushed home to seduce Beau. He was sanding the bookshelves tonight, preparing for the final varnish, which already set a seductive tone to the evening. She pictured the gleam in his eyes as his hand moved over the wood, smoothing it with his sander in that slow, thorough, purposeful way that made her skin tingle.

Which meant all she had to do was stoke the fire that already burned inside him.

Anticipation rippled through her and she attacked the financial portion of Wild Woman with a zest she'd never felt before. Her eyes didn't cross as she stared at the spreadsheets and she didn't feel sick to her stomach. She felt anxious. Excited. Eager.

As soon as five o'clock rolled around, she rushed down the hallway to the conference room and pushed open the door.

"I'm here . . ." Her words trailed off as she noted the dark room, the chairs pushed up to the table. There wasn't a candle in sight. No food. No sweet aromas. No soft, seductive music. No Albert.

She spent the next half hour going from room to room, thinking that maybe he was trying to change things and catch her off-guard. She came up empty-handed. Then she headed up to the lab to find that he'd left early for the day.

Disappointment welled inside her until she realized that it was all part of a plan. Albert was building the anticipation by acting indifferent, which meant she would do the same with Beau.

He would be fully prepared for her to seduce him tonight. Instead, she would head home, busy herself with next month's production schedule—ugh—and totally ignore him. When he realized she wasn't going to launch another attack, he would be surprised. Bewildered. And, hopefully, develop a false sense of security. Then when she seduced him again, say tomorrow or the day after, he wouldn't be expecting it. And, therefore, his defenses would be down.

It was too perfect.

Chapter Nineteen

It's the most hideous thing I've ever seen." Xandra eyed the casserole dish and the contents—a mix of brown and green that reminded her of a camouflage pattern.

"I think it's quiche," Beau said as he slid his sander over one of the shelves.

Sawdust filled the air and tickled Xandra's nostrils—a welcome relief to the aroma coming from the dish in her hands.

"It looks old," she said.

"It was piping hot when the woman dropped it off not more than fifteen minutes ago." He came up behind her and every hair on her neck went on high alert. He leaned down and peered at the dish. "Yep, I would definitely say it's quiche. Probably spinach. You should try it. It's not too bad."

"I thought real men didn't eat quiche."

"Real men eat whatever's handy."

She wasn't going to ask. Her plan was to keep her distance and she intended to follow through. So what if it was going on seven o'clock and he'd been hard at work since daybreak? He'd probably already eaten by now. And even if he hadn't, she was paying him double-and-a-half time. She didn't have to feed him, as well. Not to mention, she wasn't the least bit interested in the dish in her hands. Rather, she was going to pull the blinds in her kitchen and go searching for some real fattening food.

You ought to listen to the man. He's got the whole physical fitness thing going on.

A small grumble sounded—not her own stomach—and guilt shot through her. Okay, so she was paying him double-and-a-half time, but that didn't make up for the fact that she was working him like a slave, from sunup to sundown. Judging from the way the bookshelves were fast coming together, he seemed to be working at a rapid pace. Maybe he hadn't actually had dinner. Or lunch. Or even breakfast. Maybe he was this close to passing out on her floor.

She contemplated the notion of a very masculine Beau unconscious on her rug. While the idea held some appeal—unconscious meant his defenses would definitely be down—she had the gut feeling another part would be equally down and that wouldn't do for what she had in mind. What's more, if he passed out, she would have to get close in order to assist him. Nix the distance idea. At least with dinner, there would be a kitchen table between them.

"I don't suppose you would be interested in getting rid of this with me? I mean, probably not. You've probably already eaten and I know you're busy."

His stomach grumbled. "I *am* starved," he admitted, looking none too happy about the fact. "But I really shouldn't impose."

"It's no imposition." *Hello? You should be discouraging him.* She meant to, but her mouth seemed to move of its own accord. "I have to eat and you have to eat. Might as well kill two birds with one quiche."

"That's true." He gave her a suspicious look. "It *is* just dinner, right?"

"Of course. It's not like it's a date or anything."

It was *not* a date.

That's what she told herself as Beau went to get cleaned up and she headed for the kitchen to set the table and serve the quiche. It was simply the satisfaction of a mutual need. He was hungry. She was hungry, albeit for something other than the dish sitting on her kitchen table, but hungry nonetheless.

So hungry, in fact, that the first bite of quiche actually went down without an entire glass of water—her usual method for digesting most vegetables.

"I told you it wasn't too bad." He smiled and took a bite.

"Not too bad at all," she agreed. Thanks to him, because watching him take a bite actually made her own mouthful seem more palatable. She found herself more concerned with the way his lips moved around the fork and the way his jaw worked and the way his Adam's apple bobbed, than the way the quiche tasted.

Or the fact that it didn't taste like much of anything at all, especially a Cheez Doodle or a bite of pepperoni pizza with extra cheese or a slice of chocolate cake with double-fudge frosting.

"So how did you do it?" His question jarred her from her infatuation with his mouth. His gaze met and held hers.

"How did I do what?"

"Lose all the weight. What did you drop? Ten, maybe fifteen pounds?"

"Don't I wish. I lost an initial thirty-five, but I've inched up a little over the past year because I quit smoking. So I'm now officially twenty-five pounds lighter and holding."

"That must have been tough."

"It was, but my only regret is that I didn't lose the weight sooner."

"You didn't have a very easy time when we were kids, did you?"

"Actually, I had a great time when I was with my family. It was school that presented the problem. Not academically, of course. I'm talking socially."

"It always seemed like you had friends."

"I had a few girlfriends. No boyfriends."

"Not even one?"

She gave him a get-real look. "No guy in our school wanted to go out with the fat chick." She eyed him. "Speaking of which, I've always wondered why you said yes when I asked you to the Sadie Hawkins dance."

"Because you were nice. You always said hello. You let me copy your English assignments when I came in late every morning, because I had to open up at the gas station." His gaze caught and held hers and sincerity gleamed in the deep violet-colored depths. "You weren't ashamed to be seen with me like all the other girls, or embarrassed by the fact that I worked after school while everybody else sat in the diner and drank Cokes."

"That's because I never sat at the diner." She wasn't going to say any more, but the flash of understanding in his eyes soothed the usual hurt that came with remembering the past. "I always wanted to," she admitted. "I would always imagine what it would be like to go inside and crawl into a booth with all the cheerleaders and have them talk to me like I was actually one of them. Like I actually fit in."

She shook her head. "But I never did. Not with the in crowd, and not in my size twelve jeans."

"Not then, but you fit now."

She smiled. "Going away to college was the best thing I ever did. It gave me the chance to start fresh, without the whole fat persona hanging over my head."

"And without your virginity," he added.

The comment sent a wave of nostalgia rushing through her, but none of it had to do with the sex part of that night.

Instead, she remembered the heart-pounding excitement she'd felt when she'd first opened the door to him. The way her hand had trembled when he'd held it to walk with her to the car. The nervous flutter when he'd opened the car door and slid in next to her. The feelings had been new and wondrous, and he'd been the cause.

Despite the poor ending to that night, she couldn't help but feel grateful. She owed him. The least she could do was tell him the truth.

"I wanted to completely change my life. That meant starting fresh on the inside, as well as the outside. I wanted to be thin, pretty, desirable—all the things expected of the daughter of one of the country's most acclaimed sexologists."

"So why did you pick me?" The question hung between them for several long moments, before he broke the strange spell and wiggled his eyebrows. "Other than the fact that I was totally hot and sexy and no woman in sight could keep her hands off me."

Laughter bubbled from her lips. "I'll give you the totally hot and sexy, but that wasn't why I picked you."

"Then why?"

She shrugged as the truth found its way to her lips. "Because you complimented me once."

"I did?"

"When I wore my Cowboys sweatshirt."

"That explains it then. I've always been a huge Cowboys fan." His gaze met and held hers. "Is that the only reason?"

"You never made fun of me. While the other guys would make grunting noises back in junior high, you never did."

"They were young and stupid."

"But you weren't. Come to think of it, why weren't you?"

"Maybe because I knew what it felt like to be on the receiving end, so I never dished it out." At her surprised look, he added, "I had this big spot of oil on my shirt one morning. I didn't have time to change and so I went to school like that, and Bobby Sanders called me pit stop boy."

He smiled then, but there was a sadness in his eyes that touched something deep inside Xandra and stirred her own memories of hurt and humiliation.

"It was just a stupid name," he went on, "but I actually went home and sat in my closet." When she looked puzzled, he added, "I didn't want anyone to see me in case I cried."

"Did you?"

"Almost, but then my mom lured me out with the promise of a vanilla milkshake. She sat across from me while I drank my milkshake and told me that people are just people. We're all the same on the inside, and so it didn't matter what Bobby Sanders called me. Because he was the same as me. No better, no worse. From then on, I never let it bother me when someone said something about the way I dressed or the fact that I had to help my dad."

"My grandma told me the same thing one time—about people just being people when you peeled away all the clothes and the pretension—but I never could seem to remember it when someone was calling me a name or making *oink-oink* noises."

He grinned, but then the expression faded and a serious light touched his eyes. "I always remembered because it was the last time she made milkshakes before she went into the hospital." His gaze met hers. "It really doesn't matter what anyone thinks about you. All that matters is what you think about yourself."

She'd heard the same words more times than she could count, but they'd never really hit home until now. Until Beau Hollister stared deep into her eyes and said them. Because, unlike everyone else in her past who'd said the same thing, he truly understood. At one time, he'd felt the same hurt.

So what?

It didn't matter what he did or did not understand. This wasn't about connecting with him on some deeper level or forging an emotional bond. It was superficial. Strictly sex.

"So what happened to the station after your dad died?" she asked, determined to steer the conversation away from her inadequacy and the fact that he saw what she wanted so desperately to hide.

"When Exxon moved in around the corner, the place started to cost a lot more than it made. There was no use keeping it open when Dad died, so I boarded it up. But I still haven't put it up for sale."

"Are you going to?"

"My dad loved that place. He and my mom opened it together. I don't know if I can make myself sign the papers and give it up for good." He shrugged. "I'm hoping one of my brothers might decide to go home and set up shop. But I'm not pushing. I want them to have choices."

"Because you didn't have them."

"Because there was always something I *had* to do, no ifs, ands, or buts about it. I had to go to the only college that would accept me given my grade point average because I had to help my dad at the station before and after school. I had to bust my ass from morning until night so that I could pay for that college and send money home. I had to keep going with Hire-a-Hunk because my family came to depend on that money and I couldn't take a pay cut. I have to win this *Texas Monthly* competition now because my guys depend on me and my business."

Admiration welled inside her and sent a rush of warmth from her head to her toes. Beau Hollister might have let her down that night in the backseat of his daddy's car, but he hadn't let his family down. He never would. Determination rang in his words, despite the regret that flashed in his gaze.

"What about what you *want* to do?" She couldn't suppress the sudden need to make him forget the worry of the world, if only for a few what-if moments.

He shrugged. "I've never really thought about it."

"So think about it now. What's eating at you? What do you really want more than you've ever wanted anything in the world?"

"I want . . ."

You.

The answer was there in his gaze as he stared across the table at her, but he didn't voice it. Instead, an uneasy silence ticked by before he finally reached across the table with his fork. "I want your last bite."

"You're still hungry?"

"You don't know the half of it."

But she did. She was still hungry, as well, and it had nothing to do with food and everything to do with the man who sat across the table from her.

She wanted him and she meant to have him. Just as soon as Albert came through again.

In the meantime, she contented herself with sharing dinner and conversation with him for the next few nights. They talked about everything, from his brothers and their various careers to her sisters and the fact that Skye was now happily married to one of NASCAR's finest, despite their mother's disapproval. She told him about Skye's procreation plan, and about how she wanted a baby of her own. He told her about his plans for a family somewhere down the road, *way* down the road, after he'd established H&H as a major player in the restoration and renovation industry.

They had different opinions on most everything: he liked country music, particularly Toby Keith, while she listened to Top 40 pop; he enjoyed old westerns while she preferred the Lara Croft movies; he voted Republican while she supported the Democrats.

Oddly enough, the differences just made for an even better discussion and she found herself wanting to talk to him almost as much as she wanted to have sex with him.

Almost.

But Xandra was a woman on a mission and she wasn't falling into another rut. She'd made up her mind to get back on track professionally and personally, and she intended to do just that.

If only Albert would stop procrastinating and hurry up!

Chapter Twenty

Albert obviously didn't know the meaning of the word "hurry" and it was high time that Xandra enlightened him.

"Get on with it, would you?" she declared on Friday afternoon when he still hadn't made any attempt to seduce her.

"What are you talking about?"

"You seducing me. Where is it?" She stared around the lab. "It's been four days already. I know you're going for the element of surprise, but this is going too far. You're making me crazy. I'm looking behind every door. I even found myself peeking into the bathroom stall."

"You expect me to seduce you in a bathroom stall?"

"No. Yes. Maybe." She threw up her hands and barely ignored the urge to grab Paulie the Penis and give him a good shake. *Men.* "I don't know. That's the point. I don't know what you've got up your sleeve and the anticipation is killing me."

"But you don't want to have sex with me," he pointed out.

"I know that, but I didn't think you would give up so

easily. You're determined. Driven. When you do something, you give it your all."

"I did. I tried twice to get you to see me in a romantic light and each time you said no."

"Twice is nothing. Trust me. You should try again."

A gleam lit his blue eyes. "Does that mean you're softening?"

"No, but I think Beau may be."

"I should think so. Those two attempts focused on four out of the five senses. A double whammy each time."

"Which means there's another sense left. Another seduction attempt we haven't tried." She held her hands up. "Please, Albert. Your ideas were so good. He almost caved twice. I know I can get to him if I just have something that will really wow him. I've got him inside the house every night working on some built-in bookshelves, but it's already been four days. He's almost done. If I don't do something now, he'll be working outside the house again, and I'll be right back at square one. Please, Albert. Give me something else to use while I've got him in the house."

"You really expect me to help you seduce another guy?"

"In the interest of business."

He gave her a belligerent look. "Forget it. I won't help you sleep with someone else."

She grinned. "We're not going to sleep. Besides, you know I don't get you any more hot and bothered than you get me." When he just shrugged, she touched his shoulder. "What's all this really about anyway? What's up with you?"

He blew out a deep breath. "I'm getting old."

"You don't look old."

"I feel old. My knees creak when I sit down. And my ankle hurts when I stand too long. And I've got gray hair."

"You do not." She leaned up and ruffled his blond hair. "I can't see even one."

"That's because you're looking a little too far north."

"You mean . . ." Her gaze dropped before rushing back up to collide with his. "Oh." She didn't mean to smile, but she couldn't help herself.

His frown deepened. "Women don't have the market cornered on aging, you know."

"I know, but I didn't think men noticed things like that."

"They don't. I certainly never would have. But after you made such a big deal, I couldn't help but wonder, so I looked." He shook his head. "Why the hell did I have to look?"

She wiggled her eyebrows. "I know this girl who gives great Brazilian waxes."

"Very funny."

"I'm serious." At his horrified expression, she added, "What? You don't think men should have to sacrifice in the name of beauty?"

"I don't think *anyone* should sacrifice in the name of beauty. A person should be content with who they are and where they're at in life, and work with what they've got. In my case, I'm a successful engineer who's employed by a great company and has a wonderful rapport with his boss." He gave her a pointed look. "We do like the same things, you know."

"True."

"And we respect each other."

"True."

"We're two out of three right now. If we worked at it and gave ourselves a chance to really *like* each other— romantically speaking—we might eventually hit a home run."

"Not according to my mother. It's three out of three from the get-go, or nothing at all."

"And according to you?"

She shrugged and stared him in the eye. "When it comes to longevity, it's all of the Holy Commitment Trinity or nothing."

"Which is why we could never be together. Because we don't have enough to make it work," he told her.

"Actually, in our case, we have too much."

"Women." He shook his head. "Now you're really confusing me."

"We have three out of three right now, just not the right three. We have mutual respect, common interests, and a solid friendship. Even if we had chemistry, I don't know that I would want to act on it and risk hurting the friendship component of our relationship. You're too important to me."

He eyed her before a small smile touched his face. "You're just trying to let me down easy."

"That, too. But I'm also telling the truth." She grinned. "And while you may be thirty-five, you don't look a day over thirty. Thirty-one at the most. As for personality, you're leaning more toward the twenties on that one. You're fun and thoughtful and positively brilliant."

"Now you're just trying to butter me up for an idea."

"That, too. But I am telling the truth."

"Fun, thoughtful, and brilliant." He seemed to think. "Yep, you're definitely telling the truth."

"So wow me now with your brilliance and give me an idea. Something to really knock him out of his—" Her words stalled as the door opened and Stacey Bernard popped her head in.

"If we're going to get to the bowling alley before all the

size eight shoes are gone, we really need to leave now," she said to Albert.

"I'll just be a minute."

Stacey nodded, said hello and good-bye to Xandra, and disappeared.

Xandra turned knowing eyes on him.

"Don't look at me like that," Albert said.

"Like what?"

"Like you're about to sing the 'I Told You So' song. I hate that crappy song."

"Well, I did—"

"—tell me so. I know. But it's not like Stacey is my Holy Commitment Woman, or anything like that. This date isn't about us actually being attracted to each other. We're just two needy people who are helping each other out."

"You're both needy . . . Smacks of common interest to me."

"Hardly. We have absolutely zero in common, except that we've both fallen into a dating rut." When she gave him another look, he added, "And that's not a common interest. It's a common problem, and the Holy Commitment Trinity doesn't say anything about shared problems. There's absolutely no future for us as a couple. We're just dating in the loosest, most twisted definition of the word. End of story." She smiled and he glared. "Look, do you want my advice or not? Because I'm in a hurry."

"Shoot."

"My seduction techniques have been based on Cherry Chandler's *The Sensitive Seductress*, which basically encourages you to use the fives senses to lure a prospective mate to her or his knees. I used the chocolate the first night to wow your taste buds and the background music to seduce your ears. The massage and incense were supposed to work on your sense of touch and smell. Which means we're down four out of five, with only one left."

"Sight."

"To be honest, I was going to go for broke and try the last one, but I couldn't quite work up my nerve. Not with the newfound gray hairs."

"Those, and the fact that you've got a bowling ball waiting for you."

"Smart-ass." She smiled again and he glared even harder. "Stop digressing. Since you've done the Brazilian wax, the gray hair shouldn't be a drawback. You can let it all hang out without any worries."

Her smiled faded as the reality of his words hit home. "You don't mean . . ."

It was his turn to smile. "If you really want to wow this guy, it's time to get naked."

Beau was prepared for almost anything when he rang Xandra's doorbell on Friday evening.

The past couple of nights he'd been letting himself in to work on the bookshelves since she was rarely home by the time he finished up outside. But she'd come home early today. She'd whisked past him over an hour ago, a serious look on her face. As if she needed every ounce of concentration for what lay ahead.

She was up to something again.

He felt it deep in his bones and in the hard-on pressing tight against his jeans.

Most men would have figured she'd given up by now. After all, she'd gone four days without so much as batting an eyelash. They'd eaten together and talked, but that's as far as things had gone. No flirting, no touching, no kissing, no . . . *nothing*.

And yet Beau felt closer to her now than he'd felt that night in the backseat of his dad's car. He'd always been of a mind that sex equaled real intimacy, but he wasn't so sure now. When he looked at Xandra and she looked at him and recounted a scene from her past, like the one she'd told him the previous evening about being picked last for dodgeball, he didn't just sympathize with her, he felt her pain. He also felt an overwhelming urge to smash something with his fist on her behalf.

Crazy.

As crazy as the lust still burning in his veins for a woman who didn't lust after him. She wanted to sleep with him for one reason and one reason only—to validate her product.

The truth should have killed his desire, but it didn't. If anything, he wanted her even more. Because he actually liked her. What's more, he admired her. She had determination and vision and she wanted more out of life than what came her way. She wanted to make things happen, just like he did. He couldn't help but feel a connection to her that went beyond the physical.

Their newfound closeness was causing strange feelings to push and pull inside of him. One minute he wanted to comfort her and the next he wanted to have down and dirty, hot and sweaty sex with a capital "S."

But he couldn't allow himself to do either of those things, because their budding connection was undoubtedly a part of her overall plan to manipulate him. If he'd learned anything about her over the past few days, it was that she would never give up. But he had no intention of making it easy. Instead of being relieved each day when she paid him no mind, he found himself all the more leery. Anxious. Eager.

Eager?

Okay, so he was eager, but only because he was growing tired of always being on his guard. Tired of going home after dinner each night to a cold, empty bed. Tired of lying in that empty bed and thinking about how good she'd tasted and how he wanted to taste a hell of a lot more.

Better for her to get on with it and play her final hand. Then he could enjoy her attention for a few sweet minutes before turning up his obnoxious level and bringing the game to an end.

He needed it to end. Even though he hadn't actually slept with her, she was distracting him. The judges from *Texas Monthly* would make their inspection in less than two weeks and he still had an incredible amount of work to do. Once he finished the bookshelves, he would have no further business inside the house—Warren had finished the inside renovations early on—and he had no intention of letting her lure him back inside.

Pressing the bell again, he drew a deep breath. This was it. He was putting the final touches on the shelves, so it would be his last night inside. The end of the line for Xandra Farrel and her seduction techniques. So he had no doubt she would hit him with her best shot. She would open the door and the final round of their seduction game would begin.

Soft footsteps echoed from inside and the doorknob turned. Beau braced himself, his imagination racing at the possible scenarios waiting on the other side: Xandra dressed for sexcess in a low-cut blouse, a tight skirt, and a sex-me-up smile. Xandra in a flimsy red nightie that matched the red polish on her toes and a sex-me-up smile. Xandra decked out in a black bustier, thigh-high stockings, come-and-do-me high heels, and a sex-me-up smile. Xandra sporting a lacy black bra, and panties, and a sex-me-up smile. Xandra wearing nothing but the smile. Xandra wearing . . .

An oversized, cover-everything-up University of Texas T-shirt. The sleeves hung all the way to her elbows. The hem dropped several inches below her knees.

His gaze roamed from her head to her toes and back up again. So much for his dress for sexcess theory. She looked more comfortable than sexy. At the same time, there was just something about the sparkle in her eyes and the way her hair looked mussed, as if she'd just rolled out of bed, that made him think about tumbling her right back in.

He shook away the thought and lifted the can of varnish. "I'm ready to finish up."

"Great." She stepped back and let him step inside. The door creaked shut and his footsteps echoed as he walked into the den and over to the unfinished bookshelf.

"It's looking really good."

"Give me another hour, and it'll be finished."

"An hour? That's all you have left?"

"Maybe two. It depends on how well the wood soaks up the stain." He popped the lid on the stain and grabbed a paint stick to stir the rich mahogany color. Silence settled around him and he realized that she wasn't going to say anything.

Or do anything.

A wave of disappointment rolled through him, followed by a short rush of relief.

"The varnish goes on quick," he told her, eager to fill the silence and keep his mind fixed on the bookshelf in front of him rather than the woman standing somewhere behind. "But it needs to sit awhile. Make sure you give it plenty of time to dry before you touch it."

"No touching." Her voice sounded like it was coming from near the doorway that separated the den from the foyer. There was an unsteadiness to her tone. As if she couldn't quite make up her mind whether to follow him inside.

He was reading too much into everything. She'd given up. Plain and simple.

"Even when it's dry, you want to give it a wide berth for at least thirty-six to forty-eight hours," he went on, eager to keep his mind from wondering about why she'd finally called it quits. That would open a whole new can of worms, particularly since the obvious—she just wasn't interested anymore—bothered him a lot more than he wanted to admit. "Just to make sure the varnish is completely set."

"Completely." She was just to his left now, a few steps away from the doorway, as if she'd come to some important decision and it was just a matter of following it through. The hardwood floor squeaked as she stepped forward.

Give it a rest, man, a voice whispered. *You're imagination's definitely working overtime.*

His fingers tightened on the stir stick as he set it aside and reached for the varnish rag.

"And don't go putting anything heavy on the shelves," he went on, "because that will scratch the wood or worse, dent it."

"Forget the heavy objects." She was even closer now. Maybe an arm's length away, should he turn and reach for her.

Which he wasn't even close to doing. He was all business, his guard firmly in place, his mind made up.

"And don't use any water-based polishes. Use a natural oil that's good for wood."

"Natural's better." She was behind him now.

"And make sure you use it on a regular basis," he said as he got to his feet. Okay, so he was going to turn. But not because he'd changed his mind and had decided to reach for her. He just didn't like talking over his shoulder. "Otherwise your wood will dull."

She was directly behind him, all right, he realized as he turned to face her.

And she was naked.

Chapter Twenty-One

I'm naked," Xandra pointed out when Beau simply stood there.

Looking.

His gaze roved over her once, twice. The third time was a leisurely trek that made her heart pound even faster and her nipples stand up and beg for more.

While looking was definitely good, especially judging by the frantic tic of his jaw and the heat that blazed in his eyes, she'd expected a little more action.

"Naked," she went on. "Standing here totally au naturel. Not a stitch on."

"I know."

I know? She shook her head and ignored the urge to scream her frustration. "So what are you going to do about it?"

He looked at her for another few frantic heartbeats. Indecision glittered in his violet eyes before his mouth drew into a thin line. He peeled his T-shirt over his head and handed it to her.

"Thanks, but that's not what I had in mind." She

clutched the soft cotton and the warm musky scent of him filled her nostrils. "Though it is a very nice gesture if I happened to be naked by accident. But I'm not." When he didn't look any more ready to jump her bones, she added, "I'm naked on purpose. For you. I thought you might like it."

"I . . ." He swallowed and she could see him grappling for control. His fingers balled and he frowned. "I do," he told her, but he didn't look all that pleased about the admission. "But I don't think—"

Her fingertips went to his lips, silencing the rest of his words. "Don't think. Not tonight." And then she did what she'd been waiting for him to do—she kissed him.

Despite the fact that he'd been this close to turning her down, his lips were warm and welcoming.

He quickly took the lead, plunging his tongue into her mouth, stroking and caressing in a thorough kiss that had her breathless and shaking in a matter of seconds.

You're naked, a voice whispered. *Of course you're shaking. The air conditioner is blasting full force.*

The funny thing was, she felt hot at the same time. Hot and cold. Her skin itchy and tight. Goosebumps chased up and down her arms but they had nothing to do with the cool air rushing from the overhead vent and everything to do with the hand that slid around her waist to the small of her back to pull her closer.

The worn denim of his jeans rubbed against her tender flesh as he wrapped his arms around her. His hands stroked up and down her back, his fingers playing the grooves of her spine.

His hands slid down to cup her buttocks and rock her against the erection pressing tight beneath his jeans. Electricity sizzled along her nerve endings, making her head buzz and her heart race.

She slid her arms down his shoulders, feeling his skin against her own. His chest was hard and solid. The crisp swirls of hair created a delicious friction against her ripe nipples as she inched closer to feel more of him.

His arms tightened. He kneaded her buttocks and wetness flooded between her legs.

"I need to touch you," he murmured as his hand came around and slid between them. His fingers slid over the now bare V area between her legs and down. The rough pad of his finger moved over the soft swollen tissue and she gasped.

He caught the sound with his lips, claiming her in another kiss that took her breath away while his finger slid lower. He pushed into her just a fraction. Sensation rushed through her and her fingers curled into the dark hair at the nape of his neck. She whimpered, wanting more, needing it more than her next breath.

He gave it to her, pushing all the way inside in a swift motion that made her cry out.

He kissed her again, but his lips couldn't drown out the steady whine that filled her ears. Whine? It was more like a beep. A persistent *beep, beep, beep* that sent a rush of disappointment through her. He went stock still and the spell that had surrounded them suddenly vanished.

"Ignore it," she begged as she pressed her lips to his again, determined to recapture the moment.

But it was too late. His hands came up and he pushed her away from him. He reached for his beeper and killed the noise as he glanced at the number on the display.

"Is it an emergency?" she asked.

"It's Annabelle calling from the office." He ran a hand

through his hair. Muscles rippled and need tightened inside her. "I've got to go."

"Can't you just call her and tell her you're busy?"

"I'll call her once I'm on the road."

"Call her now and deal with it from here. Stay. Please."

He shook his head. "I can't."

"You mean you won't, even though I'm naked."

"I can't *because* you're naked." He shook his head. "Shit, I can't believe this."

She had the fleeting thought that he was more upset about being interrupted than about the fact that she'd tempted him beyond reason.

Crazy. He obviously didn't want her. She was naked, for heaven's sake, yet here he was pulling away and heading for the door, minus his shirt. As if he couldn't wait to get away from her.

It wasn't going to happen. Not tonight. Not ever.

The realization hit her as she watched him reach for the doorknob. Good riddance, she told herself. She didn't need the aggravation. She had fairly decent data from Kimmy. Enough to know that Wild Woman was on the right track with Mabel. She didn't need to waste her time with an infuriating, irritating, frustrating man like Beau Hollister.

And she certainly didn't need to cry over him.

Crying? Get real. She wasn't crying. She never cried. Crying made her face puffy, and that was the last thing she needed. But tears burned the back of her eyes and she blinked, which only made the blasted things run over. She wiped frantically as her vision blurred and she grappled for his discarded shirt.

"Shit," came the deep voice, and she knew he'd seen her. "Just my friggin' luck."

"You said it." She held the shirt up and tucked the edges

around her. She'd left her own oversized T-shirt in a puddle in the far corner.

"You're crying."

"I think I've got something in my eye."

He sighed, the sound a deep rush of surrender as he shut the door and turned toward her. "You're *crying*."

"Okay, so I'm crying. Big deal."

"Why?"

"Because I feel like it."

"Why?"

"Because . . . Because I'm frustrated and crying helps me release that frustration." She shook her head. "I've tried everything on you and nothing worked. I tried to wow your taste buds with chocolate, then I made all that food, complete with steak, which most men like, but you still managed to walk away." She sniffled. "Because I'm not the hottest, bustiest, best-looking babe in the jungle." Her vision blurred and she blinked frantically. "It's me, isn't it?"

"Damn straight, it's you," came the deep voice.

Her chest tightened and the tears spilled over. "Thanks a lot." She wiped frantically at her face before giving him the evil eye.

"You asked." Beau shrugged before his gaze met hers. "It *is* you."

"You're just not turned on, even though I've changed." she sniffled. "I mean, I'm far from skinny, but I'm certainly not as big as I was. But I might as well be because you can't get past that one night. You still see me as the awkward fat chick who put the moves on you because you weren't turned on enough to put the moves on her."

"I was scared."

"You're making me feel so much better. Why don't you just come out and say it? You don't like fat women."

"I don't."

"I knew it."

"But you're not fat. You're curvy and voluptuous and sexy. Damned sexy."

"The whole Sadie Hawkins thing was just a mercy date—What did you say?"

"I said that you're sexy." He shook his head. "Sexy as hell, which is just my rotten luck."

She eyed him. "If that's true, then why are we talking right now instead of having sex?"

He shook his head and ran a hand over his face. "You're distracting, Xandra."

"I won't be a distraction. You and me. Tonight. That's it."

"I should be so lucky." He shook his head. "I really need to go, but it's not because you don't do it for me. You're a beautiful woman and I do want you."

"Prove it."

He grabbed her hand and touched it to his crotch. "I'm about to explode right now and it's all because of you. You're hot and sexy and you look better naked than any woman I've ever seen in my life."

"Really?" She sniffled and tucked the edges of the shirt up under her arms.

He stared at her long and hard before reaching out and wiping a tear that slid from the corner of her eye. "Really," he growled before touching his lips to hers.

The kiss was hot and wet and probing, and it ended all too quickly.

"I need to leave. If I stay any longer I'm liable to take you right here, right now, and I have a feeling that would be an even bigger mistake than the first time." And then he turned and walked out so fast that he forgot his shirt, which she clutched tightly to her chest.

Xandra leaned back against the wall and tried to calm her pounding heart. Pounding because he was telling the truth.

He was attracted to her.

She'd felt it in his kiss, in the fierce way he'd held her close and devoured her for those few delicious moments.

But even more, she'd seen the desire gleaming in his eyes. And the sincerity.

He wanted her.

But he didn't *want* to want her, and it wasn't because he didn't believe a woman couldn't sleep with a man without getting ideas about the morning after. He hadn't sworn off women in general. He'd sworn off *her.*

Because she'd been such a dud the first time herself?

Before she could worry over the question, a knock sounded at the door. Her gaze went to the shirt she clutched in front of her.

Her heart started to race and her mind started working. She pushed to her feet and started for the door. Her lips tingled and her body ached and her mind reeled with the knowledge that he'd barely managed to stop.

If he saw her naked again, maybe he wouldn't be able to stop. And maybe there wouldn't be a beeper to save him this time.

Xandra held tight to the hope and tossed the T-shirt aside. Wearing nothing but a smile, she hauled open the door.

Jacqueline Farrel had seen her youngest daughter naked more times than she could count. Of course, all those times had occurred when Xandra was under the age of ten. Most had involved bath time. Or getting dressed for school in the morning. And there'd been that one time her older sisters had dared her to run naked through the sprinklers, claiming that was the only way six-year-olds could gain entrance into their sacred tree house club.

And the only man who'd ever been in the vicinity during Xandra's naked past had been Donovan. He'd given his fair share of baths and helped with the school rush every morning. He'd even been the one to toss a towel over her that time in the yard, snatch her up, and deposit her in the house before giving the other two girls a talking to about coercion.

The thought of Donovan sent a bolt of panic through her and reminded her why she'd given the slowpoke cab driver an extra fifty to get her to Xandra's as quickly as possible.

"I need to use your phone, dear. My cell isn't working." Jacqueline had been right in the middle of a conversation with Alexis when the blasted thing had conked out. Actually, it had been more of a message relay than an actual conversation. Alexis had called to tell her that Donovan had called—he couldn't reach Jacqueline's cell because of the service disruption—and said he needed to talk with her ASAP over an urgent matter.

"Urgent" as in emergency. As in one of the girls—with the exception of Xandra who stood healthy as ever right in front of her—could be injured. Or her mother could be sick. Or Donovan himself could be stretched out in a ditch somewhere, hurt and bleeding and desperate for her help.

"I have to call your father." She pushed inside the house, deposited her suitcases on the floor in the foyer, and rushed into the den.

"It's in the kitchen," Xandra said as she grabbed the T-shirt off the floor.

"I have his number on speed dial." Xandra struggled into the T-shirt as she followed.

"Do you have my L.A. number programmed in?"

"Dad's at your apartment?"

"For the past few weeks," Jacqueline replied as she retrieved the phone from the wall hook. She punched the three that Xandra indicated and held the receiver. The first ring echoed in her ear. "He thinks we need to spend more time together." *Rrring.* "Of all the crazy, absurd notions." *Rrring.* "We already see each other on a regular basis as it is and—" Her words stumbled to a halt as a *click* sounded on the other end and her answering machine picked up.

At least she thought it was her answering machine, but instead of her own voice, she heard a man's deep, familiar voice drift over the line.

"Greetings. You've reached Donovan and Jacqueline. We're not home right now, but if you leave your name and number, we'll be sure to get back with you. And if this is Jacqueline, the emergency is that I miss you, darling, and I'm counting the minutes until you get home. Give Xandra my love and hurry back. You know what to do at the beep . . ." *Beep.*

Shock gripped Jacqueline as she tried to digest what she'd just heard. A message, but not her message. This had been a new message. A *we* message.

She shook her head. She had to be hearing things. She punched the OFF button. Just to be sure that Xandra had the right number programmed, she dialed it again. The message played back and her shock faded into a wave of anger.

"This is Jacqueline Farrel," she ground out after the beep. "And I do not appreciate—"

"Hi, darling." Donovan's voice floated over the line as he picked up the other end.

"Don't *darling* me, you lying, manipulating, son-of-a-male-slave-driver—"

"I miss you, too, darling, and my father isn't a slave driver. My mother's the slave driver. My dad simply obeys."

"Obviously you didn't take after him." Accusation filled her voice. "You changed my message."

"No, I didn't."

"Yes, you did. I just heard it with my own ears."

"That wasn't your message, love. See, since I live here and you live here, it makes it *our* message. Therefore, I thought it should reflect us."

"Listen here, it's *my* message. On *my* machine. In *my* apartment."

"About that, dear. I've already called your landlord. I think we should have both our names on the apartment lease."

"I need a Tums."

"It's only fair that I share half the responsibility with you since we are a couple and I do live here now and—"

"I *really* need a Tums. I've got to go." She punched the OFF button before he could say another word.

It's okay. You're not going to throw up or break down or scream or cry. Womanists do not cry over men. Even infuriating, smothering, message-changing men. They endure and overcome. They conquer. They breathe.

That's it. Just breathe. Breathe and refocus your attention on something positive. Think about your viewers and your daters and the fact that you haven't seen your youngest daughter in weeks. Do not think about the message. Or the fact that he's taking over your life and the toilet seat is up and his dirty socks are sitting in a pile near your favorite Queen Anne coffee table.

"Mom?" Xandra's voice drifted from behind. "Are you okay?"

"I'm fine." Jacqueline drew in a deep breath, gathered her control and turned to face her youngest daughter who was now wearing a large black T-shirt and a worried expression.

"You look pale."

"And you look dressed. Unlike a few moments ago."

"I can explain that."

Jacqueline leveled a stare at her daughter and gave her best this-better-be-good-or-else smile. "I'm all ears."

Chapter Twenty-Two

There's a perfectly good reason that I answered the door naked," Xandra said as she tugged the hem of Beau's T-shirt down and tried to ignore the intoxicating aroma that teased her nostrils. "A great reason, in fact." Not that she had to give one. She was a grown woman. A grown woman with needs. She didn't have to account to anyone.

Then again, this was her *mother.* The woman who'd given birth to her. Who'd labored for hours. Who'd endured stretch marks and a stomach pooch so that Xandra could have a chance at life.

"I'm waiting. And while you're explaining about being naked, you might as well tell me who that half-dressed man was. He nearly knocked me down on your front steps."

"Half-dressed man?"

"Naked from the waist up."

"You saw him?"

"I saw him and he doesn't look a thing like Mark."

"That's because he's not Mark. Mark is, um, away right now."

"Another business trip?"

"Something like that. The man you saw is the contractor who's doing the renovations on the house. He took his shirt off while he was here working and I sort of picked it up and was going to give it back to him, but then you showed up, which means I'll just have to hold on to it until tomorrow."

"Or until you can get to your own clothes, which brings us back to why you were naked in the first place."

"Well," she started. She was going to tell her mother the truth. How Mark was history and how she was wildly attracted to Beau—in the name of research—and how she'd spent the past few weeks trying to seduce him. She had to tell her. "I'm naked because I . . ." She swallowed against the sudden lump in her throat. "Because I, um, couldn't wear clothes while I was . . . You see, I'm trying to test this new product and I needed to be naked in order to get the full effect," she blurted. "It's a body lotion."

Okay, so she owed her mother an explanation, but this was her *mother,* as in older, as in frail. She couldn't just blurt out the shocking truth when her old, frail mother already looked so pale.

"I was upstairs doing a trial test while Beau was down here working on some custom-made bookshelves I asked him to build." Her mother didn't so much as blink at the name because Jacqueline had spent most of Xandra's childhood on the lecture circuit while her grandmother had done the full-time parent thing. "He was varnishing and he had his shirt off to avoid getting it stained. So you see, he was half naked and I was totally naked, but we weren't in the various stages of nakedness at the same time, nor were we even in the same room, much less *together.* I wouldn't be naked with a man I hardly know when I have my very own Holy Commitment Man."

Jacqueline looked skeptical for a few frantic heartbeats, but then she smiled. "Of course you wouldn't, dear. You never give me a bit of trouble."

"Enough about me," Xandra rushed on. "Tell me what's going on with you. What brings you to Houston?"

"Smart Dating?" her mother prodded. "My Houston segment? Why, I told you weeks ago that I was coming. Don't tell me you forgot?"

She forgot. "I would never forget something like that."

"Of course not. I'm sure you've been looking forward to it." Her mother smiled and then she frowned. "At least I have one daughter who appreciates me."

"Skye and Eve appreciate you." Xandra followed her mother who started back up the hallway toward her luggage.

"Your sisters avoid me," Jacqueline said as she reached the briefcase she'd left on the hardwood floor. "And don't think I don't know it. Of course, they pretend that I'm a bother, but what I really am is their conscience. They're leading heathen lifestyles that totally undermine the entire womanist movement and they feel guilty. Seeing me and talking to me stirs that guilt."

"Maybe they're just busy."

"And maybe I'm actually going to give up my entire belief system and let your father buy monogrammed towels for my bathroom." She blew out an exasperated breath as she slid off her beige suit jacket to reveal an equally beige silk blouse beneath. She hooked the jacket on a nearby coatrack. "Imagine me drying my hand with your father's initials? Why, it's positively archaic. Now, if he were going to get two sets of towels, one with my initials and one with his, that would be a different matter altogether. I suggested this to him, but he's digging in his heels on this ~ouple commitment matter and driving me absolutely insane. Why, I cleared out my entire panty hose drawer to let him use it for his ties, which gives him a full four dresser drawers while I only have two. You'd think that would satisfy the man and convince him that he's my one and only, but no. He wants something more public. More permanent. More *official*." She shuddered and adjusted her glasses. "Just the thought makes me queasy. Then again, it could be that godawful Mexican food I had on the plane here."

"I think I've got Tums up in my medicine cabinet."

"Or this whole Smart Dating thing," her mother went on as if Xandra hadn't said a word. "Why, one of my young, professional, independent L.A. daters cried because no man asked her to dance while she was at this nightclub. It's society, I tell you. We're warping our female youth to believe that men can take an actual hint when a woman smiles or flirts or wears a tiny black dress cut down to there and up to here. I told her, 'You have to put it out there. Be assertive and never, ever overestimate the male species. You have to tell the man what you want if you want him to give it to you.'"

"That should work." *Yeah, right.*

"Of course it works. What amazes me is that more women haven't realized their full power in this world. And if they keep listening to lunatics like that Cherry Chandler, they never will. It's my duty as an educator and a womanist to enlighten them. Speaking of which, I have to be on the set at six in the morning. I need to get into a hot bath and then into bed as soon as possible."

"The guest room is straight up the stairs. The first door on the left. Just make yourself at home and I'll run you a nice bubble bath."

Jacqueline smiled. "That's my girl."

Xandra smiled. "That's me."

And that was the damned trouble of it all because Xandra had been playing the good daughter far too long to stop now.

Even if she suddenly wanted to.

"I'm *this* close to spending the rest of my days on death row," Annabelle declared when Beau finally called her.

"Calm down." He pressed his foot on the gas, turned off Xandra's street and resisted the urge to glance in the rearview mirror for one last look at her house.

As if he might be lucky enough to catch a glimpse of her. He was too far away, not to mention she was inside now. She had been for the past few minutes while he'd sat in his van and tried to get a grip on the push-pull of feelings undermining his control.

He'd been this close to hauling her into his arms and have the hottest, most wicked sex ever. What's more, he'd almost trampled her mother on the front steps.

He'd recognized Jacqueline Farrel right away despite the fact that he hadn't seen her in person since their high school graduation. She hadn't recognized him. He hadn't expected her to since she'd always been too busy when she pulled into his dad's gas station to do little more than hand him her credit card and ask him to check under her hood. She'd always been rushing home or rushing back out on the lecture circuit and so she didn't really know him.

But he knew her. Hell, practically everybody did.

She looked exactly the way she did in the ads that aired for her late-night talk show—so calm and cool and serious. Her lips drawn into a tight line. Her face void of any expression. Her green eyes glittering with knowledge. She wore an air of superiority that had nothing to do with the fact that she thought she was better than him, and everything to do with the fact that she *knew* she was better than him, and all his testosterone-oozing brethren.

To put it bluntly, she scared the shit out of him, and so it was a good thing that the situation had ended with Annabelle's page, otherwise he would have had to endure not only Xandra's tears, but her mother's wrath at seeing her baby girl in the arms of a man who wasn't even close to Holy Commitment material.

As it was, the only person he had to contend with was himself and the nearly overwhelming urge to haul the van around, head back to Xandra's, and finish what he'd started.

"Crazy," he muttered.

"You're telling me." Annabelle's voice drew his attention away from his racing heartbeat and throbbing lust. "If I have to talk to Savannah Sawyer one more time, I'm going to take out a contract on her."

"She called again?"

"An hour ago. She said that she's only fifty percent satisfied with her deck and since we guarantee one hundred percent satisfaction or your money back, she wants the rest of her satisfaction. She says the deck just doesn't look that good."

"Because we had our electrician doing it. Bryan's the best deck guy we have. He should have been the one finishing the job."

"I told her. I said we sent our best man, but he wasn't your idea of good-looking, so it's really your fault. That's when she pushed me to the limit."

"She used foul language?"

"She called me *hon,* for the fifth time in as many minutes. *Hon,* as in 'honey.' As in 'I'm better than you so I have to use a condescending nickname so that you feel even more inadequate.' No more," Annabelle declared. "I know this guy from my bowling club who has a cousin who knows somebody who *takes care* of people—even highly annoying people—pretty cheap."

Beau thought back to all of the trouble he'd gone to over the past few weeks to accommodate Savannah Sawyer. Rearranging people. Revamping his schedule. Inconveniencing himself. Putting the brakes on with the hottest woman he'd kissed in . . . *forever.*

"How much?" he finally asked.

"Five hundred bucks. Five fifty and we get to choose how she gets it. I say we have them tie concrete blocks to her feet and throw her into the Ship Channel. Or we could try poison, but personally I'd like something a little more painful. Maybe we could make a tape recording of her saying 'hon' and force her to listen to it over and over while we feed her a banana split. Talk about torture."

Beau entertained the notion for a full five seconds before blowing out an exasperated breath. "I'll take care of it."

"Okay, but make sure you get the real ice cream and none of that nonfat yogurt stuff. That would defeat the purpose."

"I'll call her and straighten the deck situation out. Even if I have to go out there myself and make the needed changes."

"You're not blond," she reminded him of Savannah's first complaint.

"I don't have to be." Not after next week. He was this close to giving his company a brand-new identity. He simply had to finish the job at Xandra's, kick back, and let *Texas Monthly* paint an entirely different picture of the men at Hire-a-Hunk.

Competent. Capable. Experienced. Professional.

Then customers wouldn't be calling him to hire a hunk of a man to strut around fixing things up. They'd be calling to hire a hunk of knowledge when it came to major construction and restoration.

"You're the boss," Annabelle said before she hung up. "But I still like the ice cream torture idea. She needs a few rolls here and there. No woman should be that skinny or that pretty. It's just not natural."

Amen. Natural was a real woman with full, voluptuous breasts that trembled when he rubbed the pads of his thumbs across her hard, tight nipples. A woman with rounded hips that cradled his erection when he rocked against her. A woman with lots of curves that pressed against him in all the right places when he held her tight. A woman with soft, warm skin that teased his fingertips when he stroked her.

Xandra.

He ignored the sudden image and tried to focus on the fact that he was in the home stretch. Soon there would be no more worrying about his guys and the future of his business. He would have his new image and H&H Construction would be born. Xandra would have her fully restored, prize-winning house. Their business together would be finished.

She would turn her attention back to Wild Woman.

He would turn his to the newly born H&H Construction.

Oddly enough, the thought didn't excite him half as much as the memory that rooted in his mind. Of Xandra facing him completely, gloriously naked, the T-shirt puddled at her feet, desire hot and bright in her gaze.

"Shit," he growled as he bypassed the ramp onto Interstate 59 that led to his house in the Woodlands. The last thing he needed was to go home to an empty house right now. He needed a distraction. Something to help him get his head on straight. Something to jolt some sense into a certain hard part of his anatomy that refused to listen to reason.

Fifteen minutes later, after fishing a white HIRE-A-HUNK T-shirt out of the back of his van, he walked onto the fifth floor of St. Luke's Hospital. He waved hello to Desiree who stood behind the nurses' station, a chart in hand and a smile on her face.

"How is he tonight?"

"As energetic as ever. He was up dancing around the room a few minutes ago to some MTV rap video."

"I didn't know you guys offered cable."

"We don't, but he smooth-talked the head nurse into letting him set up some elaborate computer system that has wireless Internet. So he's been tuning into the MTV Website all afternoon and bribing me for a table dance."

Beau frowned. "Shouldn't he be taking it easy?"

"I wouldn't worry. The exercise is good for him. Besides, I think it makes him feel a little more normal, which is very good."

"Look, don't say anything," Evan said when Beau walked into the room to find a table set for two, complete with a white, starched tablecloth, real china, and a bottle of wine chilling nearby. "It's nonalcoholic."

"That's good to know, but what about the rest of this stuff?"

Evan winked. "It's for Desiree. I think she likes me."

"Desiree? Your nurse?" At Evan's nod, Beau added, "It's her job to like you, buddy."

"Maybe, but maybe there's something to it."

"And maybe you're just going to make a fool of yourself."

"That never stopped me before."

"Things are different now."

"You mean I'm different now." He sank down into one of the chairs. "I know what I look like, Beau."

"I'm not talking about that. It's not about how you look. It's your attitude. Didn't you learn anything from that accident?"

"Yeah. It'll be a cold day in hell before I drive another Beamer. You can bet your ass I'll be cruising around in a Hummer next time."

Beau shook his head. "That's what I'm talking about. There shouldn't be a next time. You should have learned the first time."

"I did." A serious look came across his face and determination lit his eyes. "No more drinking and driving. I'm completely off the stuff."

"It's not just the booze. It's everything else, too. Your job. The women. You're too much of a risk-taker when it comes to *everything*. That's what the accident was really about. You weren't just drinking. You were acting on a dare. Hungry for the next rush of adrenaline. You're not just an alcoholic. You're an excitement junkie."

"What's wrong with excitement?"

"It fogs your brain and keeps you from thinking straight. It screws things up." Beau knew that firsthand. He'd spent five years working his ass off because he'd given in to a few minutes of excitement with Xandra. "And it hurts like hell." He knew that, too, because he'd walked around with that hurt for weeks, seeing her around school, wanting to talk to her, needing to tell her that he couldn't stop thinking about her, yet afraid that she didn't feel the same.

That fear had been realized each time she avoided him. If he looked at her, she looked away. If he started in her direction, she walked the other way. And so he'd finally wised up and stopped trying to talk to her.

"I know the odds of her saying yes to dinner, much less anything else. Especially with the way I look. I'm not a pretty boy anymore." He touched his face and pain flashed in his gaze. Quickly replaced by a glittering determination. "But sometimes you've got to take a chance and put yourself out there. She might really like me."

"And what if she doesn't?"

Evan's gaze met Beau's. "Then the only thing I've lost is my pride. Sure, it might hurt like hell, but at least I'll feel *something*. This playing it safe is no way to live. It's not living at all. Don't you see, buddy? Real living isn't about feeling good. It's about *feeling,* period. Because then you know you're living. Otherwise, you're just going through the motions."

Evan's words followed Beau as he left the hospital and turned onto Main Street leading away from the medical center.

Pride?

But it wasn't a matter of pride. It was all about focus. About the future.

Or was it?

Xandra had been so beautiful that night back in high school, so different, so stirring that he'd been a goner from the word "go." He'd wanted so much to make the evening perfect, to talk and laugh and dance with her. To make her feel even half of the heart-pounding attraction he'd felt.

But he'd blown it because they'd never danced. They'd

hardly talked. They *had* done the deed, but it had been a far cry from what she'd anticipated. Despite her laughter and the way she'd tried to make light of the entire thing, he'd seen the disappointment in her gaze.

The look had stayed with him long after he'd dropped her off at home. It had haunted him the rest of the night and the following day. It still stuck in his memory, resurfacing to taunt him at the worst possible moments.

Like now.

The memory rushed at him, but he didn't push it away. He welcomed it this time and finally admitted to himself what he'd known all along. His fear had nothing to do with his focus and everything to do with his damned pride. Because he feared losing control again.

She wanted him right now, but if he acted on his lust and satisfied himself, would she be disappointed again?

Maybe. Maybe not. He only knew that he would rather take a chance and risk losing his pride than live with the question for the rest of his life. The *what if* would surely haunt him even more than his past failure because he didn't have any excuses this time around. He wasn't young or inexperienced or caught off-guard.

He was a full-grown man who knew how to satisfy a woman.

But could he satisfy this particular woman?

There was only one way to find out.

"So what does Mark think about the renovations?" Jacqueline asked Xandra as she stood in the guest room in her nightgown and robe and unpacked her clothes for the following morning.

"He, um, doesn't say much about them. We don't talk that much anymore."

"Meet him at the door the way you met me tonight and that will all change. Men are such visual creatures and they interpret everything to mean sex. Why, one time I answered the door wearing nothing but a roll of Saran Wrap—I was trying to work on my middle and I read this very informative article about inexpensive ways to slim down problem areas—and your father nearly peeled off his clothes right there."

"Mom, I really don't want to hear this."

"His eyes bugged out and he started to stutter and—"

"Here's your new book," Xandra exclaimed as she grabbed a nearby copy of the best-selling *Give Me Womanhood, or Give Me Death!* "You can't leave without signing it for me."

"Of course, dear. But this is last year's release."

"I know that. What I meant was, this is your old book, but it's like a totally new book to me every time I read it. It's really an eye-opener."

"What's your favorite part?"

"The first part."

"Pre- or postorgasm?"

"Pre- and post-, and everything in between. I'll go and make you a nice hot cup of tea."

"You're too good to me. Say"—her mother eyed her—"there's something different about you." A few more seconds of scrutiny. "It's your eyes."

"I'm wearing a new eye shadow color."

"Really? And here I thought you looked different because your eyebrows are painted on."

"They're not completely painted on. I still have a few hairs of my own. The pencil is just to help me get by until they grow back. I sort of had an accident in the kitchen."

"Oh." Jacqueline turned to hang up a brown blazer and

gave a deep sigh. "I so enjoyed the bubble bath. It seems like ages since I've been in the ladies' room by myself. Your father thinks we're joined at the hip. I still can't believe he changed my message. Of all the sneaky, conniving things . . ."

While Jacqueline went on about Xandra's father, Xandra slipped from the room and went downstairs in search of tea bags. She made a mental note to add her mother's new book to her Things to Buy list and reading her mother's new book to her Things to Do list.

While the tea was steeping, she retrieved a Diet Coke. When she had guzzled enough caffeine to send her heart into major cardiac arrest, the doorbell rang. Another drink and several steps later, she found Beau standing on her doorstep.

His eyes were dark and determined, his mouth set in a thin line. His muscles were bunched and tight. He looked flushed and hot and ready for sex.

Right.

She forced the last thought aside and tried to calm the sudden pounding of her heart.

"Did you come for your shirt?" She was now wearing her own T-shirt and shorts. "Because if you did, I tossed it into the washing machine so you'll have to wait for—"

"Sex," he cut in. "I came for you and me and *sex.*"

Chapter Twenty-Three

Before Xandra had a chance to react to his words, he kissed her.

He tasted hot and wild and sweet. So sweet that she couldn't seem to get enough. Or control her hands; they clawed at his shirt, pulling and bunching until she managed to feel his skin beneath.

But the kissing and the touching and the bare shoulders beneath her fingertips weren't nearly enough to satisfy the lust raging inside of her.

She pressed herself closer and trailed her hands down his back, absorbing the heat of his skin as she opened her mouth wider.

His tongue tangled with hers, stroked and explored as the air rushed from her lungs. Her heart pounded and her knees trembled and she would have crumpled right there at his feet had he not been holding her up.

"I want you. Right here. Right now."

"For real? You're not"—she sucked in a sharp breath as his fingertips found one swollen nipple—"going to"—she gasped—"stop? Because I can't stop again," she panted.

"I won't stop." He kissed her again, hard and fierce and determined. "But you can't stop either."

"Since when did I stop?"

"You haven't, but you can't. I can't take it. It's now. Right here." He swept a hand between them to trail his fingertips down her stomach to the V of her legs. "Right now."

Here.

Now.

No.

"We can't," she blurted as his mouth swooped down for another hungry kiss. "My mother's here. Upstairs."

He looked doubtful for a heartbeat, as if the notion bothered him as much as it bothered her. He glanced past her to the staircase before his gaze shifted back and locked with hers. "Upstairs, huh?"

"The guest bedroom on the left."

"The one next to your bedroom?"

"That's the one."

"We'll keep it down."

"I can't."

"Why not?"

"Because it's my mother, for heaven's sake. She'll be right there. She could hear us or worse, see us."

"You're a grown woman. An unattached woman. We're not hurting anyone."

Just her image.

The realization hit her as she stood there holding him at arm's length when all she wanted to do was pull him close. She wasn't worried about her mother hearing for modesty's sake. She was worried about what her mother might think of her.

That her youngest daughter was a healthy grown woman who liked sex?

Exactly.

She was afraid her mother would see that she was no longer the do-no-wrong baby of the family. That she was all grown-up now and she did plenty of wrong. She didn't read her mother's best-selling books or keep up with her show topics or follow the doctrine that she preached with such conviction. The jig would be up and Jacqueline would finally know the truth about her youngest daughter—that Xandra had lost weight and changed her wardrobe and her attitude so long ago, not in the interest of personal growth but for the supreme purpose of snagging herself a boyfriend. She'd then gone on to give up Thai and Mexican food and anything else that made her scalp sweat when she took a bite just because Mark had frowned at anything that tasted better than cardboard. And she'd tamped down her own love of old houses to live in a chrome and glass mausoleum for the past eight years simply because Mark had liked the modern look.

Sure, she was gravitating back to her old self slowly but surely, but she was still going the distance for the opposite sex. She'd cooked the other night for a man. And lit candles and played seductive music and given a very erotic massage—all to entice a man.

She'd gotten naked tonight just for a man, too.

This man.

She stared up into his hungry eyes and saw the flash of desire. Her mouth went dry and her thighs trembled and warmth pooled between her legs. It was a reaction she hadn't felt in a long, long time. And one she'd never felt quite so intensely.

Her lips tingled from the feel of his mouth and her hands itched to reach out just once more . . .

Okay, so maybe she was thinking too much. They were just going to have sex, for heaven's sake. The quiet, behind-closed-doors kind of fun that was perfectly acceptable between two consenting adults. It wasn't like she was about to participate in a major life-changing event. She wasn't lobbying to kill affirmative action or subscribing to *Bride's* magazine or in any other way, shape, or form publicly advocating the enslavement of women. It was just sex, and sex in the name of research at that.

Besides, her mother was dead tired. She would probably sleep through the entire thing and all of Xandra's angst would be for nothing.

Xandra held tight to the last thought.

"What the hell," she breathed as she gave in to her lust, threw herself into his arms, and kissed him for all she was worth.

Before she knew what was happening, he picked her up and started toward the stairs, his lips never once breaking contact with hers. Several kisses later, he slid her down the length of his hard body until her feet touched the floor near her bed. He let her go long enough to close and lock the door before walking back over to her.

"Come here." But he didn't wait for her to make a move. He reached for her.

She expected him to take her with the same fast, furious pace he'd set downstairs. The same pace he'd set that night so long ago. But he didn't.

He held her face between his hands, thrust his tongue deep inside and made love to her with his mouth. Long and slow and thorough until she clung to him and clutched at his shoulders.

He pulled the T-shirt up and over her head. His fingers went to the clasp of her white lace bra. With a flick of his wrist, the cups parted and the straps sagged on her shoulders. Dipping his head, he caught one nipple between his teeth. He flicked the ripe tip with his tongue before opening his mouth wider. He drew her in, sucking her so hard and long that she gasped for air. A moan curled up in her throat.

He stopped long enough to hook his fingers beneath the elastic waistband of her shorts. He pushed the material down her thighs, his fingertips grazing her flesh and making her quiver until the soft cotton fell to her ankles. She kicked the shorts aside and stood before him wearing nothing but her panties and an open bra.

The urge to lift her arms and cover herself hit her as she stood there beneath his intense gaze. It was a habit she'd never managed to break despite the fact that she'd lost weight and, supposedly, her self-consciousness.

She lifted her hand, but he caught it midair and kept staring as if she were the most beautiful thing he'd ever seen.

A memory played at her brain and suddenly she found herself in the backseat of the Impala, staring up at him, seeing the same gaze reflected in his deep violet eyes.

Her imagination, she'd told herself back then. Wishful thinking. A fantasy.

But there was no denying the look now, or the flash of appreciation as his gaze roved from her head to her toes and back up again.

"You're beautiful," he breathed, the words washing away her anxiety and stirring a rush of confidence.

And as he stared at her for those next few moments, she actually felt beautiful. And desirable. And wanted.

It was crazy. He was just looking at her, yet her body ached even more fiercely than if he'd been touching her. Her heart pounded and her blood rushed as if she'd slathered herself with Lotion Potion—an aphrodisiac body lotion that stirred the nerve endings and increased anticipation. Her nipples tingled and heat flooded between her legs as if she'd spent the past twenty minutes with the ever-popular Clitty Kitty, a tool that teased and taunted and primed a woman when the male involved didn't quite know what to do with his hands.

She was turned on, and he hadn't really done anything. Yet.

He clasped her waist and backed her to the nearest wall. Pressing one hard thigh between her leg, he forced her wider until she rode him.

The sudden intimate contact drew a gasp from her lips. His gaze hooked on her mouth and she knew he wanted to kiss her again.

He didn't. Instead, he leaned into her, his thigh pressed against her, working her until dampness flooded the thin material of her panties and his breathing came almost as frantic as hers.

He touched her then, sliding his hand into her silk panties, into the wet and swollen folds between her legs. At the first touch of his fingers, a ragged moan curled from her lips and she shivered. She was close. So close.

"Not yet," he murmured before he scooped her up and settled her on the bed. He was about to follow her when she shook her head.

"My turn," she said, reaching for the button on his jeans. A flick of a button, a glide of a zipper, and she freed his throbbing erection. She held it in her hands and traced the bulging purple head. Dark hair curled around the base and she ruffled the soft silk, relishing his gasp as her nails grazed his testicles.

"Enough," he breathed, forcing her away. He paused to retrieve a condom from his pants pocket.

She watched him slide the sheath onto his penis, mesmerized by the sight of him touching himself before reality zapped her.

"Wait," she started. "I have to get something."

"You don't have to get anything, because I'm going to give you everything," he told her as he urged her backward and followed her down. He slid his hands under her thighs and urged them further apart.

"That's not what I meant," she started, but then he plunged into her, so fast and deep that her thoughts scattered.

Sensation overwhelmed her for a long, breathless moment, the feel of him so hot and thick pulsing inside her nearly making her scream with satisfaction right then and there. Her arms slid around his neck and her muscles clamped down around him and she closed her eyes to the delicious feel of being filled to the brim with Beau Hollister.

A feeling she expected to be all too fleeting when he withdrew and plunged back in. Once, twice and it had been over way back when. He'd groaned. She'd caught her lip to keep from crying. End of story.

He withdrew and slid back in for the second time. His hard length rasped her tender insides, creating a delicious friction that sent a dizzying heat straight to her brain. He pulled out again, then went back for a third time. A fourth.

His body pumped into hers over and over, pushing her higher with each delicious thrust until she stopped fearing it would end and started to enjoy the ride.

She lifted her hips, meeting him thrust for thrust, eager to feel more of him. Harder. Deeper. Faster. Her mind went blank as she exploded. Convulsions gripped her body and she milked his, pulling him in as he plunged one last and final time and followed her over the edge.

Several breathless moments passed as she lay there and tried to come to grips with what had just happened.

They'd had sex.

Incredible sex.

Loud incredible sex.

Worry rushed through her as she remembered her gasps. And his moans. And her cries. And his grunts. And her screams. And . . .

"You have to get out of here." She struggled to an upright position, but his arm came across and pinned her down.

"What are you talking about?"

"I didn't think it would be so loud because I didn't think I would like it so much because I didn't think it would be so good."

"You thought it was good?"

"Very good, and very noisy."

"Then I've totally blown the whole bad sex image, have I?"

"Definitely. It was way better than I— What did you just say?"

"'That you don't still think we're going to have bad sex. That is what you thought, isn't it?" He leaned on his elbow. "That I would be the perfect specimen to try out this new product of yours?" Before she could answer, he added, "The jig is up. I know. I've known all along."

"Since when?"

"Since the night you made all that food. I was working

on the staircase inside the house, your phone rang, and some guy left a message asking if you'd gotten into my pants yet."

"That was the night you burped in my face." She turned accusing eyes on him. "You did that on purpose, didn't you?"

"Maybe."

"You did. You're not really that obnoxious. You've been pretending all this time to be a first-class jerk, but it was all a lie. You lied to me."

"Well, *you* lied to me."

"I did no such thing. I was very honest about wanting to have sex with you. I just didn't say why. I sinned by omission. I didn't lie."

"Yes, you did. You told me you didn't like to dance."

"What are you talking about?"

"The night of the Sadie Hawkins dance. I asked you to dance and you turned me down. You said you didn't like to dance, but that wasn't true. I've seen you through the window dancing around when you get home from work. You obviously like to dance, so that means you lied that night."

"I can't believe you remember that."

"I remember everything. Namely, that everyone was dancing and you didn't want to dance with me."

"That's not true. I would love to have danced with you, but I didn't know how. I didn't want you to think I was even more of a geek than I was, so I said I just didn't want to." She grew silent as her mind wandered back to the swirl of colored lights and the loud music. She could still feel the frantic beat of her heart and the longing that had welled inside her when he'd asked her to dance. "You were my first date in high school, and my last. After that, I had the occasional blind date during college, but then I met Mark my sophomore year. He hated to dance, so my entire collection of moves can be attributed to getting busy on the dance floor with my girlfriends at weddings or the occasional club on a girls' night out." Her gaze met his. "I've never actually couple danced before."

"Never?"

"Not in real life." At his questioning look, she added, "I used to think about it a lot, like what I'd be wearing and how I would look and what song would be playing, but that was it."

"What would you be wearing?"

"You don't want to hear my silly thoughts."

"I do. Tell me."

She closed here eyes and remembered one fantasy in particular. "The outfit changes a lot, but my favorite is this red ball gown, with a matching corsage. One of those wrist corsages that the girls always brought to school on the Monday after a dance. I always wanted one of those."

"And how do you look?"

"I've got my hair up with all these tiny red flowers, and I look happy. And excited."

"And what song is playing?"

" 'The Time of My Life.' That song from the movie *Dirty Dancing*. The one at the end where everyone is re-united and the lead character wins everyone over with his dancing skills."

The bed shifted and she opened her eyes to see him standing in front of her, the moonlight playing his naked body. He took her hand.

"What are you doing?"

"I'm going to dance with you. The way I should have that night."

"But it wasn't your fault. I said no."

"But you're not going to say no now."

"But there's no music and we're naked . . ." Her voice trailed off as he brought her up hard against his body. Heat sizzled through her, but there was more than just a physical awareness between them now. There was a strange connection that lulled her nerves and relaxed her in his arms.

She closed her eyes and for the next few minutes, as they swayed back and forth, she actually felt the way she did in her ball gown fantasy. Alive and invigorated and special. The way she'd wanted to feel that night with him so long ago.

But this was better because it was real. And it was now.

"What are you thinking?"

His voice drew her eyes open and she leaned back to stare up at him. Desire gleamed in his eyes, along with a hint of something that sent a wave of anxiety through her and she pulled away.

"Did you hear that?" she blurted as she pulled away and made a big show of tiptoeing to the door. "I think my mother's up. She probably remembered her tea."

"I didn't hear a thing." For emphasis, he pulled open the door. The steady sound of snoring drifted from down the hallway.

"Oh. I could have sworn I heard her. We're so lucky she didn't hear us. We were much too loud."

He closed and locked the door, grinned and urged her down onto the mattress. "Then we'll just have to make a concerted effort to keep it down the next time."

"The next time?"

He grinned and kissed her belly button. "*This* time," he murmured against her stomach before his tongue dipped and he licked a path south.

"I don't know if that's such a good . . ." *Idea* was there

on the tip of her tongue, but it came out a garbled "ahhh" when he kissed the inside of her thigh. Soft hair tickled her skin as his mouth moved closer to ground zero. A little to the left . . . A little more to the north . . . *There.* He licked the sensitive swollen flesh between her legs and she forgot all about calling it quits.

"My lips are sealed," she promised herself before his tongue darted out and parted her slick folds and she gasped from the pleasure of it.

He suckled and tasted and drove her to another mind-blowing orgasm. Her body quivered and heat coiled in her stomach and she arched up off the bed. Her own voice echoed in her head as she cried out at the delicious sensation.

A split-second later, Beau's mouth covered hers, muffling her cry as his erection probed the moist heat between her legs and he slid into her again. And again. And again. And set the pace for the next few hours to come, until their night drew to a close and she rushed him off before waking her mother up for breakfast.

The last thing she needed was to have to explain Beau's presence to her mother, particularly since the woman was stressed about the morning's taping, not to mention the rush to the airport immediately after in order to catch a plane back to L.A. to check on Xandra's father.

It was just sex, Ma.

But that was the problem. It hadn't been just sex. It had been great sex. Surprisingly great sex.

One down and two to go.

The minute the thought pushed inside her head, she pushed it right back out because Beau had made it perfectly clear that he didn't want a relationship at this point in his life. And neither did she, she reminded herself. She wanted the Lust, Lust, Baby! team to come begging for her ingenuity and she wanted a baby. End of story.

At least that's what Xandra told herself the rest of the morning as she kissed her mother good-bye, wished her good luck with her Houston daters, and headed off to her office for the much needed distraction of work.

Chapter Twenty-Four

By the time Xandra reached the offices of Wild Woman, she had her priorities back in order. At the top of the list: the Sextravaganza that kicked off Thursday with a press conference at the George R. Brown Convention Center.

She wasn't going to think about last night or sex or Beau or last night's sex with Beau.

It was all about work from here on out. Or it would be as soon as she got off the phone with her father who called the minute she sat down at her desk.

"I was just calling to see if your mother got off to work okay."

"She seemed fine, in between the grumbling about messages and monogrammed towels. What did you do to her?"

"Nothing, dear. That's the problem. For the past thirty-seven years, I've done absolutely nothing to forge more of a committed relationship with your mother. Instead, I've given her space and time and the chance to realize she needs me. But she hasn't realized a thing. We're no closer to being a real couple than we were when we first met."

" 'Real,' as in legally married?"

"I don't intend to push her that far. I know her objections, particularly after witnessing your grandfather's relationship with your grandmother. But I've been hoping that we can have the complete commitment, just without the piece of paper."

"Meaning the monogrammed towels and the joint message."

"Exactly. But giving her time and space hasn't done the trick, so I'm trying a different approach."

"And what if she doesn't come around?"

"I used to think just being with your mother on whatever terms would be enough. I loved her and so I made up my mind to take what I could get. But when I walked your sister down the aisle, I couldn't help but envy Clint. Because he had what I wanted: a woman who loved him and wasn't afraid to admit as much in front of God and everybody. I want that, Xandra. I always have, I just wouldn't admit it because if I did I would have to also admit that your mother doesn't need me the way I need her. That she doesn't love me."

"She loves you, Daddy. I know she does."

"We'll soon find out, won't we?" Before she could reply, he went on, "But enough about us old folks. How's my girl? Are you gearing up for the big show at the Sextravaganza?"

"Actually, I am. I've got a really great product in the works. Revolutionary, in fact." She went on to spend the next five minutes telling him about Mabel and about the spectacular results she'd documented thanks to Kimmy. By the time she slid the phone into its cradle, she felt fully confident—despite her own failure to experience Mabel's wow-ability firsthand—that she had a winner.

A few more test runs and she would officially move

Mabel from product development to the finished product department where sales and marketing would implement a packaging concept and a trendy new name.

"Somebody looks happy," Xandra said when she walked into the outer office to find Kimmy filing.

"Happy and stylish." Kimmy fingered the red scarf draped around her neck. "It's Gucci, and just a small token of Greg's appreciation after the Swiss steak dinner I made for him last night, complete with Chocolate Love Balls for dessert." Her smiled widened. "But he isn't the only one who was totally satisfied last night. Mabel was outrageous. I was so loud that I scared his German shepherd, who spent the entire night whimpering in the corner." She handed Xandra a neatly typed sheet of paper. "I documented everything for you."

"Thanks." She took the results and perched on the edge of Kimmy's desk.

"I have to tell you, I couldn't have been more shocked. The last time Greg and I got together, it was so totally awful that I cried. He was a happy camper, of course but I cried in private in the bathroom. I was miserable. He isn't very big. Not that I'm big, mind you. It's just that he isn't even average. But last night was great anyway."

"Mabel overcomes the size dilemna." Xandra glanced over the notes and smiled. "She's certainly living up to expectations so far. Take these for your next date." She retrieved the last of the Mabel samples from her skirt pocket and handed them to Kimmy.

"I'll take them for future use—I might have a hot prospect tomorrow—he's too big and the last time we had sex I couldn't walk at all the next day."

"That's good. We can see how Mabel holds up under stressful conditions."

Kimmy sighed and slid the samples into her pocket. "As for tonight, even Mabel can't help me with this one. It's a mercy date, which means no sex. I'm going out with Theodore Zackerman, the newbie in engineering."

"The redhead with the stress penis?"

"That's him. He's my neighbor's son. Lula Zackerman. I didn't even know I was working with her son until she brought me sugar cookies this past Sunday and Theodore tagged along. Even then, I didn't recognize him until he mentioned Paulie the Penis and how you'd liked it. Then I realized, hey this is one of Albert's new guys."

"So he asked you out?"

"His mother asked me out. It seems that Theodore is shy and hasn't been on a date in forever. But all that ends tonight since I'm a sucker for homemade sugar cookies, support hose, and the smell of vanilla extract."

"Dinner and dancing?"

"Bingo and midnight fondue at the seniors center." At Xandra's raised eyebrows, she added, "We're going with his mother."

"Ah, you're testing the waters for a threesome."

"I've always wanted to try one, but I sort of pictured it a little differently."

"I think it's sweet that you're doing this for your neighbor. Who knows? Maybe you guys will actually hit it off. Stranger things have happened."

Such as Xandra Farrel having the best orgasm of her entire sexually active life with Beau Hollister, of all people, and without benefit of Mabel.

She still couldn't believe it.

Despite her poor performance expectations, Beau had lived up to every rumor she'd ever heard back in high school, and then some. It was as if she'd been with another guy that night so long ago.

Then again, ten years was a long time. She shouldn't have been so quick to think that he would be just as inept as he'd been their first night together. But she'd wanted to think that, otherwise she would have had to entertain the idea that maybe, just maybe, their one disastrous night together hadn't been his fault. But hers.

Maybe if she'd been thinner or prettier, he wouldn't have been in such a hurry. Maybe he would have been slow and thorough and determined to satisfy her the way he'd been last night.

Because she was thinner now? And prettier? Because she made a more attractive woman than an awkward, chubby teenage girl?

Yes.

She'd seen the truth blazing in his eyes when he'd looked at her naked body. She'd felt it in the reverent way he'd touched her. She'd tasted it in the fierce hunger of his kiss.

He wanted her now in a way he'd never wanted her back then. The affirmation of her worst fear should have upset her, but it didn't. Instead, it sent a surge of victory through her because she realized that she'd finally succeeded in changing her image from the dumpy and frumpy ugly duckling to a hot, sexy, vibrant swan.

Beau had not only given her a great orgasm last night, he'd given her something much more precious—a newfound sense of confidence. Not because he'd told her she was beautiful. But because he'd truly believed it. For that, she owed him, and so she intended to keep her word—she wasn't having sex with him again.

No matter how much she wanted to.

*   *   *

He wasn't having sex with her again.

No matter how much he wanted to.

That's what Beau told himself Saturday as he loaded the sandalwood latex paint into his sprayer and started painting the exterior of the house,

One night he could allow himself. He'd given in to his lust and put his pride on the line, and he'd come out victorious. He'd needed to know, to prove that he was no longer the hasty kid he'd been so long ago, and he'd done just that. He'd stopped dreaming about all the things he wanted to do to her and taken charge of the fantasy.

Now it was time to move on. To focus. On finishing the house. On winning the *Texas Monthly* renovation competition and revamping his company's image. On the future rather than the damnable fantasy that had haunted him ever since their first encounter.

Beau shifted his attention to the spray can and worked his way around the house. He'd nearly finished with the eastern side when Xandra climbed out of her car and walked up the front walk.

It wasn't so much the way she looked—dressed in a tank top and blue jean shorts—that took his breath away and made him rethink the whole no-more-sex thing. Sure, the shirt was tighter and shorter and hugged her breasts more than any he'd seen her wear in the past, and the shorts were fitted and cut midthigh rather than roomy and knee-length like the ones she usually wore. But what stopped him cold was the way she moved her body. Her steps were sure and easy, her back arched a fraction more than usual, her head held high, as if she knew she looked as sweet as a bowl of caramel popcorn.

The thought conjured an image of her as she'd been last night, so naked and soft and panting beneath him . . .

"*Shit*." The thought faded into a muttered curse as his finger faltered on the trigger of the spray can and he blasted a portion of the rain gutter with the sandalwood paint.

He stiffened, set the paint can down on a nearby canvas. After grabbing a rag soaked with paint thinner, he cleaned up the mess and pulled off his paint-splattered gloves. He met her near the front porch and reached for her briefcase. His hand brushed hers and electricity sizzled along his nerve endings, sending a blast straight to his already growing erection.

As if she sensed the response, she smiled. And he frowned.

"We really need to talk about last night. It was wonderful, but it was still just—"

"Sex."

His gaze snapped to hers. "What did you say?"

"I said last night was just sex. That's what you were going to say, wasn't it? 'Just sex.' "

His eyes sparkled. "Actually, I was thinking great sex."

She nodded. "Fantastic sex."

"Phenomenal sex."

"But still just sex." She sighed. "Look, you don't have to worry. I meant what I said; I only wanted one night. You can stop worrying that I'm going to make more out of it than it is, because I'm not. It didn't mean anything. I mean, it did. You wanted me and I wanted you, but it's over now. I don't want a relationship with you."

"Neither do I. I've got to finish the house by Friday. The inspectors from *Texas Monthly* will be here on Saturday. The office has pretty much been on hold while I've been working on this project, so I'll have a load of work waiting when I get back. Not to mention the new workload once H&H wins the competition. I'm too busy to have a woman in my life."

"And I'm too busy to have a man in my life. I've got to finish the data on Mabel and then come up with a new packaging concept and name for her before the press conference on Thursday. She's sure to have the Lust, Lust, Baby! people beating down my door to steal me away from Wild Woman, which means I'll soon be working for the top company in the business. I doubt I'll have time to breathe after that, much less make time for a man. We should just go our separate ways."

"Completely separate." He did his damnedest to keep from reaching out for her when her gaze darkened. She licked her lips and his stomach hollowed out and suddenly the thought of never seeing her again hit him hard and fast and he heard himself say, "But friends . . . Why, a man can never have too many friends." And they *were* friends, he admitted.

In between her seduction attempts, they'd actually gotten to know one another again. He liked her, and she liked him. He could see the truth in her eyes, even before he heard her words.

"Good friends are priceless."

"And there's nothing wrong with two good friends sharing a broccoli-asparagus casserole."

"Broccoli and asparagus?"

"Your neighbor dropped it off a half hour ago. It smelled pretty good and I haven't eaten all day."

"Neither have I. Let's go."

She was eating broccoli and asparagus and she wasn't gagging.

Xandra came to that realization as she sat in her kitchen across from Beau and lifted another forkful of casserole to her lips. She opened her mouth and took a bite.

Her taste buds protested for the first few seconds, but then Beau smiled at her and said something about how nice she looked in her new outfit, and she forgot everything except the man sitting across from her.

They spent the next hour eating casserole and talking about everything from the color he was painting her house to what color packaging she was planning to use for Mabel. Or Orgasma. Or The Big O. Or Shiver Me Timbers. Or any of a dozen names they brainstormed while sitting in her kitchen the way they'd done so many times over the past few days.

Despite the undercurrent of sexual tension that was always present between them, she felt a measure of comfort when she was with Beau. And kinship. She understood his drive to turn Hire-a-Hunk into H&H Construction. She knew what it was like to have goals and to work relentlessly to achieve them. Like Beau, she was *this* close to achieving her own professional goal. It was just a matter of following through and not letting herself get sidetracked by anything or anyone, particularly a good-looking man.

But a good-looking *friend* . . . Well, there was no harm in just being his friend.

At least that's what Xandra told herself over the next few days as she and Beau met for dinner every night.

"What's this?" Xandra stared at the clear plastic box that Beau handed her Thursday morning when he arrived to continue painting the trim of her house. A deep, vibrant red rose lay nestled in a bed of baby's breath and ribbon.

"It's a corsage."

"I know that." Her gaze met his. "What for?"

"You said your red dress fantasy was to get dolled up for a special occasion and wear a real corsage. I know this isn't what you meant, but today is a special occasion."

Xandra blinked back the tears in her eyes.

"What's wrong?"

"Nothing. Everything." She shook her head and pushed aside the push-pull of emotion inside her. "I'm just nervous about today, that's all."

Liar.

Better to be a liar than to tell Beau Hollister that she was a fake and a fraud. That she didn't just want sex with him. She wanted more. Much more.

She smiled. "I love it. Thanks a lot."

"I just wanted you to know that I'll be rooting for you. Not that you need it. You're a special woman, Xandra. You'll do great." He kissed her then, a slow, lingering kiss filled with warmth and passion and a strange tenderness that actually brought tears to her eyes.

"Go get 'em," he said when he finally pulled away and smiled down at her.

Xandra blinked back the tears, nodded, and left for the convention center.

An hour later, she walked up on the podium and introduced Orgasma to a throng of reporters and earned Wild Woman a huge round of applause.

"Pretty good thinking," Martin Browning's voice drew her around a few hours later as she stood near the booth and passed out Orgasma samples.

"Thanks. The new circular vibrator isn't too bad." She stared past him to the huge display set up by his company.

"It isn't fresh."

"It has been done before, though not in such an impressive shape. I would have added a softer texture to the head and given it a more vibrant, sensual color."

"Come by the office first thing Monday and we'll talk about your suggestions."

Excitement rushed through her. "Meaning you want to hear them?"

"Meaning I want to hire them. We need someone to head our female products division. Someone not afraid to put herself out there and take chances. Someone with a woman's perspective." His mouth drew into a tight line. "We need a woman."

The knowledge sang through Xandra for the next few heart-pounding moments. This was it. She was *this* close to achieving her dream. The Lust, Lust boys were making an offer.

"What about Wild Woman?"

"We'll absorb the company, as well. And your employees. They'll still work under you in your very own division."

This was it. The scenario she'd lived over and over in her mind. A win-win situation for everyone—

"Excuse me." A tap on the shoulder followed the woman's voice and Xandra turned to see a little old lady smiling up at her.

"Yes?"

"My name is Lula Zackerman. Theodore's mother."

"Theodore in engineering?" Xandra remembered Kimmy's words about his cookie-baking mother. "He's such a sweetheart."

"That's my boy." The old woman beamed. "Listen, I don't want to interrupt you, dear. I just wanted to tell you thank you. That dear, sweet Kimmy who's seeing my boy gave me one of your samples and I used it with my Bob—

we've been happily married for fifty-eight years. But while we've been happy in life, we haven't been all that happy in the bedroom. He manages to have an"—her voice lowered a notch as she whispered—"*erection,* but it all happens so fast that I haven't actually had one of those"—she pointed to the word 'Orgasma' on the overhead sign—"in nearly twenty years."

"Twenty *years*?"

She nodded and then smiled. "But I had one last night thanks to your product. And so did Myrtle Shapiro."

"Myrtle Shapiro?"

"She's president of my bingo club. Kimmy passed her last samples out to me and Myrtle and Camille and Henrietta at bingo night." She pulled a white bakery box from her large macramé bag. "You're a godsend to us, so we wanted to give you something special. It's my very own homemade chocolate fudge, along with Myrtle's rocky road fudge and Camille's peanut butter fudge and Henrietta's white chocolate fudge." She patted Xandra's cheek. "Keep up the good work, dear." The woman turned and walked away.

Xandra turned back to Martin. Warmth filled her from her head to her toes, but it had nothing to do with the imminent job proposal or the sweet, delicious smell wafting from the box in her hands. The feeling was courtesy of Lula Zackerman and her Orgasma confession, and the startling feeling of triumph that filled Xandra.

You're a special woman.

Beau's words echoed in her ears.

"You're at the top of your game, Xandra," Martin went on as she turned back to him, "but you'll never beat us. Better to join forces and play on our side."

"You're not afraid of a little competition, are you?"

What the hell was she saying? She didn't want to compete. Or did she?

You're a special woman.

"Wild Woman isn't our competition," Martin said. "You own a small niche in the market. But we own the market. We *are* sex."

Her fingers tightened on the box of homemade fudge and she smiled. "You may be sex, Martin. But I'm great sex, at least to the female population, and they're all I really care about." They were, she realized, because they made her feel even better and more complete than any job offer ever could. "I'll leave the male-oriented erotica to you."

Martin shook his head. "Am I in an alternate universe? Because I swear the last time I saw Xandra Farrel she wasn't content with owning a small portion of the market. She wanted it all."

"I already have it all."

She did, she realized as she stood there with the box in her hands, satisfaction brimming inside her. She'd felt the same feeling before when she perfected a new design or saw a small rise in sales. At the same time, there'd been something missing. She'd thought that the missing something had been a larger share of the market or more company name recognition or a better job with a bigger company, but the entire time it had been her own confidence. Her belief in herself, in her talent, in her womanhood. She'd never really felt like a woman, a real woman, until Beau Hollister had opened her eyes.

She'd taken a good look, and she'd liked what she'd seen. Even more, she liked running her own company. While her eyes often glazed when it came to the financial end, she still managed to handle the numbers and make business decisions that resulted in a growing profit margin year after year.

But Wild Woman wasn't just about making money. It was about helping women everywhere get in touch with their sexuality. It helped them appreciate and cultivate that sexuality. Wild Woman was all about making other women feel good. Satisfied. Confident. *Special.*

Exactly the way Xandra felt at the moment.

"I like working in my small niche. I like owning it. And I'm not for sale," she told Martin before handing him a batch of Orgasma samples and wishing him luck.

"You're staying with Wild Woman?" Kimmy asked when Xandra turned away from the surprised executive and opened her box of fudge.

"Of course she is. She *is* Wild Woman," Albert said as he retrieved a large piece of rocky road from the box. "And she's in love."

"Love?" Xandra shook her head. "I'm not in love." She slapped his hand. "And leave my fudge alone."

"You're wearing a cheesy corsage with a DKNY suit. You're definitely in love." He stuffed the piece into his mouth and chewed.

"It's for good luck. No way am I in love."

Love?

Why, she wasn't even sure she believed in romantic love, let alone felt it. After all, she was Jacqueline Farrel's daughter. The apple couldn't have fallen that far from the tree.

Chapter Twenty-Five

The apple hadn't just fallen. Someone had drop-kicked it from here to the next state because Xandra Farrel actually believed in romantic love.

She came to that conclusion late Saturday afternoon when Beau knocked on her door. The *Texas Monthly* team had done their walk-through early that morning while Xandra had spent most of the day at her office handling the rush of orders that had poured in immediately following Orgasma's introduction at Thursday's conference kickoff.

She'd come home a few hours ago to see his entire team loading up their vans and clearing away the remaining debris. He'd been busy talking with his crew chief and so she'd just waved and walked inside the house and tried to pretend that it was just another day.

But when she opened her front door, the truth hit home. She took one look at him standing on her doorstep, the last of his tools in hand, her porch free and clear of the construction clutter she'd dealt with for the past three weeks, and panic rushed through her.

This was it. The end of the line.

While they might remain friends, it wouldn't be the same. He wouldn't be here when she arrived home. No sharing dinner every night as they'd done for the past few nights. No seeing him every day. No talking with him.

That bothered her even more than the sudden thought that she would never, ever know the feel of his body pressing into her, loving her . . .

Loving?

Yes, she believed in romantic love, all right. She felt it. Not that the feeling changed anything. They wanted different things out of life. She wanted the Perfect Daddy prospect and a family, and he wanted his business.

She swallowed against the sudden lump that formed in her throat and held up a bottle of wine in one hand and a platter of popcorn balls in the other.

"What's this?" he asked as he followed her inside to the kitchen.

"I thought we could celebrate your *Texas Monthly* victory." She set the popcorn balls and wine bottle on the table and turned to retrieve two glasses.

"What if I didn't win?" he asked as she started to pour him a glass.

She smiled. "Then we'll console ourselves with popcorn balls, talk trash about the winner, and look on the bright side." She topped off his glass and turned to her own.

"Which is?"

"There are worse things than losing." She set the bottle down and slid into the chair across from him.

"Such as?"

"War. Famine. Pestilence. Celibacy." The last word was out before she could think better of it. "So," she rushed on, eager to change the topic before she did something really crazy like press herself into his arms and beg him to love her one last and final time before he walked away for good, "what happened?"

"You first. When do you start with Lust?"

She took a drink of her wine and blew out a deep breath. "I don't."

"*What?*" He shook his head, his expression going from outraged to angry to sympathetic. "I'm sorry."

"Don't be. I turned them down."

"But I thought you wanted to work for them?"

"I thought so, too, but I don't. I didn't realize it until the offer was on the table. There it was, but suddenly it wasn't what I wanted. I already had what I wanted. I had success. I *felt* success." She smiled. "What about you?"

"We came in second place. First place went to the old brewery over on Travis Street. Arcadian Renovation handled the job. They work closely with the historical society on all of their major renovation projects. They're really good."

"I bet they're not *that* good."

"Trust me, they are, and they deserved the award."

She eyed him and noted the gleam in his eyes. "So why don't you look disappointed?"

He shrugged. "Maybe because I'm not." He eyed her. "I should be, I know. Hells bells, we came in *second* place."

"Second place isn't that bad."

"Not in this case. The judges liked your house so much they're doing a layout on it the following month and featuring Hire-a-Hunk as one of the premier renovation teams in the South."

"You mean H&H Construction?"

"I mean Hire-a-Hunk, where a hunk of home-improvement know-how is just a phone call away."

She smiled. "I like it."

"So do I."

"Did your friend Evan come up with it?"

"Evan's busy romancing his nurse who, it turns out, likes him just as much as he likes her." He shook his head as if the fact surprised him. "They're thinking about moving in together."

"That's nice."

"I came up with the new slogan myself a few days ago. Sort of a contingency plan if things fell through with the contest. Instead of building a new image, I decided to change the company's existing one. My guys are hunks. All of them. They're beefed up with experience and knowledge."

"But things didn't fall through with the contest if they're going to feature your business."

"No, but it's not my business."

"What do you mean?"

"That I'm retiring. Annabelle and Warren bought half of the company. I'll still own the other half, but I'm stepping down as the boss. They'll run things and I'll be their silent partner."

"But why?"

"Because they don't need me. Between them, they know the business as well as I do. They eat, sleep, and breathe it, and I don't." He shook his head. "Running the company was a way to make a good living and provide for my family, but my dad's gone and my brothers are all grown-up, and my duty to them is done. Besides, I'll be too busy making my own furniture to do anything more with Hire-a-Hunk than consult on the occasional project."

"What are you talking about?"

Excitement lit his eyes. "One of the photographers for *Texas Monthly* asked about your bookshelves. When I told him I was the designer, he asked if I would be interested in doing some custom-made pieces for a new house he's building. A house that's also going to be featured in the magazine. I said yes."

"That's wonderful!"

"It's scary." His gaze met hers and a serious expression covered his face. "All this time I convinced myself that I couldn't pursue my dream because I had too many people depending on me, but the truth is, I was scared that I wouldn't be able to make it. I didn't want to trade a sure thing for possible failure. I've been playing it safe until now." He shook his head. "Until you came at me full-force, determined to get what you wanted one way or another. And you did. No fear. No hesitation."

"I was afraid, too." She was still afraid. More so because the stakes were higher now.

"But you didn't let that fear cripple you or keep you down. You faced it, and that's what I did today." He reached into his pocket and held up a DBA certificate that indicated he'd registered the name of a new business. "Meet the new owner and chief craftsman for Timelessly Texan, specializing in unique, handcrafted furniture with a Texas twang."

She smiled. "Pleased to meet you. I'm Xandra Farrel, owner and head designer for Wild Woman, Inc." She handed him a popcorn ball. "It looks like this is a double celebration. Everything worked out for both of us." She took a bite of her popcorn ball.

"Almost everything. I still have some unfinished business here."

"Just get me an invoice and I'll write you a check," she said around her mouthful.

"I was thinking we might work out a little trade agreement." His gaze glittered as it dropped to her lips. "You've got a lot to offer a man."

She swallowed as excitement bubbled inside her. "As in sex?"

"I was thinking more along the lines of a lifetime supply of popcorn balls. These are pretty good." His gaze darkened. "But sex would do just as well."

"What about us being friends?"

"I like being your friend. But I love having sex with you."

The words hung between them for a long moment before her excitement got the best of her and she smiled. "Care to prove that?"

"My pleasure." And then he kissed her so deeply and thoroughly, that it took her breath away. He swept her up into his arms, headed upstairs to her bedroom, and spent the next few hours kissing and touching and working her into a frenzy. She knew what was coming, but when it finally did, she was not prepared for the intensity of her climax. Or for the words that he whispered to her as she lay sprawled across his chest afterward.

"I lied."

"About what?"

"I don't just love the sex." She lifted her head and his gaze met hers. "I love you. That's what I really wanted to tell you when I knocked on your door tonight. To tell you that, and to see if you felt the same."

Joy rushed through her, followed by a burst of panic because Xandra had barely recognized the existence of romantic love. She certainly wasn't ready to feel such an emotion herself. And even if she did, she couldn't admit it to Beau. She was Jacqueline Farrel's daughter, after all. She had an image to maintain.

"I love you," he said again, the words hanging between them as if he expected her to reciprocate.

And so she did what any sexpert would do when faced with the "L" word—she ignored it and concentrated on kissing Beau and touching him and pleasuring him, until the only thing he wanted to hear was her scream when she came apart in his arms.

"I'm miserable," Kimmy declared when she walked into Xandra's office early Monday morning.

"No date?"

"I had a date, all right. A fourth date with Theodore."

"That explains it then. You're in sex withdrawal."

"Oh, it's not withdrawal. We've had sex already. Great sex. Awesome sex. Sex *without* Mabel." She sighed. "I think I may be falling in love."

"Just because you had great sex doesn't mean you're falling in love. Your hormones are buzzing, which creates a feeling of well-being and happiness." That's what she'd told herself since Beau had left her place early Sunday morning, after the most intense night of her life. For the past twenty-four hours, she'd avoided him. Easy considering he hadn't so much as called to say "Thanks" or "It was great" or "Can we do it again?"

As if he regretted saying those three little words that kept echoing in her head.

"I take it back," Kimmy told her after several long, silent moments. "I don't think I'm falling in love."

"That's my girl. Don't get caught up in the entire sexual zing."

"I'm already *in* love. He's goofy and dorky and he isn't even that great in bed, but when he looks at me I feel this electricity anyway."

"It's called chemistry."

"And when he touches me, I feel like I'm going up in flames."

"It's called lust."

"And when he told me that he couldn't date a girl who was so materialistic, I gathered up my Prada purses and my Anne Klein pumps and I donated them to the Star of Hope mission."

"It's called delirium." Xandra eyed her assistant. "You're kidding, right?"

"Thanks to me there's now a homeless woman pushing a grocery cart down Montrose with a hot pink Fendi bag hanging on her shoulder."

"I hate Fendi," Albert said as he walked in with a box of Orgasma samples packaged in various colors with the new logo across the front. "Too pretentious."

"If you were female, you would understand," Kimmy said. "Pretentious is the point."

"Speaking of pretentious," Albert handed Xandra the box. "I think the whole packaging concept for Orgasma needs to be more classy. Tasteful. *Pretentious*. We're selling the Lexus of sexual enhancement products. Not a souped-up Mustang with a killer sound system. We're emphasizing quality orgasm, so the packaging should say quality product."

"I agree." She peered at the neon wrapping. "This looks too cute. Get with Stacey and go over some cost-effective alternatives. Maybe miniature satin bags that look like sachets or some such."

"I'll get with her right away."

"I bet you will," Kimmy said, a knowing smile on her face.

Albert frowned. "I hate office gossip."

"Gossip is stuff that gets repeated. I didn't hear gossip. I saw Stacey memo you less than a half hour ago saying that she was headed home to a shower and that she expected you to join her since you promised to scrub her back."

"You read my memo."

"I accidentally read your memo. I was in your office dropping off the new department supply sheets and there it was on top of your desk. In plain sight. Once I accidentally pushed a few papers aside."

"A back scrub, huh?" Xandra eyed Albert.

He shrugged. "Okay, so we're having sex now, but only because we're two needy people who just happen to get along physically."

"It's just sex, as in the loosest, most twisted definition of the word, right?" Xandra eyed him.

"We don't even like each other. It's just sex."

"And bowling," Kimmy piped in.

"It's just sex and bowling. End of story," Albert said before snatching up the box and marching out.

"Enjoy your shower," Xandra called after him before turning back to Kimmy. Her smile died as she eyed her assistant. "Are you okay?"

"I don't know. I mean, I feel great. A little shell-shocked that after all this time and so many men, I could have found The One." She laughed—a warm, delighted sound that mirrored the rush of joy Xandra had felt on Friday night when Beau had made his declaration. "Can you believe I've actually fallen for *Theodore,* of all people. Even more, I'm happy about it. Ecstatic. Can you believe that?"

Xandra smiled as she thought about Beau, and the fact that she missed him and wanted to see him even more than she wanted to start in on the new vibrator design for next season. "Stranger things have happened."

Namely, Xandra Farrel falling hard and fast for the one man in her past she'd vowed never to fall for ever again. She was hopelessly, desperately in "like" with Beau Hollister.

And love?

She forced the question aside. She didn't know, she only knew that she liked him. She truly liked him, and he liked her. He loved her, or so he'd said.

So why hadn't he called?

He's waiting for you to make the next move.

Maybe. And maybe he'd changed his mind. Or maybe he'd simply said the words in the heat of the moment and he hadn't really meant anything by them.

If he really loved her, he would call.

He didn't love her.

Xandra made the decision on Friday afternoon as she finished her work and packed up her briefcase. She'd never been one to sit around and wait for something to happen, and now she knew why.

She'd waited all week for his phone call. And worried. And agonized. She was this close to going off the deep end and calling him herself, regardless of the outcome. Better to hear him tell her in no uncertain terms that it was over and to get lost. At least then she would know for sure and she could stop hoping and fantasizing that he was going to show up and whisk her up into his arms in a scene straight out of *An Officer and a Gentleman.*

At the same time, the thought terrified her.

Then again . . .

Her thoughts were about to start another push-pull when Albert walked in.

"Here's the new package sample."

She took the small white satin bag that was tied with a matching ribbon. The word "Orgasma" had been imprinted on the satin in pink calligraphy. She smiled. "This looks great. You did a great job."

"It wasn't me. I mean, it was me. I had the initial idea, but it was Stacey who brought the concept to life." As if his words had conjured her, the door opened and she peeked in.

"I hate to hurry you up, but we're already fifteen mintues late. We promised your parents we would be at their place for dinner no later than six."

"Give me a few seconds."

She smiled and waved to Xandra before closing the door.

"You two are having dinner with your parents," Xandra said as Albert turned back to her. "But I'm sure it doesn't mean anything, right?"

Albert didn't frown this time. Instead, he shrugged. "Actually, it does. Stacey could be it. The One."

"But you guys don't have anything in common. You said so yourself."

"I know. That's the thing. We don't like the same things and we argue about everything, from who bowls a better strike to how long she should be on top during sex, but that's what makes it fun. She keeps me stirred up. Excited. *Alive.*" He smiled and shook his head. "I thought I was too old to feel this way, but here I am feeling like a teenager with his first girlfriend. Crazy, huh?"

"Yes, and I think the condition's contagious." Xandra

felt the same way when she was with Beau. Even worse, she felt the same way when she just thought about him.

Albert's gaze met hers. "You mean you and Beau Hollister?"

She nodded. "I can't stop thinking about him, but he hasn't called and I want to call him, but I don't know if I should and if I do, I'm not really sure what to say because I'm not really sure what I feel, if it's the same as what he feels or if it's just—" She shook her head. "I'm sorry. You don't need to hear any of this right now. You've got someone waiting for you."

He glanced at the door, then back to her. "I can't leave you like this."

"You can and you will." She squared her shoulders. "I'll be fine."

"You need a friend."

"I don't need a friend. I need Beau." The words were out before she could stop them. "Ohmigod, did I just say that?" She shook her head. "I did. I just said I *needed* him, and it didn't feel creepy or weird. It felt good." Her gaze met Albert's. "It felt right. I need him. I love him."

She'd said it. What's more, she felt it deep in her bones. "I really *love* him."

"That's great, Xandra. There's just one problem."

"What's that?"

"You're telling the wrong person. You should tell him."

"I think I just might do that." She smiled and reached for the phone.

Chapter Twenty-Six

Beau didn't answer his cell phone.

Not when Xandra called him from her office, or at the first red light en route home, or when she stopped at an intersection just shy of her neighborhood. She left him messages each time asking him to call her—she couldn't say the "L" word in a message, for heaven's sake. Gathering her briefcase and purse, she climbed out of her car.

She *loved* him.

The knowledge sang inside of her and made her smile, even when she saw Katy wave from her front porch before rushing down the steps, a casserole dish in her hand.

"It smells yummy," Xandra said as she met the woman on the sidewalk in front of her house and reached for the white Pyrex bowl. "What is it?"

"Asparagus and Spinach Delight." Katy held the dish out of reach. "And it isn't for you this time. It's for Chantal. Bill left her after sixteen years yesterday. She's devastated."

"Chantal?"

"Chantal Williamson." When Xandra didn't look any more enlightened, Katy added, "The big colonial three houses up with the green and white gingerbread trim."

"Oh, Chantal." She made a sympathetic face. "That's terrible."

"You're telling me." Her voice lowered a notch. "This one's a red alert. She's already gained fifteen pounds during the marriage, so we're bringing out the big guns. It's not just a veggie fest like we did for you. We're doing low-fat and low-carb. You're up for tomorrow night. That's what I wanted to tell you."

"You mean I'm no longer the official neighborhood project?"

Katy smiled. "You're past the danger zone." Her eyes twinkled. "Everyone's seen that you've been getting pretty friendly with that construction hunk, which means that you're not pining away for what's-his-name, which means that you're not going to go off the deep end and binge. At least not any more than the rest of us at this point. So remember: tomorrow night. Your dish should be there when she gets home from work, and make it something healthy."

But Xandra didn't do healthy, she realized as she stood in her kitchen and stared at the contents of her refrigerator. Other than a bite or two left over in the various casserole dishes supplied by her neighbors, the contents of her refrigerator included a two-liter bottle of Diet Coke, a six-pack of chocolate puddings, a bag of half-eaten candy corn, and two slices of leftover pizza so old there were things she didn't recognize growing on them.

She hadn't bought groceries in forever—not counting the seductive feast she'd made for Beau. But those things had been ingredient-specific and she'd used them all for the recipes.

But even if her fridge had been fully stocked, it wouldn't have contained anything healthful because Xandra lived for fast food and Doritos and, heaven help her, everything in the chocolate family. Sure, she controlled her intake quantity, which helped keep her weight down, but she didn't give a fig about quality. The only reason she'd been eating the veggie casseroles was because Beau liked them.

The truth hit her as she stood in front of her open refrigerator. The cold air drafted out and sent a jolt of awareness up her spine.

She was pretending again, putting up a front, trying to be what she thought Beau wanted. Just as she pretended to be the sweet, angelic baby of the family for her mother. Just the way she'd pretended to be everything Mark had wanted her to be. She'd eaten tofu and quit smoking and given up her sense of self, and she was still doing it now.

She was still putting up a front, because she was afraid. She feared Beau wouldn't like the real woman. She feared losing his friendship, his acceptance, his love.

But she couldn't lose something she'd never had. Beau didn't love her. He loved the Xandra she was pretending to be.

She didn't want that. She wanted someone to love and accept her for who she was: a once-upon-a-time chubby girl who still battled with her weight and her insecurity. While she'd changed on the outside, deep down she was still the same.

She didn't just want love. She'd had that, but it had always come with conditions. She wanted unconditional love.

That's why she'd been so determined to have a baby. She'd wanted someone to love her regardless of the way she looked or what food she liked or what music she listened to. Someone who didn't care if she'd read the latest womanist book or watched the most recent episode of *Get Sexed Up!* She wanted the lasting, forever and ever kind of love celebrated in romance novels.

The kind that didn't fade at the first sign of gray hair or wrinkles. The kind that her sister Skye seemed to have found with Clint.

Xandra wanted something real. Something solid. And she wanted it with Beau. She loved Beau.

The trouble was, he loved an illusion.

And everyone knew an illusion couldn't last.

"You're alive," Beau declared when she answered his knock late that night. Relief glimmered in his eyes as he swept a gaze over her. "I tried calling so many times that my finger has a blister from hitting the damned redial button." Anger lit his eyes. "Why didn't you answer?"

"This will never work." She stuffed the spoon she'd been holding into the quart of Baskin-Robbins ice cream she held in the other hand and wiped at her puffy eyes.

"What are you talking about?"

"Us. You. Me." She shook her head and spooned another bite of ice cream into her mouth. "It won't work," she said around the mouthful.

Where the cold comfort had gone down easy since she'd collapsed onto the sofa with the carton in hand— after a thorough trip to the grocery store where she'd bought every comfort food from ice cream to brownies to Doritos to chocolate milk—she had trouble swallowing now. Her head hurt and her chest hurt and her stomach hurt. Everything hurt—and not because she'd been bingeing all evening—but because she knew what she had to do. She had to come clean with Beau.

She swallowed the last of her bite and drew in a deep, shaky breath. "There are some things you need to know."

His expression darkened. "You're involved with someone else, aren't you? That's why you didn't call all week."

"Of course not, and I didn't call because I wasn't sure of my feelings. I mean, I was sure, but I was scared because I thought it couldn't work. But then I realized that it could. But now I know it can't."

"You're confusing the hell out of me."

"And you're missing the point."

"Which is?"

"I'm eating ice cream." She held up the quart of Chocolate Explosion.

"And?"

"And you don't like ice cream."

"Ice cream's all right."

"You don't like Chocolate Explosion. You're not into chocolate, but I am. I live for it. I could eat it every day, several times a day." There. She'd said it.

He didn't so much as bat an eye. "And?"

"And I just might."

"Baby, you're not making any sense."

"This is me," she said, stepping back so he could see her favorite gray sweats and her oversized white T-shirt with the small pizza stain all the bleach in the world hadn't managed to fade completely. "This is what I look like when I'm not at the office. I like to be comfortable. I do get dressed up on occasion, but I hate it. I can't wait to peel off my panty hose and loosen my bra and undo the button on my skirt."

"I can't wait either."

"And that thong you saw in my bathroom, it's not mine. It's my sister's." Bomb number two. She eyed him and waited for the fallout.

"Do you normally share underwear with your sister?"

"I didn't mean that. It is mine, but it's not a real thong. It's a favor from Skye's bachelorette party. It's half the size of a real thong, not that I would wear it if it were larger. I tried one once. It felt like I was flossing between my butt cheeks, and so I stick to briefs. I'm just not a thong person."

"Neither am I."

"And I'm not a vegetable person. I don't like jazz. I don't smoke anymore, but I think about it. I dream about it. And one day, I may backslide and start puffing away again."

"What are you trying to tell me?"

"That *this* is me. The real me. This is what you get if you love me." Tears burned the back of her eyes, but she blinked them away, determined to follow this through to the very end without falling apart. "I don't have a perfect body and I never will because I get hives just thinking about the exercise machines at the gym. I do like sports, particularly racquetball, but that's because I get to gossip with Albert—he's my chief engineer and best friend at Wild Woman. I'll never be the perfect housekeeper because I hate to dust. I can cook, but only rich, fatty, melt-in-your-mouth stuff that isn't heart-smart or low-carb or low-fat. And I didn't make those popcorn balls yesterday." *Take that.* "I tried, but I ended up with a gooey mess, so I went to Eula's candy shop over on Louisiana.

She's got everything from caramel apples to popcorn balls."

"I already knew that. I've tasted Eula's popcorn balls more times than you can count."

"I was just trying to impress you."

"You did."

"How's that possible if you knew I didn't make them?"

"The thought impressed me. Very few women have ever gone to such trouble for me before. In bed, yes. But they get as good as they give. But for me personally"— he shook his head—"you're one of the first, sweetheart."

She wanted so much to believe him. Maybe Albert was right when it came to relationships. Maybe a little opposition spiced up the mix rather than doomed it to failure. Maybe Beau would still love her regardless of who she really was.

Maybe he would love her because of who she really was.

Maybe not.

Either way, she was determined to let it all hang out. For better or worse.

"I can sew on a button," she rushed on, "but that's the extent of my expertise with a needle. I don't mend socks or knit or crochet. I can't stand Howard Stern. I love Top Forty music and I love to sing along with the radio even though my voice sounds like a teenage boy going through the change."

He grinned. "Is there anything else I should know?"

"I snore sometimes."

"I already knew that."

Her cheeks burned, but she kept going. "I like to stay up and watch cheesy late-night dating shows. I'm not a big crier, but I do break down sometimes during an old movie or when I've had a particularly bad day at the office. And speaking of movies, I actually like those teenage high school flicks and"—she drew in a deep breath and gathered her courage—"I like Freddie Prinze, Jr."

"We can't all be perfect." When she frowned, he grinned again and reached for her spoon. He took a bite of ice cream. "Not bad."

"But you don't love it."

"I don't have to. I love you, Xandra."

"But I've got gray hair." There. She'd said it.

"I don't see any gray."

"Not there." Her glance went south. *"There."*

"Welcome to the club."

"You're saying that you have gray hair down south?"

"I'm saying that I'm getting older. We both are. It's nothing to be ashamed of."

"Maybe so, but I'm still far from the perfect woman."

"So am I."

She couldn't help but smile. "I'm being serious. I'm going to get old and I might get fat or lose my hair, or all three."

"And I'll love you anyway."

"You say that now, but—"

"But nothing. I'm not just saying it. I mean it."

"How do I know that? How can I really know? And even if you do feel it now, maybe it won't last. Maybe your feelings will fade. How can I know that it's for real, and it's forever?"

"I guess you'll just have to trust me. Just like I'll have to trust you. Unless you don't love me." Worry touched his gaze and his mouth drew into a thin line. "Is that what all this is about?"

She shook her head. "I just want you to see the real me."

"I see the real you. I always have. Ever since that night in the back of my daddy's Impala. I took one look at you and said, here's the most beautiful woman I've ever seen."

"Right. You were in a hurry to get it over with."

"Is that what you think?" He shook his head. "Baby, I took one look at you and you looked so hot that I couldn't control myself. You looked so curvy and sexy in that miniskirt." He shook his head. "I'd never seen you wear a miniskirt before. You'd always been all covered up with those baggy clothes, he admitted."

"I'd always been fat. But then I lost twenty-five pounds on my going-away diet. Not that anybody noticed."

"I did, but not until you peeled off those clothes," he admitted. "That's when I saw you in a different light. It shook me up and turned me on and that's why I was so quick on the trigger."

"Because you wanted me?"

"Because I wanted you. I still do."

"I'm wearing baggy clothes now."

"It doesn't matter, because I don't see the clothes. I see what's underneath. I see the woman. In the gleam of your eyes. The fullness of your lips. I feel her in the softness of your skin and the tremble of your hands." He kissed her then, just a feather-light press of his lips on hers. He tasted like warm male and sweet chocolate.

Her heart pounded and her blood rushed and her knees

actually trembled. But there was more, as well. There was a warmth in her chest, a certainty deep in her gut.

"Now say it. Say that you love me."

"I do."

"I want to hear the words." His expression grew serious. "I need to hear them."

She stared into his eyes and saw the emotion there that mirrored her own, and that's when she knew beyond a doubt that he was it. The One. Then again, she'd always known it because he'd looked at her just the same on that dark moonlit night, she'd just been too young and naive to recognize it.

She saw clearly now. This was the real thing. Him. Her. The two of them. Forever and ever.

"I love you," she told him. "I love you so much."

"Now that's all I really needed to know." And then he pulled her into his arms and gave her a real kiss.

Epilogue

It won't work this time," Jacqueline told her executive producer after listening to the woman recite viewer statistics for every hit reality show, from *The Bachelor* to the entire *Survivor* series, to *American Idol*. "I'm not doing it."

"There's nothing to do," Barbara told her. "The damage is already done. Like it or not, the Smart Dating series was a huge success. So much so that we've got thousands of entries pouring in every day for the next round. Women nationwide want to utilize the Jacqueline Farrel method to find their own happily ever after."

"But I don't do happily ever after." She shook her head. "I will not be a party to any sort of wedding, reality or otherwise."

"You don't have to do anything. Just show up, smile, and be a fixture, like you're about to do right now." She motioned to the open ballroom doorway and the festivities going on inside. The live broadcast of the official engagement party for the ten out of sixteen women who met their soul mates utilizing Jacqueline's Smart Dating advice. Inside, several cameras rolled, broadcasting the official announcement to millions of viewers. Five-and-a-half million—two million more than Cherry's average viewing audience for her Mr. Perfect series.

She shook her head. "I won't do it. I don't now, nor have I ever, condoned marriage. It would make me a hypocrite. A fraud. A liar. A—"

"—good mother," Donovan finished for her as he came up next to her. "She'll do it," he told Barbara. "Just give us a few minutes, then she'll make an appearance."

"What are you talking about?"

"Xandra is inside." He motioned to the ballroom. "Xandra and Beau, and they're waiting to tell us something."

"What could possibly be that important that they would come on national television just to tell us . . ." The question trailed off as she had the sudden image of her little girl standing on top of a wedding cake. But not just any cake. A big frosty white number with lots of tulle and bows and a tiny little noose strung around the little bride's neck. "I think I need a drink of water."

Donovan signaled a nearby waiter while Jacqueline fought for a deep breath. Okay, so maybe she didn't need water. She needed air. Lots and lots of air.

"This can't be happening."

"It's happening, darling. So just calm down and accept it. Your youngest daughter is getting married, and she's announcing it on live national television with the other daters. It's her way of standing up and saying that she believes in marriage."

"But I don't."

"She's not you, dear. She's entitled to her own beliefs

and she's proud of the fact that she loves Beau and he loves her."

"That's no reason to do something so foolish."

"Maybe it is." At her sharp look, he shrugged. "Maybe marriage isn't so bad." He motioned toward the festivities inside and Jacqueline turned to catch a glimpse of her youngest daughter standing with the tall, dark, handsome man who'd nearly run her over on the front porch. "Xandra certainly looks happy with Beau."

"She *does* look happy," Jacqueline admitted as Donovan's hands worked their magic on her tired, stressed shoulders. "Of course, it could just be an illusion. Or brainwashing. Or simply sex. It's all so new to her so maybe they've got just a bad case of lust for one another."

"If that's the case, then what's Skye's excuse? She looks every bit as happy as her sister."

Jacqueline's gaze shifted to Skye who held on to her husband's arm and laughed at something he said. "It's the brainwashing, I tell you. That Clint is a smooth operator. He's still got her under his spell."

"I don't know. She looks genuinely happy to me. Radiant even."

"Nonsense. Only pregnant women look . . ." Her gaze swiveled to Donovan's. "You mean she's—"

"—pregnant." He smiled. "That was the other reason you have to make an appearance tonight. She plans on making the announcement and she wants you there."

"Why, that's wonderful! And, of course, I'll be there. Why didn't you just say so in the first place? I can endure anything, even an engagement party, for the sake of my future granddaughter."

"What about for the sake of your future grandson?"

"Are you trying to tell me she's having a boy?"

"She's not having *a* boy."

"Thank God." She waved a hand at her flushed cheeks. "For a second there, I thought I might faint."

"She's having two boys. Twins."

The word echoed in Jacqueline's head. Boys. As in *not* girls. As in . . . *Oh, no.*

The floor tilted and everything swam, and then Jacqueline felt herself falling. She never reached the floor, however. Two strong arms swept her up and a few heart-pounding moments later, she felt the soft cushions of a nearby sofa.

Everything was so soft and warm and male, that she stopped thinking for the next few minutes and she simply lay there, her eyes closed, her nostrils tuned in to the musky scent of Donovan. She heard voices, but they seemed so far away and it really was better just to keep her eyes closed. She concentrated on breathing while Donovan instructed a waiter to bring some smelling salts.

Good. She needed to smell something besides the delicious scent of cologne. Because if she smelled it for much longer, she would be lulled into submission and she might even believe that everything would be all right as long as she had him by her side.

"Here are the smelling salts, sir." The deep voice drew her attention away from her frantic thoughts and she waited for the sour smell to bring her to her senses. But instead of a smell, it was the waiter's next words that did the trick. "I hope your wife is okay."

Jacqueline cracked one eye open and glared at the waiter. "I am not his wife.

The waiter blushed and Donovan grinned and Jacqueline opened her other eye to glare full force at the young man.

"I'm sorry," the boy stammered. "I mean, I just figured you guys were married."

"We are no such thing." She struggled into an upright position. "We coexist in peace and harmony and mutual respect, which is more than I can say for most married couples."

"I think we've been straining the peace and harmony aspect lately," Donovan said as he stepped back and extended a hand to help her up. "Then again, we could get back to the peace and harmony if you would just admit that you need me."

"I do not need you." She ignored his help and pushed to her feet, grasping at the edge of the sofa when the floor seemed to tilt. "I need food," she said when she managed to regain her balance. "I need water." Her gaze met his. "But I do not *need* you." She gave him a look that would have sent most men running, but he simply smiled at her.

"Careful, honey, you're liable to kill me with all this sweet talk."

"I should be so lucky." She ignored the urge to smack his smiling face, or worse, kiss him right then and there in front of God and a dozen television cameras. She was Jacqueline Farrel, acclaimed sexologist and womanist, and she didn't go around leaning on men or kissing them or needing them, for heaven's sake.

She celebrated her femininity and gave advice to women regarding the same, and reality engagements and weddings aside, this was still her show, and there was still hope. Eve had yet to buy into the whole marriage propaganda thing. Xandra getting married meant that she would probably be giving Jacqueline grandbabies in the not too distant future. Possibly *girl* grandbabies. And Donovan could still learn to put down the damned toilet seat and pick up his socks.

Okay, so maybe that was stretching the whole hope concept a bit far.

"Shall we go join our daughters?"

"On one condition." She eyed him.

"What's that?"

"You learn how to put the toilet seat down, or I'm buying a case of super glue." Where she lacked in faith, she made up for in coercion skills.

"Maybe you just need to learn how to put the seat up."

"And maybe you'll be living by yourself because I'll be moving in with my mother."

"I suppose I could make an effort. You have been washing my back here lately and while that isn't exactly what I had in mind when I moved in with you, I'm all for compromise."

"Dare I ask what you *did* have in mind?"

"Dare away, but I don't think you really want to know. Or do you?"

The seconds ticked by as she stared up at him and into him and saw . . . Uh-uh. No way. No how. Not this woman. Not *ever.*

"We really should get inside," she blurted. "The girls are waiting." She slid her arm into his.

As they stepped forward, Jacqueline could have sworn she heard him hum the wedding march. She was this close to pulling away and running for her life, but then his hand closed over hers and everything faded except the warmth of Donovan just to her right and the sight of her three beautiful daughters just up ahead.

And for the first time in a long time, Jacqueline Farrel felt like smiling.

About the Author

Award-winning author Kimberly Raye lives deep in the heart of Texas with her very own cowboy, Curt, and her young children. She's an incurable romantic who loves Sugar Babies, Toby Keith, and dancing to Barney videos with her toddler. You can reach Kimberly on-line at www.kimberlyraye.com, or write to her c/o Warner Books, 1271 Avenue of the Americas, New York, NY 10020.

More
Kimberly Raye!

Please turn this page
for a preview of

*Sweet as Sugar,
Hot as Spice*

AVAILABLE IN MASS MARKET
AUGUST 2005.

Chapter One

She was totally screwed.

The truth struck Eve Farrel as she stood beneath the blazing spotlights near center stage and listened to her youngest sister vow to "love, honor and cherish . . ."

This revelation had nothing to do with the fact that she was wearing a tea-length yellow tulle dress and matching satin pumps in front of both a live television audience and several million dedicated *Get Sexed Up!* home viewers; and everything to do with her mother, the show's host and, like Eve, an unwilling witness to the enslavement ceremony being broadcast in the name of ratings. Jacqueline Farrel sat in the front row and stared at Eve as if she were the last pair of Anne Klein slingbacks at a Macy's half-off sale.

Make that a very bright, peppy, vibrant, *yellow* pair of slingbacks.

Okay, so maybe the get-up had just a little to do with the sick feeling in the pit of Eve's stomach. She didn't do bright or peppy or vibrant. Rather, she lived in black, from her thigh-high patent leather boots and her favorite Elvira dress, to the usual thick layer of eyeliner rimming her eyes and the nail polish dulling her fingertips. Black reflected her artsy personality, and her unconventional attitude.

Even more, her mother hated black.

Which was why it had become Eve's signature color at the age of fourteen, when she'd dyed her platinum hair Clairol's Raven No. 102 just an hour before the family's annual Christmas picture. Jacqueline had turned the same shade of red caused by her severe allergic reaction to shellfish. Then she'd rushed off in a huff to rethink her decision to have children in the first place. And to contemplate lawsuits against the hospital that obviously had switched her second daughter at birth. And to plot revenge against her life partner and the man obviously responsible—Jacqueline didn't have any loose screws on *her* side of the family—for their oddball daughter.

Thoughts aside, controlling Jacqueline had been so dismayed she'd run the other way and given her daughter some much-needed space.

Needless to say, Eve had been shocking her mother ever since.

Up until last year, that is, when her oldest sister, Skye, had one-upped Eve by doing the unthinkable—she'd waltzed down the aisle with the hottest NASCAR driver to ever do a Pep Boys commercial. Now her youngest sister, Xandra, was smiling and letting her significant other slide a platinum wedding band onto her ring finger on live television.

Xandra had planned to hold the ceremony at a hotel in Houston, but then the producers of *Get Sexed Up!* had approached her with an offer she couldn't refuse. The "Smart Dating" segment they had recently aired, which featured Jacqueline giving dating advice to single women, had been so successful that several of the participants had not only nabbed a man, but were on their way to the altar. The producers had asked Xandra and her fiancé, Beau, to take part in the show's Valentine's Day special—a reality multi-wedding, complete with an in-studio ceremony and a complimentary reception at the posh Beverly Hills Hotel. Xandra had agreed because it would guarantee her mother's presence on the most important day in her life.

Jacqueline Farrel was the show's host, after all. Contractually, she *had* to attend, even if it went against her entire philosophy—namely that marriage was the worst evil, second only to terminal illness. Lasting relationships weren't built on a flimsy piece of paper but a solid foundation of shared interests, mutual respect and great sex—the infamous Holy Commitment Trinity for which she'd become famous. Obviously, however, she'd failed to enlighten two of her three offspring.

But all was not lost. She had one single daughter left to save the Farrel name and serve as a shining example to Womanists everywhere. She had Eve.

And Eve had a massive migraine the size of Paris Hilton's ego.

She was screwed, all right.

The floor tilted just enough to make her sway. Sweat beaded on her upper lip. Her hands went damp and she had to readjust her grip on the heavy bridesmaid's bouquet.

Geez, it was hot. And stuffy. And bright.

She blinked away the tiny black dots dancing in front of her eyes and swallowed against a rising wave of nausea.

"Are you all right?" The whispered question came from the woman who stood just to Eve's left. Skye Farrel-MacAllister was the matron of honor and the expectant mother of twin boys.

"I'm fine." Eve swallowed again as reality weighed down on her.

She had *definitely* been drop-kicked into an alternate universe. It seemed like just yesterday her oldest sister had been as anti-marriage as their mother. Even more, while Skye had always liked kids, they'd been just a far-off, *maybe someday* thought. Skye hadn't been able to keep a boyfriend long enough to add his name to her electric bill, much less start a family.

"You don't look fine," Skye said under her breath as the exchange of rings finished and the minister declared, "What God hath joined together, let no man put asunder." Skye caught Eve's trembling hand in a gesture that looked more like an older sibling's sign of affection rather than the subtle, but crystal clear *screw-this-up-now-and-I'll-kick-your-ass* warning it truly was. "You look like you're going to throw up."

Big Brother had nothing on Big Sister.

"I'm fine." Eve swallowed and cleared her throat. "Really." She drew a deep breath and gave her older sister a reassuring squeeze before disengaging her fingers.

Pulling her shoulders back, she clutched the monstrous blend of yellow roses, buttercups and daffodils stem-wrapped in ribbon and sweetheart lace. Lace that matched the trim on her dress. Which matched the color of the tulle and bunting draped around the set. Which matched the giant satin bows marking each row of chairs. Which matched the hue of the daisy petals sprinkled on every aisle.

". . . marriage is a joyous union that marks the beginning of a new life together . . ." The minister's voice droned on.

A drop of sweat tickled its way down her right temple

and heat smothered her. The razor burn under her arms prickled and she damned herself for not toughening up her skin by shaving for more than just special occasions.

"... and now by the power vested in me ..."

She blew out a deep breath and inhaled again. Her nostrils burned with the sickeningly sweet scent of flowers coupled with the half gallon of perfume the wedding coordinator had spritzed her with prior to the walk down the studio aisle. Her stomach pitched and rolled.

"... I now pronounce you man and wife ..."

Get it together, Eve told herself. *Now.*

She hadn't made a huge name for herself in the erotic video market by upchucking every time a difficult situation arose.

She was *Eve Farrel*, for heaven's sake—the ballsy, headstrong producer and owner of Sugar & Spice Sinema, the fastest growing production company in L.A. and the only one that specialized in how-to sex videos for couples. Her life was one crisis after another. She worked with temperamental actors and actresses. She endured the endless pressure caused by tight production schedules and small budgets. She dealt with know-it-all cameramen and clueless production assistants and snotty set caterers who couldn't tell a blueberry bagel from a raisin and cinnamon.

"... and now let us seal this blessed union with a kiss ..."

She was *not* going to throw up, despite the hot lights and the horrible dress and the overwhelming smell and her mother's adoring stare.

Rather, she was going to paste a smile on her face and make it through the few minutes it would take to waltz back up the aisle. Then she was going to head for the reception like the headstrong, confident, capable woman that she was. And then she was going to do what any head-strong, confident, capable woman would do in her present situation.

She was going to drink.

Heavily.

Three hours later, after an endless stream of pictures, a question-and-answer session with several local radio shows and an interview for *Entertainment Tonight*—they weren't about to miss out on the biggest reality event of the year—Eve finally walked into the Crystal Ballroom of the Beverly Hills Hotel.

The reception was already in full swing, the room packed with guests. The live band belted out Kool & the Gang's classic "Celebration" for a dance floor full of people. Waiters squeezed this way and that, carrying silver serving trays offering everything from appetizers to champagne. Candelabra towered over the banquet tables and flickered with candlelight. Large sprays of flowers filled every nook and cranny. French doors opened out into a garden filled with more tables and people.

The place was nearly bursting at the seams.

Thankfully.

While Eve would have given her right eye—her throbbing eye thanks to a headache from hell—for some peace and quiet, chaos was preferable at the moment. The more people, the easier it would be to steer clear of her mother.

Or so she hoped.

She retrieved a frozen margarita, bypassed the seats reserved for the wedding party and headed for a round banquet table in the farthest corner of the ballroom.

Eve had just downed half the icy drink and slid off her shoes when a six-foot plus, sometimes green-eyed, sometimes blue—depending on her contact supply—woman collapsed into the seat next to her. Trina Carlington had gone for the green tonight, and had her long hair dyed a vibrant red to complete the look.

"I am *so* glad you invited me," Trina declared in a breathless, excited voice. Trina was the chief marketing director for Sugar & Spice Sinema, a go-getter when it came to advertising and product perception, and an ex–Playboy Playmate. She had an impressive background that included a degree from Stanford University and an internship with the prestigious Bart & Baxter Ad Agency, and an equally impressive list of measurements, thanks to L.A.'s leading plastic surgeon. She wore a slinky, strappy dress that clung to her shapely body and made Eve seriously consider torturing her own body with a Pilates class.

"Weddings aren't usually my thing," Trina went on as she pulled out a mirrored tube from her gold Fendi bag and retouched her flaming red lipstick, "I always end up dancing with somebody's dorky cousin or drooling uncle." She licked her lips. "But I've already done the Macarena with the vice president of a major network, the Electric Slide with one of the cameramen from *The Today Show* and the Twist with some rich guy who's staying in the hotel's penthouse suite and just popped in because he's in the mood for wedding cake. Speaking of which, why aren't you dancing and having fun?"

"I'm too busy having a nervous breakdown." Eve scooted her chair even further into the shadows of a huge potted palm that sat next to the table and effectively hid her from full view of the rest of the ballroom. Namely, from the woman seated across the sea of wedding guests, near a silver fountain flowing with champagne punch.

"I'm actually the good daughter now! Can you imagine

that?" She shook her head. "I've never been the good daughter. I *can't* be the good daughter. Then I'll have to put up with more than one visit a week from my mother and I can barely handle that."

"She's a busy lady. Do you really think she'll try to spend more time with you?"

Eve watched as Jacqueline Farrel downed her fourth glass of punch and glanced around for the countless time, as if searching for someone. Her gaze paused on the potted palm.

Eve ducked to the side and grabbed her friend's arm. "My mother didn't see you come over here, did she?"

"How would I know?" Trina wiggled her perfectly arched eyebrows. "I have much more interesting people to watch besides your mother." She smiled. "Check out those hot bodies over there."

Eve's gaze shifted to the four tuxedo-clad hotties who stood near the bar. They talked and laughed, seemingly oblivious to the cameras that clicked around them and captured each of their expressions on film.

"They must be actors or stuntmen or something," Trina said.

"NASCAR drivers." At Trina's questioning look, Eve added, "Since Clint was attending the wedding with Skye, the show's producers decided to tape a "Hot New Men of NASCAR" interview for their brother channel—Spike TV."

"Clint's been racing forever. He isn't exactly a NASCAR virgin."

"No, but three out of the four drivers for his race team are. He must have invited them to tag along to the reception."

"I've never been into NASCAR—Sunday is my day to catch up on all the reality shows I tape during the week—

but I'll have to start watching." Trina's eyes gleamed as she pointed a red-tipped nail. "I'd definitely trade the last three Bachelors for that one cutie right over there."

Eve's gaze shifted to the blond hunk who stood near a giant ice sculpture shaped like a hammer (made in honor of her new brother-in-law, who was the founder and owner of Hire-a-Hunk Construction). The man looked mouthwatering in a black tuxedo. He had his arms draped around two different women—a brunette on one side and a strawberry blonde on the other—while he smiled and flirted with a very attentive female reporter who was holding a microphone in front of him.

"It's all good, sunshine."

The deep, rich southern drawl echoed in Eve's memory and awareness skittered up her spine. She frowned and ignored the crazy sensation. "I might trade in that football-playing Bachelor—he *did* pick the wrong woman—but the rest of those drivers are definitely preferable to Linc Adams."

She watched as the reporter laughed at something he said and leaned in even closer. Eve's frown deepened. "He is every womanist's worst nightmare." Which was why, when her newly married sister had mentioned a fix-up with Clint's new driver, Eve had actually agreed. She'd needed to do something to win back the Rebellious Daughter title she'd held for so many years. Big mistake. "He guzzled beer out of a bra cup at the Victoria's Secret after-show party."

"That was *him*? I saw that on *E!*" Trina shook her head. "He looked a little . . . different."

"He doesn't usually dress this well. He lives in board shorts and T-shirts and a very inebriated grin." When he wasn't wearing his racing suit, that is.

Eve's thoughts rushed back to the Napa Valley race she'd attended, where the first race car designed and manufactured by and for the MacAllister Magic Race Team had been introduced.

She hadn't felt near the rush when she'd seen her brother-in-law's groundbreaking car as she'd felt when she'd glimpsed his new driver. The after-race date had taken on a different meaning when he'd climbed from behind the wheel and smiled at her. Forget about pissing off her mother. Eve had thought that she might actually have a great time. Linc *was* a handsome guy, in a blond, blue-eyed, All-American sort of way.

While Eve didn't usually do the All-American type—she gravitated more toward dark, brooding, deep men with tortured souls and non existent bank accounts—she'd been ready to make an exception. Until the race had ended, and her fantasy of stimulating conversation, followed by hot, wild sex on the hood of Linc's car had melted away.

He'd shed his racing suit, pulled on a worn, ripped pair of shorts and a T-shirt that read, I BRAKE FOR BEER, BABES & AMMO, and proceeded to flirt with every female within hearing range during their dinner date. She'd promptly told him off in a voice that made most men tremble, but he'd simply smiled at her and murmured, *"It's all good, sunshine."* She'd called him a colorful name, tossed a breadstick at him and walked away, and that had been that.

"I can't remember," Trina's voice pulled her back to the present. "What sort of bra did he drink out of?"

"What?" Eve's attention shifted back to her friend and the familiar predatory light in her eyes. Trina was a go-getter, all right, even when it came to men.

Especially when it came to men.

"What sort of bra?" she asked again.

"What difference does it make?"

"I'm wearing a Very Sexy Body Bra. Double D." She grinned. "That should hold a lot of beer, don't you think?"

"He might not be in a beer mood tonight," Eve heard herself say. "He might not be drinking at all, for that matter."

Yeah, right.

From the rumors being printed in the tabloids and broadcast on every major show from the fun CMT's *Celebrity Homes* to the more serious ESPN's *Live and In Color*, NASCAR'S latest and greatest wasn't just racing for the championship. He was drinking and partying his way into the Bad Boys Hall of Fame. Undoubtedly he was drinking tonight, and doing any and everything else Trina might have in mind.

Trina pulled her shoulders back, pushed out her ample chest and grinned. "You never know when thirst will strike. I think I'll walk over and introduce him to Pam and Dolly." She cast one last glance at Eve. "You'll never hook up sitting in this corner. Men are visual."

"So is my mother, which is why I'm staying right here."

For the next five minutes she watched as Trina made her way through the crowd toward Linc Adams. When her friend reached him and drew his attention away from the reporter, Eve downed the rest of her margarita in one long gulp.

Linc's gaze swept over Trina and he smiled, and Eve pushed to her feet. He was obviously drinking tonight, and so was she.

"I'll have another margarita," she said when she reached the bar a few minutes later.

The rumors circulating about him *had* to be true. He was a dog, all right. The hound of all hounds. Mr. Tramp himself. Number one on the pound's Most Wanted—

"There you are!" The familiar female voice shattered her thoughts. "I've been looking all over for you."

"Make that two," Eve said to the bartender before turning to greet the woman who'd stepped up behind her. "Hi, Mom."

THE EDITOR'S DIARY

Dear Reader,

All work and no play make for dull romance. But what if you could combine work and play and get more romance and excitement than you ever dreamed possible? Find out in our two Warner Forever titles this October.

Publishers Weekly raves that **Karen Rose's** previous work "offers heart-racing thrills, both in the bedroom and the forensics lab" and that "readers will . . . rush to the novel's thrilling conclusion". Well, fasten your seatbelt— her latest, **I'M WATCHING YOU**, is going to take your breath away. With the highest conviction rate of any prosecutor in the state, Kristen Mayhew is passionately devoted to locking criminals up. It isn't just a job to her—it's the most important thing in her life. But one night, she opens the trunk of her car and discovers pictures of three dead bodies with a cryptic note that vows retribution on the few criminals that have gotten away, signed "Your Humble Servant". As the death toll rises, Kristen and broad-shouldered Homicide detective Abe Reagan follow the clues to the serial killer while finding comfort—and love—in one another's arms.

Journeying from heart-stopping suspense to sugar, spice and everything nice, we present **Kimberly Raye's** **SOMETIMES NAUGHTY, SOMETIMES NICE.** Vicki Lewis Thompson raves "Kimberly Raye is hot, hot, hot!" So good luck trying to cool down! Xandra Farrel knows men are only good for two things: sexual pleasure and procreation. As the owner of Wild Woman, Inc., the largest erotic aid manufacturer, Xandra is about to launch her best product yet that promises mind-numbing pleasure for women. One problem: she needs a guinea pig for a test drive. So when Beau Hollister reappears, she thanks her lucky stars. Beau is a blast from her past, responsible for her absolute worst sexual experience ever, and she's certain that if she can have a deliciously naughty night with him, her product's success is a sure thing. But after one kiss, it's romance—not work—that's on her mind.

To find out more about Warner Forever, these October titles, and the author, visit us at www.warnerforever.com.

With warmest wishes,

Karen Kosztolnyik

Karen Kosztolnyik, Senior Editor

P.S. The holidays are right around the corner so put down that turkey baster and enjoy these two reasons to give thanks. **Amanda Scott** pens a sexy and magical Scottish medieval of two devoted lovers overcoming their warring clans and the betrayal that threatens to rip them apart in **HIGHLAND PRINCESS**; and **Diane Perkins** delivers the poignant and evocative story of a man who returns from war only to discover that a beautiful, pregnant stranger is claiming to be his wife in **THE IMPROPER WIFE**.